KATE CARLISLE

The Twelve Books of Christmas

A Bibliophile Mystery

BERKLEY PRIME CRIME
New York

BERKLEY PRIME CRIME
Published by Berkley
An imprint of Penguin Random House LLC
penguinrandomhouse.com

Copyright © 2023 by Kathleen Beaver
Penguin Random House supports copyright. Copyright fuels creativity,
encourages diverse voices, promotes free speech, and creates a vibrant culture.
Thank you for buying an authorized edition of this book and for complying with
copyright laws by not reproducing, scanning, or distributing any part of it in any
form without permission. You are supporting writers and allowing Penguin
Random House to continue to publish books for every reader.

BERKLEY and the BERKLEY & B colophon are registered trademarks and
BERKLEY PRIME CRIME is a trademark of Penguin Random House LLC.

Library of Congress Cataloging-in-Publication Data

Names: Carlisle, Kate, 1951– author.
Title: The twelve books of Christmas / Kate Carlisle.
Description: New York : Berkley Prime Crime, [2023] | Series: A Bibliophile mystery
Identifiers: LCCN 2023013961 (print) | LCCN 2023013962 (ebook) |
ISBN 9780593637685 (hardcover) | ISBN 9780593637692 (ebook)
Subjects: LCGFT: Detective and mystery fiction. | Novels.
Classification: LCC PS3603.A7527 T94 2023 (print) |
LCC PS3603.A7527 (ebook) | DDC 813/.6—dc23/eng/20230327
LC record available at https://lccn.loc.gov/2023013961
LC ebook record available at https://lccn.loc.gov/2023013962

Printed in the United States of America
1st Printing

For Jenel Looney,
my fearless assistant and wonderful friend.
Thank you for your warm sense of humor,
your amazingly organized mind,
your generous spirit, and your invaluable
help in whipping this book into shape.
I couldn't have done it without you.
Merry Christmas and Happy Hogmanay!
May your troubles be less and your blessings be more,
and nothing but happiness come through your door.

The Twelve Books
of Christmas

Chapter 1

I stared out the wide kitchen window as a black stretch limousine pulled to a stop in front of our new second home in Dharma. Less than two minutes later, another limo arrived, and I had to take a few bracing breaths. "Have we done the right thing?"

My darkly handsome husband Derek quirked an eyebrow. "Regrets already, darling?"

"God, yes." I tried to laugh, but the sound bordered on hysterical. "We couldn't settle for a cozy dinner for four, could we? No way. We had to invite thirty-four people for dinner on Christmas Eve. Thirty-four people! Or is it thirty-five?" Did it really matter? Either way, we were about to be besieged in our brand-new house. With family and friends, but still. "Are we crazy?"

"Of course not," he said, his distinguished British accent lending extra credibility to the statement. "It's a perfectly respectable thing to invite favorite friends and family members over for Christmas Eve dinner."

"Is it?" I wondered. "We're likely to cause a frenzy."

He laughed. "Would that be so bad?"

I gaped at him.

"Maybe they won't all show up," he said, but he was still laughing.

"Oh, please," I said. "You know they'll all be here."

He gently rubbed my shoulders. "All the people we love best."

His kind words calmed me down a smidge, as they usually did. It would all work out and we would have a good time. After all, this was the reason we'd built our second home in Dharma, the small town in the Sonoma wine country where I'd grown up. We wanted to be close to family, so now we were about to welcome my parents, two brothers, three sisters, various spouses, and lots of children to spend Christmas Eve with us. Derek's parents were coming, too, along with several of his brothers, their wives, and more children. We were also expecting our good friends Gabriel and Alex, along with my parents' guru, Robson Benedict, and Derek's aunt Trudy. It was going to be an interesting evening.

"It'll be lovely," Derek insisted.

"It'll be chaos."

He chuckled and rubbed his hands up and down my arms. "As it should be, darling. After all, it's Christmas."

I tried to remember to breathe. "Christmas. Right." I watched another limo drive up and park. It sounded extravagant, but we had gone ahead and ordered a number of limousines so our friends wouldn't have to drive through the hills after a long night of good food and lots of wine. It just made sense.

Derek kissed me, then slowly let me go and gazed out the window. "Look on the bright side. At least you don't have to cook."

"Good point." I was the absolute worst cook in the world, and everybody knew it. Happily the entire evening was being catered by my sister Savannah's fabulous restaurant in downtown Dharma. Most of her staff had been here all day prepping and cooking a huge feast, using our brand-new clean garage as their backstage area. Across the living and dining rooms, tables had been beautifully set for dinner. Tasting stations had been arranged outside on the terrace, where Savannah's staff would serve cocktails, wine, and a number of yummy hors d'oeuvres and munchies before the dinner began.

The entire house looked festive and smelled wonderful. Our Christmas tree was magical, with flickering fairy lights and at least a hundred handmade ornaments covering its boughs. I had to admit I'd gotten carried away with crafting dozens of tiny three-dimensional books—with tiny first-chapter pages included!—that we would be giving to our guests as Christmas ornament takeaways. As a bookbinder specializing in rare book restoration, I considered it my duty to always give books as gifts, and I tried to be creative about it.

Scattered under the tree and spreading nearly halfway across the living room were oodles of beautifully wrapped gifts. Most were for the children, and yes, we had gone overboard, but why not? This was our first time hosting Christmas Eve, and we wanted it to be special.

When the front doorbell finally rang, I took a few more seconds to silently freak out, then rested my head on Derek's strong shoulder. Smiling bravely, I said, "I'll get it."

He reached for my hand. "We'll go together."

*A*n hour later, the chaos that I'd warned Derek about was upon us. But, okay, it wasn't quite as horrifying as I'd imagined. People were chatting and laughing while enjoying the wine and appetizers. Christmas carols were playing in the background, and the children were sneaking peeks at all the goodies under the tree. For the most part, everyone was having a lovely time.

My oldest friend Robin held court on the living room couch with baby Jamie, my darling new nephew. There was some minor controversy brewing since Jamie's dad—my brother Austin—had taken to calling the little guy Jake. But whatever they decided to call him, the wee one was constantly being whisked away by anyone with an urge to cuddle an adorable baby boy. And who didn't have that urge once in a while? He was such a good baby and was just one more reason why Derek and I had decided to build a home here in Dharma. I loved all my brothers and sisters and their kids, but I'd especially wanted to be near Robin when she had her first child. Derek and I both wanted to be a part of their lives, and that wasn't always easy to do while living and working in San Francisco. This way, we could have the best of both worlds.

A few years ago, Derek's parents had surprised us all by buying a vacation home in Dharma after we'd introduced them to my parents before our wedding. Now the four of them were best friends and part-time neighbors, too.

My sister China, who was seven months pregnant with her second child, sat down next to Robin, and the two began exchanging childbirth horror stories. Anyone was welcome to join in, but seriously? I loved them both, but I was steering clear. Mainly because I'd heard the worst of their stories before, but also because, yuck. Am I right?

From across the room, I met Robin's gaze, and her eyes gleamed with mischief, knowing that all the childbirth talk tended to make me a little queasy. I was pretty sure she did it on purpose, but I loved her anyway. Even when she regularly warned me, "You're next," which was often followed by a spine-chilling, bloodcurdling laugh.

I regularly assured her that I *wasn't* next, but she still enjoyed taunting me with all the grisly details of her labor pains as though that might be some kind of temptation. I personally thought she spiced up the stories just for me. We had been besties from day one, when my family and I arrived in Dharma and I first saw her, a skinny little eight-year-old clutching her bald Barbie doll. Even at that early age, I recognized a fellow misfit when I saw one.

I smiled at the memory, took a sip of champagne, and nibbled on a melted brie mini-quesadilla as I made my way across the room, checking that everyone was enjoying themselves. I savored the brie as well as the eclectic bits of conversation I overheard as I moved through the crowd. I couldn't wait for everyone to open their presents, especially the ones I'd made. In the past my sisters had given me some grief for always giving books as gifts. But what did they expect? Books were my life. I made my living by restoring rare books. What else would I give as a special gift to the people I love?

I was happy to hear that this was the year that everyone finally wanted books again, especially the parents of the youngsters who were just learning to read. Both Derek's and my family members were voracious readers, so they had made it clear that books as gifts were once again in vogue.

Still, I had decided to venture a bit farther afield with my gift giving, especially for the adults in the family. It had taken me months to complete everything, but I had managed to make every gift by hand, mostly using recycled books, and I was excited to see the reactions they got.

A few of my sisters would be receiving something I called a Butterfly Book—an old book that, when opened, revealed dozens of delicate paper butterflies flitting out from the pages. It was charming, if I did say so myself.

For each of my brothers, I'd fashioned a night-light by taking pages torn from an old book, singeing the edges, and placing a red light in the middle so that when it was turned on, it looked like the pages were on fire. I knew they would love it.

For Robin, who had every intention of returning to her sculpting work eventually, I had taken an old Barbie doll and manipulated it into a sitting position, then used my old decoupage training to cover the doll entirely with text from the pages of another old book. The final touch was to give Barbie her own little book to read. Again, it was book-oriented but whimsical enough that I thought Robin would get a kick out of it.

I stopped at one of the food mini-stations, and a waiter poured me another glass of champagne. I took a sip and happened to glance at the front door, which was standing open to let in the cool evening breeze. I saw my mother perched on the railing of the front porch talking to her friend Ginny Morrison. I'd only met Ginny twice, but I liked her. A little girl with curly blond hair was huddled against Ginny's legs, and I wondered if she was too frightened to venture inside to meet anyone else.

"Oh, Brooklyn," Mom said, waving me over. "You remember my friend Ginny?"

"Of course." I walked out to the porch and gave the woman a brief hug. "Merry Christmas, Ginny. And who is this?"

The three of us stared at the little girl clutching Ginny's legs. "This is my daughter, Charlotte," she said, stroking the child's hair.

"Hi, Charlotte," Mom and I said in unison.

She gazed up at both of us. "Hi."

"Merry Christmas," I said.

Her smile was tentative. "Yesterday was my birthday."

"My goodness," Mom said. "Happy birthday, sweetie."

"Happy birthday, Charlotte," I said. "How old are you?"

"I'm five years old." She held up five fingers.

"Isn't that wonderful?" Mom said softly.

"Would you both like to come inside and sit by the Christmas tree?" I asked. "It's so pretty and it smells really good. And we have lots of tasty food if you'd like something to eat."

Charlotte said nothing but stared up at her mother. I could tell she was intrigued.

"That's sweet of you," Ginny said quickly. "And I think Charlotte is very tempted. But we really can't take up any more of your time. I just wanted to stop by and give your mother a little Christmas gift."

"And I love it." Mom whipped out a skinny little tree branch and whisked it back and forth through the air. I figured it had to be some kind of a wand, since Ginny was a fellow member of Mom's local druidic Wiccan group. Mom had recently been reelected Grand Raven Mistress of the coven, and Ginny had been elected treasurer.

I had no idea what the treasurer of a coven did, but I suppose it meant that she was good with numbers.

"It's pretty." I reached out and touched the wand. "It feels good. Stronger than I thought it would be."

"It's cherrywood," Ginny said. "It has a warm feminine energy, and it's good for healing."

"And it's especially excellent for detecting other magical properties," Mom added, and her eyes narrowed. "Can't wait to put that to the test."

Ginny smiled at me. "And a cherrywood wand doesn't mind being shared."

"Yeah?" I said, my tongue planted firmly in my cheek. "Maybe I'll take it for a spin sometime."

"That would make me very happy," Mom said. "But I know you're just teasing me."

I gave her a one-armed hug. "Sorry, Mom. You know it's not my thing."

She kissed my cheek. "I love you anyway." Then she turned back to Ginny. "Now, we have plenty of room at the table and lots of food. We would love to have you join us."

"That's very sweet," she said. "But I think we're just going to go home. We've had a long day."

Gazing up at me, Charlotte whispered, "My daddy went to heaven."

"Oh no." Tears instantly filled my eyes, and without another thought, I knelt down and met the little girl on her level. "I'm so sorry, honey."

She said nothing, simply wrapped her arms around my neck and began to cry.

I was well-known for my sympathetic tear ducts, but even my tough big brothers wouldn't have been able to withstand this little girl's pain.

I wondered how her father had died, but now wasn't the time to inquire.

Ginny placed her hand on my shoulder and quietly explained, "We picked up Hank's ashes today. Charlotte wants to buy a pretty box to put them in."

"She's a sweet little girl," I murmured.

Mom gave her friend a hug. "Why don't we all go inside and warm up around the Christmas tree? Just for a few minutes."

After another sniffle, Charlotte loosened her grasp and looked up at me. "Mommy said you have a cat."

I smiled. "I do. Would you like to meet her?"

"Is it a girl cat?"

"Yes. Her name is Charlie."

She managed a watery giggle. "It sounds a little like my name, except Charlie is for a boy."

I smiled at her. "I think some girls might like the name, too."

She thought about it and nodded. "Maybe so." Without consulting her mother, Charlotte took my hand, and we walked into the house and headed for the stairs. I took a quick look back at her mother and got a nod of approval.

"Your cat isn't coming to the party?" Charlotte asked.

"No, she's pretty shy. She likes to stay upstairs when there's a lot of people in the house."

"I can stay with her," she whispered.

"Okay. Let's go find her." In the bedroom, I sat down on the floor next to the bed and whispered Charlie's name.

"Is she under there?" Charlotte asked.

I nodded. "This is where she usually hides."

"Do you think she'll come if I call her?"

"Maybe," I said. "Give it a try."

Charlotte nodded, then whispered, "Charlie? Hello? Charlie?"

Sure enough, after a few seconds the cat peeked out from under the bedspread. "There she is."

Charlotte flashed me a tremulous grin. "She came out."

"She must like you," I said, then reached for the cat. "Come on, sweetie. I want you to meet my friend Charlotte."

Charlie came into my arms and draped herself bonelessly over my shoulder. I stroked her soft fur, then angled her toward Charlotte. "Charlie, this is Charlotte. She wants to say hello to you."

The little girl tried to follow my lead by patting Charlie's back. It was an awkward move, but the cat didn't seem to mind.

"Hi, Charlie," Charlotte said tentatively. "Hi, Charlie." She looked at me. "Will she let me hold her?"

"I think she'd like that. Why don't you sit down on the floor and lean back against the bed? I'll put her in your lap."

"Okay."

I stroked Charlie a few more times, then gently passed her over to Charlotte, who wrapped herself around the cat.

"Hi, hi," she whispered in Charlie's ear. "Hi, Charlie." She closed her eyes and swayed slightly from side to side, as though she were rocking the cat to sleep. Charlie seemed to like it, because I could hear her purring. She was such a good cat.

I glanced at the doorway and saw that my mother and Ginny had followed us upstairs. They stood by the door, watching the action, and I could see tears in both their eyes.

I quietly pushed myself off the floor and walked over to my mom. "I was thinking of getting something to eat. Do you think Charlotte would like some hot chocolate if I brought it up here?"

Ginny looked from me to Mom and took hold of our hands in hers. "You are both so kind. Thank you. I'm sure Charlotte would love it."

The little girl was still clutching the cat, so I said, "I'll be right back."

Downstairs in the kitchen, I ran into my sister Savannah. "One of Mom's Wiccan friends and her little girl came by to give Mom a present."

"Aw, that's nice."

"Yeah. Turns out her husband just died."

Savannah exhaled. "Oh, Brooklyn. That's terrible."

"I know. So they might stay for dinner if you can make room. Or if they're just not up for it, I'd like to give them a little something to take home. Is that okay?"

"Of course. We can make room for them at one of the tables, or we can pack a to-go box for them. Either way is fine."

"Thanks, Bug." She rolled her eyes at the nickname and went dashing off. My parents had come up with quirky middle names for each of us, and Savannah's was Dragonfly. At some point in her early childhood, *Dragonfly* had become *Bug*, and we still called her that.

I pulled a packet of hot chocolate mix from the cupboard, then filled a mug with water and heated it for two minutes in the microwave. I poured in the powder and mixed it well, then I walked back upstairs and stopped when I noticed that my bedroom door was closed. Mom and Ginny stood in the hallway talking quietly.

"Everything okay?" I asked, warming my hands around the mug of chocolate.

Mom nodded. "Charlotte was curled up on the carpet with Charlie and fell right to sleep."

"The poor thing is exhausted," Ginny said. "We've had a long, sad day."

"I'm so sorry," I said. "Do you think she'll still want the chocolate when she wakes up?"

Ginny smiled softly. "Oh, trust me. She'll drink it even if it's ice cold."

I turned to Mom. "Charlie stayed right with her?"

"She hasn't left Charlotte's side."

I noticed Ginny's eyes fill again. "What a dear creature she is."

I was ridiculously proud of Charlie for keeping watch over Charlotte. She seemed to have an innate sense of the child's needs.

Ginny reached for the mug. "Let me hold that for you. You must want to go down and mingle with your guests."

Mom jumped in. "Yes, Brooklyn, you go find Derek and enjoy your party. We'll be down shortly."

I chuckled. "It's everybody's party, Mom. But I should go make sure everything's running smoothly."

"You've planned this party down to the matching tartan napkin rings," Mom said with a laugh. "What could possibly go wrong?"

A shiver ran across my shoulders. I gave her a look as I rubbed the chill from my arms. "Don't go tempting fate, Mom."

And that's when my phone began to ring.

Who in the world would be calling me on Christmas Eve? I wondered, and considered ignoring it. But I'm only human. I stared at the phone and was delighted to see my friend Claire's name appear on the screen. Calling all the way from Scotland? Just to wish us a Merry Christmas? Sweet!

I pressed the button and said, "Claire! Merry Christmas! How are you? How's Cameron?"

"Brooklyn! Is it really you?"

"Of course it's me." I laughed. She sounded almost frantic. "Are you all right?"

"Yes, of course!"

But there was a slight hysterical edge to her voice, so I decided not to push her and to bide my time until she was ready to tell me what was going on. "So, how are you? How's Cameron? How's life in Castle MacKinnon?"

"Everything is wonderful. Cameron is wonderful. I'm so glad to hear your voice. I remembered that you were having a holiday party, but I really needed to talk to ye. I'm so glad you picked up the phone."

"So, what's up?"

"Is Derek there with ye?"

I had to smile. Since moving back to Scotland, her brogue was growing stronger every day. "He's here somewhere. I'll go get him."

"No, no. That's all right."

Mom caught my eye. "I'll go find Derek," she whispered, and tiptoed toward the stairs.

"Thanks, Mom." I turned back to the phone. "Now, come on. What's up, Claire? Something's going on. Is Cameron okay?"

She began to laugh. "He's fine. He's wonderful. If you must know, he just asked me to marry him."

I had to take a breath, then I began to bounce up and down like a kid. "Oh-my-God-oh-my-God! Oh, Claire, I'm so happy for you! I knew it! I could tell he was smitten with you from the first day we all met. I'm happy for him, too. What a wonderful surprise. Have you set a date yet?"

"Brooklyn, slow down!" She giggled. "Yes, we've set a date. That's why I'm calling. He wants to get married on New Year's Eve. Well, after midnight, so technically it'll be New Year's Day."

"New Year's Eve? But . . ." I mentally pictured my calendar and blinked. "Claire, that's only a week away. You can't pull off a wedding in one week . . ." I stopped and sucked in a breath. "Wait. What I meant to say was, how wonderful! I'm absolutely thrilled for you."

"Thank you." She was laughing again. "I know it's crazy. But, yes, of course I can pull it off, because I have Mrs. Buchanan to help me. The woman is a magician, as you know."

Mrs. Buchanan was the head housekeeper and resident miracle worker of Castle MacKinnon.

"She really is," I agreed.

"But here's the real question, Brooklyn," she said slyly. "Can *you* pull it off?"

I frowned at the phone. "Beg your pardon?"

"The reason we're calling you on Christmas Eve is because Cameron and I would love it if you and Derek would stand as our witnesses."

"You . . . you're flying to San Francisco to get married?"

Her laugh was musical. "Oh, Brooklyn, no! We want you and Derek to come to Scotland. We'll take care of the expense, and of course, you'll stay in the castle. We'll have so much fun!"

"You . . . you want Derek and me to fly to Scotland?"

"Yes? Doesn't that sound wonderful?"

"It does. I mean, it really does." I took a steadying breath. It honestly did sound wonderful. "I'm so honored and grateful that you thought of us." I glanced around. "You know, I should track down Derek and let him in on your big news." I took another deep breath and exhaled slowly. "I should mention that there's one little glitch. You see, we were planning to hang out with my mom and dad over New Year's since we really haven't been able to spend much quality time with them this whole year."

Saying it out loud, it sounded ridiculous. From our home in San Francisco to my parents in Sonoma was less than an hour. We could visit them anytime we wanted to. But the fact was, we hadn't been able to really get together in months, and now I felt like we'd be deserting them if we simply flew off to Scotland.

And, yes, it really did sound ridiculous. I mean, who wouldn't want to fly off to Scotland? With all expenses paid? It was nice that Claire had offered, even though it wasn't necessary. Mom and Dad would understand, wouldn't they? I quickly tried to calculate the logistics of flying to Scotland in the next few days to make it in time for their wedding. We would have to drive back to San Francisco for our passports and our heavy winter clothing. I assumed it would be snowing in Scotland or at least extremely cold.

I pictured my mother's expression as I announced that we were flying off to Scotland instead of spending the week with her and my dad. The four of us had planned to visit some new wineries and also check out a goat farm near Petaluma that made the most delicious cheeses in the world.

All these thoughts sped through my head in a matter of seconds. And now I didn't know what to say.

"But that's perfect!" Claire cried. "You must bring them along! I would love to see your mum and dad again, and I know Cameron will adore them the instant they all meet." She hesitated, then added, "That is, if they'd like to come for a visit."

"Oh. Well. Hmm," I said with my usual flair.

"We'd love to come!" Mom shouted from the hallway.

"Hoorah!" Claire cried.

"I guess you heard that," I said dryly.

"Yes, and I'm so happy!" Claire raised her voice to add, "Becky, that's lovely! We'll have a grand time!"

"We can be packed in one hour," Mom added cheerfully.

Claire laughed. "Wonderful."

Apparently my mother had been hovering at the top of the stairs, listening to every word of our conversation. Why was I surprised?

And she wasn't the only one tuned in to our chat. I spied Derek standing a few steps down on the stairway wearing a smirk as he watched me.

"Did you hear what we were talking about?" I asked.

"I caught the gist of it." He held up his phone. "And I also took a brief call from Cameron."

"Ah." But of course Cameron would've called Derek. The two men had bonded over the discovery of a secret passage under the castle. "And what do you think?"

"Daphne and Duncan are here for two more days," Derek said. "We can hitch a ride to Inverness from them."

Daphne's family owned an airline company, and their planes flew for the British military. "Including my parents?"

He winked at my mother. "Naturally."

I spoke into my phone. "Did you hear all that?"

"Yes," Claire said, "and I'm beyond ecstatic."

"So, I guess we're flying to Scotland."

"Wonderful! Now, we can work out the logistics later, but I did want to pass on some details while I've got you on the phone."

I wasn't sure why, but there went that shiver across my shoulders again.

"What are those details?"

"Well, first, I'm hoping you can bring your bookbinding tools. I have a gift for Cameron that needs some refurbishing."

I smiled. "A book, I assume."

"Of course."

"That's no problem," I said, since I brought my tools with me whenever I traveled anywhere.

She hesitated, then added, "And second, I may need your help in solving a wee mystery in the castle library."

"Brooklyn does love a good library mystery," Mom said.

It was true, but still. "What's the mystery?" I asked.

"It seems we've a few books gone missing."

"A few missing books?" I said. "How many?"

"Um." Claire was hesitant, but then admitted, "Twelve."

Twelve books were missing? That was very specific. "Any idea what happened to them?"

Derek was more to the point. "And how do you know there are exactly *twelve* books missing?"

"Good question," she said with a smile in her voice. "I recently hired a part-time librarian to inventory and organize the books."

I hesitated, then asked, "Do you trust her?"

"Yes, of course. She works part time at the village library."

"So, she knows what she's doing."

There was the briefest hesitation, then she said, "Absolutely."

"Okay, good," I said, but wondered why she hesitated. Maybe I was imagining things. "That was smart of you to hire a professional librarian."

"It was your idea," she said brightly. "Remember?"

"Hmm. Vaguely."

"Very smart, darling," Derek said, grinning at me.

"Okay," I said. "If the books are still in the castle, I can try to track them down. Do you have titles?"

"Yes, of course," Claire said. She hesitated before adding, "Believe it or not, at least half of them are Christmas books."

I frowned. "Do you think that's why they were taken?"

"I have no idea."

"Are they simply missing? Or do you think they were stolen?"

"Honestly, I haven't a clue. But maybe you can look into it when you get here."

I mulled over that. "And some of them are Christmas books?"

"Yes. Isn't that fun?"

Fun? It would be more fun if they weren't missing, but I didn't say it aloud. Was Claire suffering from wedding-induced delirium? If half of the books were related to Christmas, I had to wonder who would steal them from the castle library. Maybe the Grinch was alive and well and living on a mountaintop nearby the tiny village of Oddlochen, Scotland.

One look at Derek's clenched jaw, and I knew he agreed with me.

"*Fun* wasn't the word I was thinking of," he said.

Claire chuckled. "Oh, I know. But I'm certain Brooklyn can solve the mystery."

"I'll do what I can," I said. "Are the books valuable?"

She hesitated again, then said, "Yes. Our copy of *A Christmas Carol* was recently valued at twenty-five thousand pounds."

"And it's one of the missing?"

"Yes."

I felt my stomach sink. "Can you e-mail me a list of the titles and any details you know about the books?"

Chances were, most of the books had already been sold to a collector, and we would never find them. *But we might find the thief*, I thought brightly, because I was a glass-half-full kind of girl.

We spoke for another minute, and I promised to call tomorrow with our flight information. We ended the phone call shortly after that.

"That's exciting, isn't it?" Mom said. "They're getting married! And you two were there right from the start."

"Yes, we were." I gazed at Derek and got the feeling we were both experiencing the same memories. Hunting down a missing person. Confronting a killer in the tower of the castle. Finding a dead body on the Clava Cairns. There were happier memories, but those were the ones that brought me back to Scotland.

"It'll be nice to see Claire again," Mom said. "And I'm looking forward to meeting her Laird."

"I'm so happy for them," I said, then rubbed my hands together and tried to think positively. "And I can't wait to track down all those missing books."

"Talk about a mystery," Mom said with a cheery smile. "And as we all know, any mystery that involves Brooklyn and books invariably ends in murder."

Derek's expression was suddenly as grim as I'd ever seen it.

And there went those shivers again.

Chapter 2

After some discussion, Derek, Mom, and I helped Ginny bundle a sleepy Charlotte up in a warm blanket, and while Derek carried the little one out to their car, I quickly packed two full meals, plus several desserts and plenty of extra appetizers, in some plastic containers for them to enjoy over the next few days. Mom gave Ginny a big hug and promised to call her tomorrow. Ginny meanwhile couldn't stop thanking us, but I felt like we were the ones who should've been thanking her for bringing us such a sweet little visitor on Christmas Eve. I knew that Charlie had enjoyed Charlotte's company, too. And we all promised to get together once we returned from Scotland.

It felt as if we'd been gone for an hour, but the time spent upstairs with little Charlotte and then the phone call with Claire had only taken about a half hour altogether. In that short time, though, our plans for the rest of the holiday had completely changed.

Derek and I were able to enjoy our friends and family and all that beautiful food that Savannah and her staff had prepared. Her restaurant had earned a Michelin star a few years ago, and her food was always fantastic, despite being a fully vegetarian menu. Somehow she made it so delectable and fabulous that even if you were a die-hard meat eater, you would love it. Everyone loved it. Tonight's meal was no exception.

It wasn't a formal sit-down affair. Everyone was welcome to graze all evening or fill their plates and enjoy the meal in one sitting. We could start with dessert and finish with soup, or any other way we chose.

Savannah started things off with an elaborate salad bar, and lucky for me, I loved salads. Especially when she included all the basic greens along with cold pasta salads, three different kinds of spring rolls, and an incredible potato salad.

After that, she served stuffed porcini mushrooms that melted in my mouth, followed by two kinds of soup: a creamy roasted butternut squash and a rich French onion soup served with lots of cheese melted over thick sourdough toast. The incredibly lush melted cheese reminded me to say a little prayer of thanks to the dairy gods that my vegetarian sister hadn't yet gone full vegan and still approved of goodies like cheese and ice cream.

The soups were followed by three of the most incredible pasta dishes I'd ever tasted. First came a thick, rich fettucine Alfredo; next, there was pasta with pesto and peas; and finally, orecchiette with mixed greens and goat cheese.

While some of us sat inside by the fire, other guests roamed and chatted and walked outside to stare at the stars. It was an incredibly clear night and the moon was full.

I had a brief chat with Robson Benedict, my parents' guru and the man who had lured them to the wine country all those years ago. He was a kind man and very quiet. Sometimes I didn't even realize he was standing right next to me.

"I understand you will be traveling to Scotland for a wedding soon."

I didn't exactly jump at the sound of his voice, but it was close.

"Oh, Robson." I patted my chest to calm myself down. The man really could sneak up on you if you weren't paying attention. Maybe that was the lesson he was trying to impart. *Pay attention.*

"Yes," I said. "My friend Claire and her fiancé Cameron are getting married. Do you remember meeting Claire?"

"Of course. She was quite experienced in the art and practice of weaponry."

"That's right."

He thought for a moment. "There were several unfortunate events that took place while she was here."

"Yes." *Murder is always unfortunate*, I thought. "Two men were after her. Both ended up getting killed."

He said nothing for a moment, just nodded slowly. "You will take care while visiting your friends. And you will be mindful of your parents."

"Absolutely," I assured him.

He smiled. "And you will have a wonderful time."

I smiled back at him, amused by his declaration. "I certainly hope so."

"Please convey my very best wishes to Claire and her fiancé."

"I will."

"And take care, dear one."

"Thank you, Robson. Merry Christmas."

He beamed at me and bowed his head slightly. Then he disappeared into the crowd of partygoers.

I gazed at his retreating back, knowing that many people would consider him odd. But I just simply loved the man.

. . .

*T*he next three days were filled with visits from family and friends, more Christmas dinners, and even more leftovers. There were several wine tastings, a bocce ball competition, and lots of football games on television, as always.

On the day before our flight, Derek and I drove back to San Francisco to retrieve our passports and pack for the trip to Scotland. Our friend Alex had also returned to town and had generously offered to take care of Charlie and keep an eye on our apartment. I had complete confidence in her abilities, both as a cat sitter and a house sitter, first because Charlie loved her, but more importantly because her résumé included her years as a CIA operative and she had a fifth-degree black belt in tae kwon do and Kenpo. She also taught Krav Maga and Brazilian jujitsu. Best of all, she was a master cupcake baker. If we were lucky, there would be cupcakes waiting for us when we got home.

While we were gone, Alex's gorgeous hunky boyfriend Gabriel, who also happened to be our very good friend, would be staying with her, so we would have two seriously awesome warriors watching over Charlie and our apartment.

The next afternoon, Gabriel drove us to a private terminal at San Francisco Airport, where we met Mom, Dad, Daphne, Duncan, and Daphne and Duncan's three ridiculously well-behaved children. We all boarded one of the family's well-appointed jets that would take us to Inverness.

Mom and Dad were clearly thrilled to be traveling in a deluxe private jet. "It's the only way to fly," Dad said, as he and Mom celebrated with vintage champagne.

On the long flight to Scotland, I had time to wrap a last-minute present for Cameron and Claire. It was a book, of course, a beautifully illustrated version of *The Twelve Days of Christmas* by the artist

David Delamare that I thought they would enjoy. I just hoped it wouldn't turn out to be a bittersweet reminder of the twelve library books that were lost. I was determined to hunt them down—if there was any chance that they were still somewhere in the castle.

With all of the holiday festivities, I had only done a few minutes of research on the list of books Claire had e-mailed me. But I happened to know that Castle MacKinnon had a strong Wi-Fi signal, so I'd be able to access all the information I would need from there.

I pulled the list out of my purse. It was an odd combination of books, some of them very short stories, some classics, some not-so-classics, and despite Claire's belief that half of them were Christmas related, I knew that, in fact, every one of them had a Christmas connection.

I read over the list a few more times and reminded myself of the plots and the main ideas. I had always been a voracious reader, but there were a few I'd never read before. It was easy enough to look up the basic plotlines in those cases. The books she listed were:

- *A Christmas Carol*
- *The Gift of the Magi*
- *The Little Match Girl*
- *A Christmas Memory*
- *Little Women*
- *A Christmas Story*
- *The Tailor of Gloucester*
- *Afterward: A Ghost Story for Christmas*
- *A Child's Christmas in Wales*
- *The Velveteen Rabbit*
- *How the Grinch Stole Christmas!*
- *The Greatest Gift*

I didn't expect to sleep on the plane, but staring at the list for a full hour did it for me. It was a big surprise and a relief to wake up and realize that I'd slept for five hours and that the plane was only a little less than sixty minutes from Inverness.

"Good morning, sleepyhead," Mom said, brushing my hair back from my face.

"Hi, Mom," I managed. "Were you able to sleep for a while?"

"I did and it was blissful." She stood in the aisle. "There's coffee. You want some?"

"Desperately," I whispered.

She walked to the galley at the back of the cabin, and I took the opportunity to rub my eyes and blink a couple of times to clear my vision. How was it that my mother could look so bright-eyed and ready to hit the ground running when I felt like a wrung-out dishrag?

And wasn't that an attractive image?

Mom returned with a coffee mug. "You'll love this coffee. It's dark and rich and strong."

"Mmm." I took hold of the mug and carefully sipped. "Ohhhh. Oh, yes. Thank you."

She smiled. "Good, huh?"

"It's heaven," I murmured, blowing softly on the liquid's surface.

She patted my shoulder. "The flight attendant said that the plane is about to make its final descent into Inverness."

"Thanks for the intel. I'll be ready."

She went back to her seat, and a few minutes later, Derek sat down beside me.

"You're awake," he said, and pressed a kiss to my temple.

I leaned my head against his shoulder. "What have you been doing?"

"Just chatting with Duncan and the pilot."

I sat up and studied his expression. "Everything okay?"

"I hope so. We were discussing football." He lowered his voice. "The pilot is a rabid Manchester City fan. There was a moment there when I worried that he and Duncan would come to blows."

When we discussed football with Derek's family, it was understood that we weren't talking American football. I was aware that Duncan was a die-hard Liverpool fan, although I had no clue if that was a good thing or not. "Surely the pilot knows better than to argue with his boss's husband."

He grinned. "His restraint was admirable."

The flight attendant moved down the aisle collecting our dishes, glasses, and utensils. She returned with a large plastic bag for any candy wrappers and potato chip bags we'd emptied during the flight. When she reached the front of the section, she said, "Ladies and gentlemen, we'll be landing in approximately twenty minutes, so kindly put away your tray tables, bring your seats to the upright position, and be sure your purses and backpacks are stowed safely under the seat in front of you." She gazed down at Daphne's youngest daughter. "And what else?"

"Buckle your seat belts!" the little girl cried.

"Very good, sweetie," Daphne said, patting her daughter's knee while flashing the flight attendant a grateful smile.

Looking out the window, I could see the beautiful blue water of Moray Firth up ahead on the right. The hills surrounding the Firth and the town of Inverness were brown because of the cold winter weather, but I didn't see any snow. And there were still some patches of green farmland as we approached the runway.

The town of Inverness took over the view with its homes and buildings spreading out in a wide arc. The next thing I knew, the plane had smoothly touched ground, and minutes later, we all stood on the tarmac.

It was a beautifully sunny day, and the air was as cold as I could ever remember. We all exchanged hugs and good wishes since Duncan and Daphne and the kids would soon be reboarding the plane and continuing on to Oxford. Two burly airport workers retrieved our luggage from the belly of the plane and loaded it into the back of an SUV limousine parked nearby.

"Thanks for ordering the limo," Dad said to Derek when we were all seated inside the spacious car. "This is nifty."

"Of course," Derek said. "I didn't think we'd want to deal with a crowded taxicab after a ten-hour plane ride."

"That plane ride was super deluxe," Mom said.

I had to agree. "Completely deluxe." On the drive to Oddlochen, I could've dozed off again, but the weather and the views were so beautiful that I couldn't look away. The highway ran along the River Ness, which soon widened to become Loch Ness. A thin layer of fog hovered over the water, and on the opposite side of the loch, dark pine forests covered the hillsides.

"It's stunning," Mom said in awe. "Every direction I look is picture perfect."

"How far to the castle?" Dad asked.

"About thirty miles," Derek said.

"We'll be there in no time, sir," Timothy the driver said.

"Jim, look," Mom said to Dad, and pointed to a rolling hillside dotted with woolly sheep. "Aren't they sweet?"

"They're probably cold." Dad grinned. "That reminds me, we should all buy sweaters while we're here."

I smiled, leaned against the window, and closed my eyes. "I don't know why I'm so sleepy."

Mom frowned. "I hope you're not coming down with something."

I sat up straight. "Absolutely not."

She glanced at Derek. "When she was younger, she would fall asleep when she was nervous about something."

"She still does," Derek said.

I scowled at both of them. "I do not."

Mom and Derek shared a wry look.

"Stop that, you two," I said.

Now they were grinning.

Maybe they were right to tease me. After all, the last time we visited Oddlochen, there was plenty of danger, including at least one murder and several attempts on my life.

I shrugged. "Okay, maybe I'm a little anxious about the missing books. And about the wedding."

Mom patted my shoulder. "Nothing bad is going to happen. We're going to a wedding! It's going to be lovely and happy and fun." She gazed more carefully at me, then reached up and rubbed my forehead—or more accurately, my third eye. "Om, shanti, shanti, shanti."

"I'm okay, Mom."

She flashed a determined smile. "And I'd like to make sure you stay that way."

I could hear her whispering the chant as I closed my eyes. I could hardly be mad at her when she was wishing me peace in mind, body, and spirit.

I knew that she and Claire had become close after my friend visited us earlier this year. Claire had lost her mother at an early age and Mom had taken her under her wing. I also knew that one of the items the two of them had chatted about were the various murders that had taken place while Claire and I had been together. I was pretty sure my mother would have contributed to the conversation by filling Claire in on all the murders that I'd been involved with in

San Francisco and Dharma over the past few years. It was disconcerting, to say the least. But at least Mom and Claire were bonding.

Glancing out the window, I could see clouds forming overhead. It looked as though it might rain.

I guess I had to admit, privately, that I was a little anxious about returning to the scene of several murders, but I would just have to get over it. If I freaked out over every murder scene I'd ever come across, I wouldn't be able to function. Which was to say, I seemed to come across quite a lot of murder scenes. It wasn't my fault; I just couldn't seem to help myself.

When Mom finished chanting, she said, "Hey, let's talk about the wedding. I still can't believe it's going to happen in a castle with a real live Laird."

That perked me up. "It's very exciting, isn't it? You met Claire, so you know she's wonderful, and Cameron is, well, he's very impressive. It's going to be a fabulous ceremony."

Derek nodded his agreement. "Cameron's a good man."

"Sounds like we'll have a blast," Dad said, always agreeable.

I had to smile. Mom liked to say that Dad resembled Jimmy Stewart in both looks and temperament: tall, good-looking, and relentlessly cheerful.

"We absolutely will," Mom agreed. "And don't forget, sweetie. We'd love a chance to visit the Clava Cairns if there's time."

"I haven't forgotten," I said. "I'll set it up for you. And I'm sure we'll all have plenty of time to do some other sightseeing while we're here."

"You weren't planning on going with them to the Cairns, were you?" Derek asked me. His tone was mild, but he looked concerned.

I appreciated his concern. The last time we'd visited the site, we'd discovered the body of a young woman, a member of Cameron's housekeeping staff who'd been brutally murdered.

Just remembering the sight of the young woman's body spread out on the rocks made my stomach lurch. I never wanted to go through that again.

"No, I won't be going with them." Still, I knew Mom would love it. The grounds were simply fascinating, with different types of burial sites from the Bronze Age spread across many acres. There were standing stones, pyramids, spirals, underground crypts, and so many other examples of entombments, Mom would be blown away. She would pick up all sorts of odd vibes out there and get a real kick out of it.

Dad always enjoyed watching Mom in her element. And knowing my father, I had no doubt that on the drive back, they would stop at one of the many pubs in the area to give Dad a chance to sample the local lager.

"I imagine Cameron can recommend a driver to take you there," Derek said. "It shouldn't be a problem."

"I'll leave my card with you, sir," Timothy the driver said. "Feel free to call me if you need transport."

"Thank you, Timothy," Derek said, grateful for the offer.

From the back seat, Dad patted the driver's shoulder. "Yeah, man, thanks a lot." Then he sat back, wrapped his arm around Mom, and gave her a little squeeze.

I knew I wouldn't have to worry about them. They always managed to have a good time wherever they went.

"Look, there's Loch Ness," I murmured, and Mom and Dad whipped around to watch as the massive body of water came into view.

"Oh," Mom whispered. The surface gleamed darkly against the cold blue of the winter sky. Off in the distance, on the western side of the loch, stood the imposing ruins of Urquhart Castle.

"What castle is that?" Mom asked.

"It's Urquhart Castle and 'tis one of our most famous sites," Timothy said proudly. "Its history is important to all Scotsmen."

"It's a magnificent site," Dad said.

"Beautiful," Mom agreed. "So stark against the horizon."

"We'll be sure to visit while we're here," I said.

"Oh, yes," Mom said. "I'd like to see it up close."

We chatted for another few minutes. Then glancing around, Mom said, "This loch is so big."

"Aye," Timothy said. "'Tisn't the biggest of our lochs, but it's the deepest, leaving lots of room down there for our Nessie."

"The monster," Dad said.

Mom grinned. "I hope we see her."

"With the winter weather upon us," Timothy said with a sigh, "she's taken to hiding. But come the spring, she'll likely show herself again."

The Loch Ness Monster, affectionately known as Nessie, was as famous as any human being who ever lived in this part of Scotland. There was even a theme park known as Nessieland, where tourists could cruise the Loch and hear the myths and legends of the monster. Afterward, you could shop for monster swag and dine at the Nessieland Restaurant. Or stop in at the bar, if you preferred.

We drove for a few more miles, and suddenly I sat up as Castle MacKinnon came into view. "Here we are."

"Ah," Mom whispered.

"Oh, hey." Dad broke into a big smile at the sight of the stunning castle, with its soft coral exterior and at least a dozen odd towers and turrets and gables.

We all stared at the imposing fortress that fronted the loch for a hundred yards or so. Its other three sides were surrounded by acres of evergreen woodlands. If you wandered in almost any direction, you would find woods and gardens of some kind or another: herb gardens and roses and a wonderful vegetable garden that fed the castle inhabitants and half the village. I thought it must be dormant right now with the winter weather.

Mom sighed. "It's like Sleeping Beauty's castle come to life."

A minute later, the car pulled into the wide circular drive and stopped in front of the tall, thick double doors that led into the castle. A few yards farther along was a six-car garage with apartments above it that had been built in the same whimsical style as the castle.

As we stepped down from the SUV, the front doors flew open and Claire rushed out to greet us. "You're here."

Cameron followed at a more sedate pace, but he looked equally pleased to see us. And more handsome than the last time I'd seen him, if that was possible. And more . . . elegant. More polished. Even in casual cargo pants, a thick fisherman's sweater, and old work boots, Cameron MacKinnon was an imposing sight. Perhaps the months he'd spent as Laird had raised his awareness of his position and his responsibilities. It looked good on him.

Claire grabbed me in a fierce hug. "I'm so happy. You look wonderful."

"I was about to say the same for you. You look beautiful." I held her at arm's length to take a good look at her. Her dark red hair was longer than it had been the last time I saw her. Her skin was clear and radiant, with happiness, I guessed. "You're glowing."

"Possibly from terror," she whispered. "I can't quite believe I'm attempting to pull off this outrageous event."

"But the terror is bringing roses to your cheeks," I said, making her laugh.

Cameron stepped forward and wrapped me in a big hug. "Marvelous to see you, Brooklyn. Thank you for coming."

"It's wonderful to see you, too," I said. "Both of you."

"Commander." Cameron reached out and gave Derek a hearty

handshake. "We're honored to have you visit and very pleased that you've consented to be a part of our wedding celebration."

"We wouldn't have missed it for anything," Derek said.

Seeing the two men together gave me a chance to compare and contrast. They were both over six feet tall, with Derek being an inch or two taller. Cameron was a bit more muscular, with thick arms and strong legs. He looked as though he could easily compete in the caber toss at the Highland Games. His hair was red but darker than Claire's, and he still wore the closely cropped beard he'd had since we'd all met the first time.

Needless to say, they were both seriously gorgeous men.

"We're thrilled to be included," I said, and reached for my mother's hand to pull her forward. "Cameron, allow me to introduce my parents, Becky and Jim Wainwright. Mom and Dad, this is Cameron MacKinnon, Laird of Castle MacKinnon."

"Ach," Cameron protested as he began to shake their hands. "We'll have none of that. Please call me Cameron."

"And you must call me Becky," Mom said, gripping his hand.

"And I'm Jim." Dad shook his hand. "Good to meet you, Cameron. Thanks for allowing us to invade your beautiful home."

"It's our pleasure," Cameron insisted, then pointed at the door. "Let's go inside and get out of the cold."

"Great idea," Dad said, and reached for one of the carry-on bags.

"I'll take care of that, sir," Timothy said quickly, already pulling out our luggage and stacking it next to the car.

Derek clutched his own satchel and slipped my heavy tote bag over his shoulder. "We're glad to lend a hand."

"Isna a problem, sir," Timothy protested. "Get the ladies out of the cauld, and I'll have yer bags inside in a jiffy."

"Thank you, Timothy," I said, but still managed to grab hold of my bookbinding tool case before being ushered inside.

We stepped into the massive central foyer, and I felt warmer instantly. The room smelled pleasantly of beeswax and the faintest hint of lemon. The marble floor was polished to a fine shine. I glanced up at the elaborate crystal chandelier hanging over the highly polished dark wood table that always held an exquisite flower arrangement. This time, there was a Christmas theme to the colors of the flowers, and a bright red-and-green tartan ribbon wound its way through the leaves and around the vase.

Beautifully painted porcelain figures were placed in front of the flower arrangement. I leaned in for a closer look and realized that each of the figures represented one verse of the song "The Twelve Days of Christmas." So far, there was a partridge in a pear tree, two turtledoves, three French hens, four calling birds, five gold rings, and six geese a-laying. It was the perfect accompaniment to the Christmas book I had brought for Claire and Cameron.

Tiny Christmas lights were strung along the crown molding of the high ceiling and draped at intervals like ribbons toward the plaster medallion that held the chandelier.

"How wonderfully festive," Mom declared, turning in a circle to take it all in.

An older woman stepped into the foyer from the dining room, and I couldn't help but smile.

"Mrs. Buchanan!" I gave her a light hug. "It's so good to see you."

"Brooklyn, dear, you're looking as smart and beautiful as ever." She gave my shoulders a quick pat.

"Thank you." I pointed to the figurines. "Are you the one responsible for this beautiful display of the twelve days of Christmas?"

"Guilty as charged," she said jovially. "We put one figure out each evening until Twelfth Night."

"It's charming," I said.

"We enjoy it," Mrs. B said. "'Tis a way to extend the Christmas holiday for as long as possible, so I hope you enjoy it, too."

"We will."

She turned to Derek with a more formal nod of her head. "Commander Stone, welcome back to Castle MacKinnon."

"Thank you, Mrs. B," he said, and surprised her with a hug. "It's lovely to see you again."

"Ah, well, my goodness." Her cheeks turned light pink and I couldn't blame her. She gave me a quick wink, then peered over my shoulder. "And these must be your parents."

"They are," I said. "Becky and Jim Wainwright, this is Mrs. Buchanan."

They all shook hands, and finally the housekeeper said, "Now, you must all call me Mrs. B. So much easier to remember."

Cameron added, "You'll soon learn that everything works better with Mrs. B in charge. If you need anything, you'll be wise to see her first, before any of the rest of us have a chance to muck it up."

"That's true," Claire said, laughing.

Mrs. B beamed with pleasure at the accolades, and I could see and feel the easy affection between the three of them. She turned to the young man standing just behind her and pulled him into the circle. "This is my nephew, Angus Buchanan. He came to work with us four months ago after a two-year course in hotel management in Switzerland. We're very proud of him."

"Ach now, Aunt," Angus said, beginning to blush at her words. He gave a slight bow in our direction. "How do you do?"

Cameron made the introductions.

"It's great to meet you," Dad said, and reached to shake Angus's hand.

Derek followed. "Good to meet you, Angus."

"Thank you, sir," the younger man said. He was in his mid-twenties, tall and thin, and his thick brown hair fell in a mop across his forehead. He was awfully cute.

But cute or not, the fact that he'd been living here for four months meant that he could've had plenty of time to pilfer a few books from the library. I hated to be so suspicious, but Claire had asked me to look for the books, and that meant I would be keeping an eye on young Angus.

"Very nice to meet you, Angus," Mom and I said in unison.

I gazed up at Cameron. "It's probably none of my business, but are you thinking of turning the castle into a hotel?"

He looked confused at first, then chuckled. "Because of Angus, you mean? No, absolutely not. But I'm considering leasing a few of the outer buildings to some of the local farmers. I might include some acreage if they can promise to grow sustainable crops and share a bit of it with the castle and the village. Angus has given me some interesting ideas."

The young man smiled broadly. "I took an ecological farming course a few years ago, before I went into hotel management. I like to be helpful."

"I imagine some of the farmers will take you up on that offer," Dad said to Cameron, then turned to Angus. "I'd like to hear some of those ideas of yours. I grow a few crops myself, you know."

I had to laugh at Dad's description of our vineyards. "We grow grapes. For wine."

Cameron chuckled. "I understand you have a beautiful winery and thousands of acres of vineyards."

Dad grinned. "It's true."

"We do hope you'll come and visit someday," Derek said.

"That would be wonderful," Claire said, gazing up at Cameron.

"And I'd be honored to share my meager knowledge with you, sir," Angus said.

"We'll talk," Dad said amiably.

And I knew he would make a point of sitting down with Angus to chat about such things.

Mrs. B happily changed the subject. "Now, Cameron and Claire want to take you to the pub tonight, but that won't be for another two hours or so. I thought you all might care for a light nibble before I show you to your rooms."

"A nibble, Mrs. B?" Cameron teased her. "Not a formal tea?"

"There will be tea, but it won't be formal," she said primly, slanting a look at him. "Tea and some savory snacks to tide you over before you unpack your bags and then take your trek into the village."

"It all sounds wonderful," Mom said.

"It sure does." I could feel my own stomach starting to growl. I was familiar with Mrs. B's idea of "snacks" and knew that we wouldn't starve—far from it.

"If tea isn't to your liking," Cameron said, "I've a local IPA that you might enjoy."

"Now that sounds right up my alley," Dad said.

"Then let's proceed to the blue parlor," Cameron said jovially, taking hold of Claire's hand. They led the way through the foyer and turned left at a wide hallway.

I started to follow the others but was distracted by a movement behind me. Our luggage had been piled near the main staircase that led up to our rooms. Mrs. B's nephew, Angus, was standing by the luggage, turning over the baggage tags. To see who they belonged to? But why? Simple curiosity? Or something more sinister?

But again, why? And why did I always attach an ominous motive to the most innocent acts? "Everything all right?" I asked.

Angus looked up, saw me staring, and grinned. "I'm to carry your luggage up to your rooms, and I'm trying to figure out whose goes where. But while I was checking the tags, it occurred to me that American penmanship is most fascinating."

I smiled. "I suppose we might find yours equally fascinating."

He chuckled. "Indeed."

"If you're not sure which goes in which room, you might just leave it outside the door, and we'll sort it out."

"I'm determined to get it right, but just in case I'm stymied, I'll do as you say. Thank you."

I walked away, wondering if I was being paranoid for suspecting foul play. Well, yes, of course I was. But I couldn't help myself. Paranoia was ingrained in my psyche after years of being confronted by various suspicious characters.

I sighed, hating this feeling. I really could use that beer. Continuing down to the end of the foyer, I stopped and stared at the closed door that I knew led to the library.

I walked to the door and grabbed the knob. It was locked. Disappointed, I figured I would just have to wait until Claire had a moment to open the door for me. I really wanted to get to work solving the puzzle of the missing books.

"Is it still locked, then?"

I turned at the sound of the voice behind me. "Yes."

"Och," the young man said, and his shoulders slumped. "I'll come back later." He turned to walk away, then stopped. "Beg your pardon, ma'am. I'm Willy, a friend of Angus's, and also a friend of Olivia, the librarian. Would you be the Yanks coming for the wedding?"

I smiled. He was young and so good-looking, I almost did a double take. His black hair was combed back, and he was twice as cute as Keanu Reeves. "Yes, my name is Brooklyn. My husband Derek and I have just arrived from San Francisco."

"Yaldi!" he said. "We've been champing at the bit for your arrival."

"Yaldi?" I said.

"Sorry. It means, 'We're very excited.'"

"Oh, that's nice. Thanks. We're happy to be here."

"Well, I'll be off, then. Enjoy your day. Bye."

"Bye, Willy." I watched him walk down the hall, then he picked up speed and ran for the front door.

"Perhaps the librarian is on a break," Derek suggested. "She might show up at any minute."

I smiled up at him. "If she knows Willy is waiting for her, she'll be here."

He raised one eyebrow and I had to laugh. But my good humor fell as I stared at the locked door.

I recalled how dusty and disorganized the room had looked last time, but now Claire had hired her friend Olivia, who had apparently organized everything. I wanted to see how it looked. I also wanted to meet Olivia. After all, the twelve books had gone missing on her watch. Not that Claire would blame her, but I might. Not right away, of course. I would wait to see if she deserved to be blamed. For now, I would refrain from judging her.

I almost laughed. What was wrong with me? I was seeing suspicion and fault everywhere I looked.

"What are you thinking, darling?" Derek asked quietly, as if he didn't know.

"I'm going to ask Claire to unlock the door so I can take a quick look inside the library." I frowned at him. "Why would they lock the library?"

"They've already lost twelve books, several that seem quite valuable," he reasoned. "Perhaps they'd rather not lose any others."

"Of course not," I whispered. "But do you think they suspect someone from inside the castle?"

"I have no idea. But I doubt it. We both know that Mrs. B leaves the kitchen door unlocked during the day. Anyone from the village can wander inside, pick up a book, and walk right out. They probably wouldn't think anything of it."

"But twelve books?" I said. "And by the way, after looking at the list Claire sent me, I realize that all of them have Christmas themes. What's that all about?"

"I didn't say it made sense," he said.

I thought about it for a moment. "Actually, it does make a strange sort of sense. Someone in the village could be presenting a Christmas-themed reading program. Maybe they thought nothing of walking into the castle and taking some books for that purpose."

"Maybe." But now he looked doubtful, too.

I supposed it made as much sense as anything else. Meaning it made no sense at all.

I glanced down the hall toward the blue parlor. Claire and Cameron had already gone inside, and it appeared that Mom and Dad had followed them, too.

"Let's go get the key from Claire," Derek said.

"My partner in crime." I smiled. "Thanks."

"Let's try to avoid any reference to crime," he said. "But I know you won't be satisfied until you can take a look inside."

"Right you are."

We headed for the blue parlor, but as we passed the great hall on our left, we had to stop. "Wow. It looks amazing."

"This is Claire's doing, obviously," Derek said. "It's quite impressive."

"It's definitely Claire's work," I said. "She really pulled it together." Like so many rooms in the castle, the great hall had been a jumbled mess the first time we saw it. Now it was beautifully organized and smart looking. I was so proud of my friend.

Many of the castle's historically significant weapons—the broadswords, spears, longbows, and swords—were now tastefully displayed along two walls. The smaller weapons—the daggers, stilettos, and dirks—were neatly lined up inside six glass cabinets. Elaborate descriptions of each item were written on cards and placed next to the item. The lighting was subtle, with individual pinspots highlighting each weapon. It looked like a very well-organized museum.

Claire and I had met a few years ago on *This Old Attic*, the popular television show that traveled around the country and featured local people who brought family antiques to be appraised on camera. When the show came to San Francisco, I had been hired to evaluate the antiquarian books that people brought to the show. Claire's field of knowledge, of course, was antique weaponry.

The main reason Cameron had invited Claire to live at the castle was to organize the vast weaponry collection that had been moldering in the cellars for the past century or two. She was an expert on the subject, after all.

When I heard they were getting married, I was absolutely thrilled—but not surprised. I had seen the attraction from the very first moment Cameron met Claire. And it didn't have anything to do with her expertise in weaponry. Although, that was the perfect excuse for Cameron to ask her to move into the castle.

The great hall, despite the weaponry, looked festive with sparkly Christmas lights wrapped around the heavy wooden beams and the wide circular lighting fixtures. In one corner was a gigantic Christmas tree, at least twelve feet tall, decorated with dozens of tiny colorful lights and hundreds of delicate glass ornaments.

The massive open fireplace, big enough to roast an entire ox inside its walls, now held the largest poinsettia plant I'd ever seen, its gleaming red leaves brightening the cavernous space. The mantel was festooned with holly leaves and evergreen boughs and more of the tiny colorful lights.

"Isn't this beautiful?" Mom whispered. She'd popped out from the blue parlor to join us in front of the great hall. "Did Claire have a hand in arranging all of these weapons?"

"Yes," I said. "And she outdid herself."

"She sure did." Mom slipped her arm around mine. "Come join us in the blue parlor. It's a beautiful room, and you've got to see the light reflecting off the loch. It's spectacular."

We walked down the hall and into the blue parlor. I knew there were a number of sitting rooms—or parlors—in the castle, and they were each delineated by color. The room was as I remembered, large and bright with several picture windows and an amazing view of Loch Ness. The walls were painted a pretty cornflower blue, and the elaborate window treatments came close to matching the shade. The comfortable furniture was arranged to accommodate several different conversation groupings, and in the corner was a full bar with six stools.

Mrs. B had worked her Christmas magic in here, too. Delicate cutout snowmen and snowflakes hung from the lighting fixtures, and tiny white lights outlined each of the windows, as well as the elegant mirror behind the bar.

"There you are," Claire said.

"We were admiring your work in the weapons hall," Derek said. "It's quite impressive."

"Thank you, Derek," Claire said. "I'm very proud of it."

"And so am I," Cameron said, his gaze focused on his fiancée.

"Very smart of you to marry a weapons expert," I teased.

Cameron grinned. "I'm a smart man." He leaned closer. "We're currently debating whether to open the great hall to the entire town."

"How do you feel about that?" I asked.

"The jury's still out, although we've already opened the library to the public." He took a sip from the bottle of beer he held. "For now, though, our biggest decision is whether to be married in the great hall or the dungeon."

I stared at him, then glanced at Claire. "He's kidding, right?"

She sniffed. "I happen to think the great hall is the perfect setting, despite the weaponry. There's plenty of room for everyone, and it's right down the hall from the kitchen, which makes it convenient for the servers." Her eyes narrowed on him. "The dungeon is not up for discussion."

"I should think you'd feel nostalgic about the old jail cell since it's where we discovered a certain beloved relative of yours."

"I do love it for that reason alone, but nevertheless . . ." Claire rolled her eyes. "He's teasing me, obviously."

I laughed. The very idea was crazy. Derek and I had been here when that relative of hers was discovered, after hiding out in the castle dungeon to evade capture by some local evildoers. In the end, we had all been confronted by one of those same evildoers, and Claire's weapons expertise had saved the day.

I decided to change the subject. "By the way, Claire, the library door is locked. I was hoping to take a quick peek inside, if you have the key."

She cleared her throat self-consciously. "I'm afraid I gave my key to Olivia, so we'll have to wait until tomorrow morning when she comes to work."

I studied her expression. "Olivia has the only key?"

"Yes." She smiled weakly. "She's quite protective of her space."

I looked at Derek and saw that he was wondering the same thing I was: Twelve books had gone missing on her watch. Just how protective had she been?

Claire's expression lightened. "But wait till you see the library, Brooklyn. It's completely reorganized and clean as can be, thanks to Olivia."

"I'm looking forward to seeing it. And meeting Olivia."

"She's interesting," Claire said. "I hope you'll like her."

"I'm sure I will. Especially because she obviously loves books." And yet, I really wasn't sure I would like her, although I didn't say it aloud. I didn't like the fact that Olivia alone controlled the key to the library. Apparently she held a proprietary interest in the room, which was just weird since the books belonged to the Laird and the library was inside a private home. But I couldn't talk to Claire about it, not yet. I didn't want to upset her with my suspicions after only being here an hour or so. I'd give her time. And I'd give myself time. Maybe I was wrong. Maybe I'd jumped to the wrong conclusion. It happened.

But I did know that two generations of MacKinnon Lairds had neglected the castle and, in some cases, had plundered some of its many riches, including books. Now twelve valuable books were missing, so something was clearly off. Still, I couldn't do anything about it today. I took a deep breath, let it go, and decided the locked library door wasn't that big of a deal. I would simply wait until tomorrow.

But tomorrow I would act on my own proprietary interests, the ones I had felt months ago when I entered the castle library for the first time. Cameron had just become the new Laird, and the entire castle was in dire need of a good cleaning. Many of the rooms had been badly neglected; some needed a new coat of paint, floors sanded and varnished, windows replaced. The library mainly needed sweeping and dusting and polishing. The books had to be inventoried and reorganized. I had offered to clean it up, but at the time, Cameron hadn't considered it the highest priority. Nevertheless, I insisted on taking a few badly treated books home with me to refurbish before sending them back to Claire.

Claire could tell I was troubled by the locked library door and tried to cajole me. "Brooklyn, you've got to try some of our chef's holiday treats."

"Are they similar to Mrs. B's nibbles?"

She grinned. "Yes, and you'll adore them all."

She lured me over to the bar, where Mrs. B had placed a large platter of wonderful-looking pastries. And, yes, there were nibbles as well.

"We have a lovely new chef in the kitchen," Claire said. "She made the holiday pastries and put together this spread for all of us."

"Everything looks and smells delicious," Mom said. "Come see, Brooklyn. They're little Christmas trees."

"And your chef made these?" I wondered.

"Yes," Claire said enthusiastically. "Aren't they sweet?"

"They're beautiful."

"She's an astonishingly good baker as well as a cook," Cameron said, already halfway through his first Christmas tree.

I reached for a puff pastry Christmas tree and bit off the powdered sugar star. "Wow."

"Isn't it yummy?" Mom asked.

"The puff pastry is baked to perfection," I said. "The wiggly tree part is smothered in cinnamon sugar, which I can't get enough of."

Thanks to a hard chocolate square that worked as a tree stand, the little trees stood up and stayed in place.

"It just may be the perfect food," Mom said.

"It absolutely is," I said with a laugh as I nibbled the rest of the Christmas tree.

"She makes them savory, too," Claire said.

"Wait," I said. "What?"

"The other tray is all savory goodies."

"Oh, I like the sound of that," Mom said, moving to the coffee table, where she reached for one of the savory trees.

Claire was clearly pleased that we were so excited. "It's made with goat cheese, sun-dried tomato pesto, garlic, and oregano, among other ingredients."

I stared at Mom. Unlike me, she was a really good cook. "Why haven't you made these?"

"I've never even heard of them." She bit off the top half of the tree. "But I plan on making them from now on. Delicious."

"You won't hear me complain," Dad said, and popped another one into his mouth.

"The recipe is all over the Internet this season," Claire said. "But we all come to them in our own time."

Mom smiled at her. "Isn't that the truth?"

"Now, since I don't want to spoil my dinner," I said, "I'm only having two more."

"She's very strong-willed," Mom said, winking at Claire.

I shrugged. "I remember the food at the pub, so I have to save room."

Claire checked her wristwatch. "We'll leave for the pub in about two hours, while it's still light out. I'd like to drive through the village so you can see our little town."

"Wonderful idea," Mom said.

"Does that give you all enough time to unpack and get settled in your rooms?"

"Works for me," Dad said jovially. "I'm all about the early bird special these days."

I had to smile at that. So, for now, I would try to relax and enjoy the moment. Tomorrow I would meet Olivia, get a good look at the library, and try to solve the weird mystery of the missing books. But even as I thought it, I still considered it odd that the woman in charge of the castle library had taken the key with her. I hoped I could talk Claire into turning the key over to me for as long as we were here. After all, if she wanted me to figure out the puzzle of the missing books, I would need to have full control of the crime scene.

And mentally uttering these thoughts made me shake my head. Me? Full control? Over the crime scene? It was just some missing books!

My good friend Detective Inspector Janice Lee back in San Francisco would probably say, "You need to chill out, girl." And she'd follow that up with a swift kick in the butt on general principle.

Chapter 3

"We've given you the same rooms here in the east wing that you had the last time," Claire said, opening the door to our room.

"Wonderful," I said, and we stepped inside the room. Mom and Dad were right next door, so I felt good about that.

Across the wide hallway from our doors stood a nine-foot Christmas tree decorated in a few hundred vintage ornaments, strings of twinkling multicolored lights, and sparkly gold bands of garland.

Delighted, I said, "We have our own Christmas tree."

"We thought you'd enjoy it," Claire said.

"We will, all of us," I said. "Everything is perfect."

"And this is a lovely suite," Derek agreed.

And as promised, our luggage sat neatly inside the door.

I walked over to the wide picture window with a table and two chairs placed in front of it. "I remember this amazing view of the loch. And this table is perfect for my work."

"I'm so glad." Claire glanced around to make sure the three of us were alone, then she pulled a small volume from under her shirt. "This is the book I want to give Cameron. I hope you can repair it."

She handed it to me and I glanced at the spine. The title of the book was *The Merry Muses of Caledonia*. Since I'd never heard of it before, I opened the book and turned to the title page where I found this subtitle: *A Choice Collection of Songs Gathered from Many Sources. By* Robert Burns.

"Robert Burns," I murmured. "How perfect."

There was an additional subtitle that read, *To which are added two of his Letters and a Poem—hitherto suppressed—never before reprinted.*

It made me smile. "This is so cool."

"And I'm quite certain Cameron doesn't have a copy," she said.

"Then that makes it doubly cool." I closed the book and studied the front cover for another moment. It was slim, about a half inch thick, and approximately eight inches tall by five inches wide. It was covered in three-quarter burgundy morocco leather, which meant that the leather wrapped around the spine to about halfway across the front and back, then each corner was covered with the same leather for a triangle effect. The remaining sections were covered in high-quality burgundy cloth. Those triangles were decorative as well as protective since the corners of books tended to take a lot of abuse.

I looked up. "It's a sweet book."

"I'm not sure how sweet it is," Claire said dryly. "If you noticed that line on the title page, it explains that the book is 'Not for Maids, Ministers, or Striplings.'"

I laughed. "Now that's the Robbie Burns we all know and love." I stared at the spine with its elegantly gilded letters. That section wouldn't need any repairing. "It's very handsome, isn't it?"

"I think so," Claire said. "I know Cameron will love it. It's his favorite author, after all."

I turned the book over to examine the back cover. "Oh. Ouch." This is where the damage had occurred. It had a badly dented top corner and serious scuff marks on the leather.

I opened my tool kit and pulled out my magnifying glass to study the destruction up close. Not just scuff marks, I realized, but there were actual thin gouges cut into the corner leather piece. "Ugh." I wondered how it had happened.

Claire's expression turned to borderline panic. "Can you fix it? Because if you can't fix it, I'll have to—"

"Of course I can fix it." I continued to stare through my magnifying glass at the dented corner. "I didn't mean to freak you out. The front is pristine, so I wasn't expecting to see the damage in the back. But no worries. The damage is concentrated in this one section. I can definitely fix it." I smiled at her. "It's what I do."

Claire slid down into a chair and blew out a breath. "All right. Good. Sorry to be such a twit."

I patted her shoulder. "I've been a twit once or twice myself, so I know what that looks like. You're not being a twit."

She chuckled weakly. "Thank you."

Derek stepped closer. "May I see the book?"

"Of course," I said, and handed it to him.

After taking a minute to check out the problem area, he smiled at Claire. "Do you know how it happened?"

Her cheeks reddened, and she had to take a long breath in and out. "I'm so mortified. I bought the book at Gwyneth's shop last month, and as I was walking back to my car, a hard glass object came flying out of a doorway right toward me."

"How awful!" I said.

"Yes, it was awful and it took me by surprise. I wasn't thinking straight, but I immediately managed to hold the book up to protect my face."

"That was fast thinking," Derek murmured. "What happened?"

"The glass hit the book and fell on the ground. It broke, of course. And I was in such a frantic state, I dropped the book right onto the broken glass. When I picked it up, I accidentally scraped it across the jagged edges." She scowled. "I felt like such a radge. Cut my finger, too, when I was picking up the glass pieces."

"You must've been frightened to death," I said. "But what's a radge?"

"Oh, well, it's rather beyond an idiot," she explained.

"Do you know who threw the glass?" Derek asked, getting more to the point.

"I've no idea." She exhaled slowly. "I didn't see anyone and finally decided it must've been a freak accident."

"Of course it was," I said. But looking at Derek, I could tell he had second thoughts. And I did, too.

"Which of the shops was it thrown from?" he persisted.

"I can't be certain because it truly caught me by surprise. But I think it came from a place two doors down from Aunt Gwyneth's. It's changed hands a few times over the past few years, but right now it's a Pilates studio. They do yoga as well. Very posh."

Derek nodded and set the book down on the table. "However the damage occurred, Brooklyn can fix this."

I smiled at Claire. "See?"

She looked from Derek to me. "You're both so wonderful. I'm awfully glad you're here."

"We're glad to be here, too," Derek said.

"I'll work on the book tomorrow," I said. "It should only take me a few hours."

"Are you sure?" Claire asked. "Do you have all the supplies you need?"

"Yes. In fact, I've got a piece of burgundy morocco leather that might match almost perfectly. And I always travel with my tools and supplies, of course."

"I'm very grateful," Claire said.

"We're just happy to be here. And it's wonderful to see you and Cameron again."

Claire stood and gave me a hug. "I'll let you get settled. If there's anything you need . . ."

Derek smiled slyly. "We'll call Mrs. B."

Claire laughed. "Exactly. Oh, wait. Almost forgot." She pulled two keys from her pocket and handed them to us. They both had a pretty piece of blue ribbon attached to them for easy carrying.

"We rarely lock our doors," she said, "but there will be dozens of outsiders visiting this week for the wedding, so to be on the safe side, I would recommend it."

"Thank you," I said.

"Of course." She walked to the door, turned, and thanked us once more. "I'll see you downstairs in a bit."

"See you," I said, then closed the door and turned to Derek. "We'll check out the Pilates studio before we go to the pub."

He raised one eyebrow. "We?"

I smiled. "If you walk into that Pilates studio by yourself, I can't be responsible for what happens to you."

"Darling, there are plenty of men who take Pilates. But I'm willing to concede that you may have a point."

"Thank you." I laughed and changed the subject. "Now, since we know what Claire's giving Cameron as a wedding gift, do you know what Cameron's planning to give Claire?"

"No. And if I did, I wouldn't tell you." He began to unpack, first strolling to the closet to hang up the suit he would wear to the wedding. "There are rules about these things."

"Are there now?"

"Yes indeed."

"I thought the rule was that you told me everything all the time."

He laughed but quickly sobered. "I'm Cameron's best man. I owe all my allegiance to him."

I wrapped my arms around his waist. "All your allegiance?"

"Well, at least when it comes to his wedding gift."

"Ah." I smiled up at him. "I'm glad I found that out before I told you any of Claire's secrets."

His lips twisted into a smirk. "Claire is rather more open about her secrets."

"That's true. And very unfair."

"Not to worry, love." He pulled me closer and slowly ran his hands up and down my back. "In two days, we'll know exactly what each of them is giving the other."

I rested my head on his chest and closed my eyes. "Good point." I suddenly wanted more than anything to give in to the need to take a nap. But we didn't have time. I yawned, then stepped back from him. "I'd better wash my face and wake myself up if I want to last through the evening."

He stared into my eyes. "Are you still anxious about the missing books?"

I didn't like being so transparent, but this was Derek, after all. "Of course. But I'm also pretty flipped out about this thing that happened to Claire."

"So am I," he said.

"But you were right the first time. That locked library door is disturbing. And so is the fact that Claire gave Olivia the one key that opens the door. I don't like it, mainly because I don't know the woman and I'm not sure I trust her."

"Why would you? The library is this woman's domain, and these books have gone missing on her watch."

I smiled. "I know what will ease my anxiety."

"I'm afraid to ask."

"I'll just toss an axe around tonight."

He stared at me with concern. "Perhaps we ought to stay here and grab something from the kitchen."

I laughed. "I was sort of kidding."

"I wasn't."

The last time we'd visited, we threw axes in the back room of the pub. It was great fun and I actually got pretty good at it. "Seriously, though, don't you find it weird?" I asked. "The fact that twelve valuable books are missing, and the person in charge of those missing books is the only one holding the key?" I gazed up at him. "I'm not sure what Claire was thinking."

Derek thought about it. "It's possible she wasn't really thinking at all. She has quite a bit on her mind, including her wedding preparations and her out-of-town guests. And apparently half the village is showing up to help celebrate the nuptials. Perhaps handing the library duties over to someone else was the best way for her to deal with it. And surely it's only a temporary situation."

"I hope so."

"And another thing," he added. "You, of all people, should have complete confidence in anyone who works as a librarian."

"You're right about that." I smiled up at him. "In fact, I'm going to go with that theory. I'm tired of worrying about it."

"Good. Maybe you'll be able to enjoy the evening."

"That's the plan."

"And if you're tired and want to leave earlier than the others, we can always walk home."

"True." Although the thought of walking through the freezing cold dark woods was not appealing at all. But I could do it if I had to.

When Cameron parked the car and led the way to the pub, Derek and I told the others we would meet them there shortly. Then we took a quick trip up the high street to take a look at the shop Claire had described. The Pilates and yoga studio also offered various types of massage, including deep tissue massage and shiatsu, according to the sign above the wide plate glass window. Once a week they offered acupuncture and cupping therapy.

Derek and I stepped inside the studio. Bamboo curtains hung halfway down the window, allowing passersby to partially observe the classes in session. On one side of the studio was a hardwood floor with room for at least six clients doing floor work. The other side held two of the Pilates Reformer machines. In the far corner was a desk and two chairs, and there were more chairs scattered along the walls. It was fairly typical of other Pilates studios I'd been in. There were two doors along the back wall. One said MASSAGE and the other said EXIT.

I wondered if whoever threw the glass object at Claire had escaped through that exit door.

A woman seated at the desk approached us. "May I help you?"

Derek smiled. "I see that you offer cupping therapy."

She smiled brightly. "We do. I can make an appointment for you, or you can call our office anytime."

"Thank you. I'll call."

She nodded and walked back to her desk.

Derek snuck a few photos with his phone, then we walked down to the pub to join the others.

I grabbed his arm. "Those cups they use for that therapy are often made of heavy glass."

"Yes, they are," he said.

"I'll bet they could really pack a wallop."

"My thought exactly," he murmured.

When we walked into the pub a few minutes later, it looked as though everyone in Oddlochen might be into the early bird special, just like Dad. The place was packed even though it was barely five o'clock at night.

The music was lively and every seat at the bar was filled. Despite the line at the door, Cameron and the rest of our party were already seated in a wide comfortable booth. I wondered if the Laird always got a primo booth or if we just lucked out. It was the perfect spot to observe the entire restaurant, the bar, and the bartender, Claire's best friend Sophie.

"There's Sophie!" I said, recalling that her parents owned the pub.

"I let her know we were coming," Claire said. "She'll try to join us for a few minutes."

I managed to make eye contact and waved at Sophie. She immediately returned my wave and smiled happily. "I'd love to introduce her to my parents," I said to Claire as I watched the woman work. "How's she doing?"

"She's doing fine," Claire said, pronouncing it more like *Shay's daein fain*. Her brogue had thickened just by stepping into the pub. "If she's too busy to talk tonight, we'll see her tomorrow when she comes to the castle."

"That works for me."

When our waitress arrived at the table, Cameron recommended another local IPA, and since Claire approved of it, too, we all ordered a pint. Cameron, Derek, and Dad added a shot of whiskey—a "wee dram"—to their orders, and we settled into studying the menus.

After we put in our dinner order and our drinks arrived, the men began the inevitable discussion of which single malt Scotches were the best while Claire, Mom, and I began to check out the crowd. Claire knew almost everyone in town and pointed out a few key people to us. "The blonde in the corner booth is an old friend of Cameron's."

"An old friend or an old *girl*friend?" I asked, thinking he must have legions.

"Actually." Claire lowered her voice. "He claims he didn't date a lot growing up. Seems his father, the old Laird, warned him about dating the local girls."

"Interesting advice," Mom said, then turned to check out the blonde. "She's pretty enough. But she's got a rough edge."

"What do you mean, Becky?" Claire asked.

"She's not soft," Mom explained. "She's, um, a tough cookie."

"I think I know what you mean." Claire frowned and added, "She doesn't like me."

"Of course not," Mom said.

I laughed. "You're lovely and kind and smart, and you won the grand prize. She lost."

"You mean Cameron?" she whispered.

Mom nodded. "Exactly."

Claire glanced at Cameron, then shook her head in resignation. "He is quite a prize. And I'm fairly certain several of the ladies around town would've liked to have won him instead of me."

"That's human nature," Mom said philosophically.

I leaned in closer. "Do you think the glass thrower is one of those ladies?"

"I don't know." She took a furtive glance at Cameron, who was deep in conversation with Dad and Derek. "That's what Sophie thinks, but I can't imagine it."

"Imagine it," Mom said briskly. "It has to be one of them."

I glanced around. "Who's the cutie flirting with Sophie?"

"Ah." Now she grinned. "That's Gregory James. He's the vicar at St. Tristan's."

Mom and I stared at the tall, well-built, sandy-haired man in his late thirties enjoying a pale ale and laughing with Sophie and a couple of men sitting nearby.

"The vicar," Mom said. As a huge fan of British mysteries, she was clearly intrigued. "He's very handsome."

As we watched, Sophie set a dinner plate down in front of the vicar. He beamed at her and grabbed her hand to thank her. Sophie laughed at something he said, and he let go of her hand.

"He's a bit of a flirt," Mom declared.

"He likes Sophie," I said.

"Everybody likes Sophie," Claire said with affection.

"Does everybody like the vicar?" Mom asked.

"Aye, he's a lovely man," Claire said. "We'll go say hello to him later."

"Which church is his?" I asked.

"It's the one on the hill with the white steeple."

"I saw that one on the drive over. It's so pretty," Mom said. "Very charming."

"Isn't it?" Claire nodded. "That's the church we go to. They just had a rummage sale, and we donated a number of items we found in the cellar. Aunt Gwyneth was in charge of the donations."

"You must've found a lot of good stuff to sell."

"We did," Claire said. "Mostly clothing, but also a few interesting pieces, including an entire set of dinnerware that Cameron swears he's never seen before."

"It must be old if he's never seen it," Mom said.

"One of the ladies working at the auction thought it might be World War II vintage."

Mom nodded. "I hope they got a good price for it."

I took a sip of beer, and my gaze wandered over to the bar. "Sophie looks swamped."

Claire frowned. "Yes. Well, as I said, if we don't talk tonight, she'll come over tomorrow. She's my wedding planner. Did I tell you that?"

"You did," I said.

"She must be a miracle worker," Mom said.

"She is that," Claire said. "And she has a lot of good ideas for ways to streamline things. We're inviting everyone in the village, but she insisted that we didn't have to send out invitations. Instead, whenever someone walks into the pub, she hands them a card with the time and date and tells them to spread the word and wear something fancy."

I laughed. "That's one way to get the word out."

"Everyone must go to the pub at some point during the week, and everyone knows Sophie." She sipped her lager. "We don't need gifts. We just want people to show up and be happy for us. Everything else is being handled by Mrs. B and her housekeeping staff. Flowers, decorating. And of course, Tamara will take care of the food and the cake."

"It'll have to be a huge cake."

"It will be. And she and her team are making hundreds of biscuits, too. Or cookies, as you say in the States." She chuckled. "Cameron really likes cookies."

"Who doesn't?" Mom said. "And Tamara's your chef, I assume."

"Yes. She's wonderful."

"If those little Christmas tree pastries are any indication of her abilities, then I agree," Mom said.

"Do you have your dress?" I asked.

"Yes, and it's so pretty." Her smile grew misty. "It was my mother's. Aunt Gwyneth saved it for me."

"How thoughtful of her," Mom said. "That's very sweet."

"There was a veil that went with it, but we can't find it." She shrugged. "But that's okay."

"Is there anything else I can do to help you prepare?" I asked.

Claire gave me a shy smile. "Just fix Cameron's book."

I patted her hand. "I'm on it."

"Thank you." She looked a little dazed. "Am I crazy?"

"Of course not," I said, then flashed a smile. "Well, maybe just a little. But it makes you more intriguing."

That forced a laugh out of her. "If I'm crazy, then so are you."

"Oh, absolutely."

At that moment, I noticed a young man waiting by the hostess stand and waved. "It's Angus."

Angus waved back, and he and another fellow walked over to our table. I recognized him from earlier. The one who wanted to get into the library. "Hello. This is my good mate, Willy Smith."

"Hello, Willy," I said, and everyone chimed in.

"Willy's helping me with the gardening and fieldwork at the castle."

"That's great," I said. "Did you grow up here in Oddlochen, Willy?"

"Aye," he said. "Yes, ma'am."

"So, you must know everyone in the village."

"I do. I know most everyone." He shoved his hands into his pockets. "My father owns a fishing boat, and I grew up near the loch."

"I got to go fishing with them every summer," Angus said. "It was a belter, aye."

"Aye," Willy said. "We'll do it again when the weather turns."

"So, you still work on your father's boat?" Derek asked.

"I went to the agriculture school in Ayr, so I'm splitting my time now."

"Right now he's working for Cameron," Angus explained. "He's helping me clear out the acreage beyond the outbuildings."

"And gathering up extra wood for the bonfire," Willy added.

"We'll be working with Cameron, building the bonfire," Angus said.

"Willy's a good worker." Cameron smiled.

"Aye, he is." Angus gave him an elbow in his side, and Willy faked a punch.

Cameron glanced at my father. "I'd like to put them both to work, turning that acreage on the eastern slope into barley and wheat fields."

"Those can be lucrative crops," Dad said.

"That's what I'm aiming for," Cameron said. "We can bring others from the village into the mix."

"That helps everyone," Claire said.

"Aye," said Willy.

Angus waved to the hostess. "We've got a table."

"I'm glad we'll see you at the bonfire," I said, though I had no idea where that was, or when.

"Yes." Mom smiled up at them both. "It's good to meet you, Willy. And good to see you, Angus."

"Enjoy your evening," Angus said, and the two young men strolled back to the hostess stand.

We watched them tease the hostess as she picked up menus.

I smiled at Claire. "They're both so cute."

"Aye," she said. "And the girls seem to agree. I've seen them lately in the library flirting with Olivia."

"They're not reading?" Mom asked, and we laughed.

"I wish," Claire said. "But no. It's Olivia they're interested in, not the books."

"I'd like to meet Olivia myself," I said. "I'd like to find out more about those books."

"Maybe tomorrow," Claire said, her tone suddenly vague.

Mom had returned to study the vicar. "Is this the vicar who's performing your ceremony?"

Claire perked up. "Yes, he is. Cameron's family has attended that church for decades."

"It's nice to have that kind of connection to your community," Mom said.

"I think so, too," Claire said.

"And did I mention that he's awfully handsome?"

She smiled. "I believe you did."

"Mom, leave the vicar alone."

Claire laughed. "I'm quite sure he'd be flattered by the attention."

"Oh, sure," Mom said, rolling her eyes. "But let's get back to the old girlfriend."

"Yes, let's," I chimed in.

Claire waved her hands to shush us both, then checked to make sure Cameron and the men had begun another intense conversation, this one concerning the best type of cigars to hand out after the wedding.

Claire spoke in whispers. "I wouldn't call her a girlfriend, because Cameron insists they never dated. But he's known her forever, and they've been each other's plus-one on some occasions. I've only actually met her twice. She wasn't very nice to me."

"Of course not," I said, and Mom nodded her agreement. "She probably thinks you stole her man away."

Claire grimaced. "I didn't, of course, because Cameron tells me they never really dated. Still, they did go out together on occasion."

"She probably considered that dating even if he didn't," I said.

"Why don't you know her better?" Mom wondered. "Didn't you both grow up here?"

"It's a long story, but essentially I went away to boarding school while she grew up here. And every summer when I was here, her parents took her on a grand tour, always visiting different cities throughout Europe and the Middle East. I heard they even went to the Indian Ocean one year. Madagascar or Mauritius or some exotic place like that."

"Adventurous," Mom said.

We both tried to get another look at the woman without being too obvious. "She's pretty," I said.

"But nowhere near as beautiful as you, Claire," Mom added.

"What's her name?" I asked.

Claire lowered her voice even more. "Bitsy."

My mother made a face. "Bitsy?"

I sat back in the booth, trying to make sense of that one.

"Her name is Elizabeth," she explained, "but everyone calls her Bitsy."

Mom shrugged. "It's a cute name. For a five-year-old."

We all laughed, then immediately shushed each other.

I shook my head. "I can't quite picture Cameron with a woman named Bitsy. It's no wonder they never dated." I suddenly froze. "Oh, that was so rude. I'm sorry. It's none of our business."

"That's right," Mom said. "So let's get back to the vicar."

We all giggled some more.

At that moment, the front door of the pub swung open, and

another attractive young woman rushed in on a wave of freezing cold air. Her long dark hair was windblown, and she glanced around slowly as though she expected lots of attention, which she seemed to be getting. After a moment, she turned and headed straight for Bitsy's table.

"Who's that?" I asked.

"It's Bitsy's younger sister."

Mom looked hesitant to even ask. "What's her name?"

"Her name is Fleur, but they call her Fluff," Claire said.

I looked at her sideways. "Now you're just pulling our legs."

"No." Claire held up her hand in a pledge. "As God is my witness, that's what they call her."

"Fluff and Bitsy," Mom murmured. "Good grief."

"And now we've exhausted the subject of so-called girlfriends," Claire said.

I swallowed my last sip of beer, knowing Mom and I had not even come close to exhausting the topic.

Claire glanced at Cameron, who was still deep in conversation with Derek and Dad, discussing the merits of Highland Scotches versus Lowland and Islay and every other kind. "I hope he didn't hear any of that."

"He didn't," I said confidently. "When men are discussing Scotch or wine or beer or cars or cigars or whatever, they seem to think their opinions come straight from the mouth of God. Nothing else matters." I glanced at Mom. "At least, that's how my brothers and their friends are. And Derek and his brothers, too."

"And your father," Mom admitted.

"There you go." I held up my empty glass. "Shall we order another round?"

"We'd better," Mom said. "Our dinners will be coming any minute, and we'll need drinks to go with the food."

Claire patted Mom's shoulder. "Becky, you're so smart."

"I know."

I wasn't sure why, but we all laughed at that.

"Have you noticed how beer makes everything funnier?" I asked.

"And it makes us all smarter, too," Mom said, and we giggled at that.

I sighed. "I guess I won't be throwing axes around tonight."

Mom giggled, thinking I was kidding, but Claire shook her head. "They won't let you. The first rule of axe throwing is *No Alcohol*."

"Darn," I said. But it was just as well. And given the way we'd been carrying on, I was pretty sure the second rule of axe throwing would be *No Giggling*.

Dinner was fabulous. Dad, Derek, and I had the fish and chips, and I couldn't remember anything tasting better or crispier or more succulent, ever. Cameron and Mom had cheeseburgers that looked mouthwatering. And Claire ordered a bountiful chef's salad. Everything looked fresh and delicious.

As we were digging into our dinners, I noticed the blonde, Bitsy, headed our way. She had a look on her face that spelled trouble in any language.

She stopped at our table and struck a pose by placing one hand on her hip and flipping her hair back with the other. "Hi, Cameron. Haven't seen you around lately."

Cameron stared at the woman while he chewed a French fry. Finally he said, "Hello, Bitsy."

There was an awkward pause, then she said, "Well, aren't you going to introduce me to your friends?"

He didn't give a hint of his annoyance, but I watched as he transformed himself into the Laird of the castle. His shoulders broadened, and he sat taller and managed to look down his nose at her while gazing up at her. "These are my friends from America: Brooklyn, Derek, Becky, and Jim. Everyone, this is Bitsy."

Catching Cameron's vibe, we all acknowledged her with nods and weak smiles. Dad waved.

Bitsy ignored us and continued to bat her eyelashes at Cameron. "Will you be building the bonfire tomorrow?"

"Yes. Of course."

She gave him a little smirk. "Remember that time I helped you build it? We had fun, didn't we?"

"The time you fell in the loch, you mean?" he said easily. "Who could forget it?"

Her eyes narrowed and her lips thinned in anger. "I didn't fall in. Someone pushed me."

"Of course," he said. "Well, we'll see you tomorrow night, then."

She returned to her flirty pose and twirled a strand of hair around her finger. "You definitely will. And if you want to play darts later tonight, you know I'm available. I promise not to whip you too badly."

She turned and strolled away, swinging her hips as though she knew every man in the room was watching her.

I glanced around and confirmed that several men were doing just that, but none of them were sitting at our table.

"That was awkward," Mom murmured.

I glanced at Claire. "She didn't even look at you."

She exhaled slowly and deliberately, as if trying to rid herself of the irritation she clearly felt. "Welcome to my world."

*A*fter dinner, we stopped at the bar to say a quick hello to Sophie, and I introduced my parents.

She shook both of their hands and then said, "It's good to see you again, Brooklyn."

"You, too."

"I thought I might make it over to your table, but as ya can see, we're slammed tonight."

"It's all right," Claire said. "We'll see you tomorrow morning."

"I'll be there for breakfast," Sophie said with a wink. "And fair warning, I'm bringing a list of last-minute details."

"Another list?" Claire moaned.

Cameron wrapped his arm around her shoulders. "It'll all be over in a few days, my love."

"But in the meantime," Sophie said, "it's my job to torment you."

Claire scowled. "You're awfully good at it."

"Thanks," Sophie said, chuckling. We all joined her.

After Sophie wished us a good evening and went back to work, Claire walked us over to meet the vicar. He had moved to a small table on the other side of the bar and was just finishing an order of fish and chips.

"Gregory," Cameron said. "I mean to say, Vicar James, I'm sorry to interrupt your meal, but Claire and I wanted to introduce you to our American friends who are visiting for the wedding."

The vicar stood to greet us. "How delightful," he said, shaking my hand because I was nearest to him. "I'm Gregory James, vicar at St. Tristan's."

"I'm Brooklyn Wainwright. This is my mother Rebecca Wainwright."

He went around the group and shook each of our hands, telling us how nice it was to meet us and welcoming us to Oddlochen.

He returned to me. "Brooklyn. What an interesting name."

"Thank you. My parents named me after the New York borough they visited while my mother was pregnant with me."

I exchanged a quick glance with my mom. I had actually been *conceived* in Brooklyn while my parents were following the Grateful

Dead on tour, but we didn't need to plant an image in the vicar's mind of my not-so-immaculate conception. Frankly, I didn't need that image in my mind, either, but I'd been living with it my entire life.

His eyes widened, and then he grinned at my mother and father. "Isn't that fascinating?"

"We have six children, all named after various cities that we loved to travel to."

"Wonderful," he said. "Well, I look forward to seeing you at the wedding. And I do hope you enjoy your visit to Oddlochen." He brightened. "Any chance you'd name your next child after our wee village?"

"We would if we could," Dad said.

Mom glanced around. "It's quite charming."

Cameron laughed, then reached out to shake the vicar's hand. "We'll see you tomorrow night, Gregory."

"Aye, looking forward to it," he said.

"Goodnight, Vicar," Claire said.

As we drove back to the castle, I said, "Mom, Dad, I would truly love to have a little brother named Oddlochen."

"I was thinking the name would better suit a little girl," Dad said.

"Oh, dear Lord," Derek muttered.

"Sweet Oddie," I said, suppressing yet another giggle.

"That's got a nice ring," Dad said.

"Our little Lochie," Mom suggested.

"Stop!" Claire was laughing too hard. "You people are crazy!"

"Best get used to it," Derek said. "It never stops."

*B*ack at the castle, Derek and I walked Mom and Dad upstairs to their room. We planned to meet Claire and Cameron in the blue parlor for a nightcap. Mom and Dad were ready for bed after a long day of travel and fun.

"You don't have to walk up with us," Mom said.

"Just want to make sure everything's copacetic," I said easily.

Mom gave me a quick peck on the cheek. "Thank you, sweetie."

"Your room is all right?" Derek asked.

"It's fantastic," Dad said. "Big and comfortable. We've got a view of the loch out one window and the hills over the village out the other."

"Perfect." I gave them both a hug. "Sleep well, you two."

"You, too, kids," Dad said, and they both walked into their room.

"Goodnight," Derek said. He took my hand, and we started to head for the stairs.

Suddenly we heard an intense scraping sound followed by a loud bump.

Mom poked her head out of their doorway. "What was that?"

I turned at the same time. "Did you drop something?"

"No," she said.

Derek was already running past Mom and Dad's door to the opposite end of the hall. He stopped to listen, then looked at Dad. "Can you tell where the sounds came from?"

"Definitely came from this end," Dad said.

Suddenly there was a clank, as though someone had dropped a heavy chain.

Startled, Mom jolted. "What in the world?"

Then something scraped along the floor. At least, that was what it sounded like.

Dad joined Derek. "It definitely came from this end of the hall."

The two of them followed the hall to the opposite end of the east wing and disappeared around a corner.

"Maybe it was the cat," I said, but seriously? There was no way a small animal would make that chain-dragging sound.

"Maybe it's the plumbing," Mom suggested half-heartedly.

"That's possible," I said. "These old houses, or castles, make a lot of odd noises."

"It could be the Ghost of Christmas Past," Mom said hopefully. "He's the one with all the chains, right?"

"Umm." I frowned at her. "I think that's Marley."

"Oh." She shook her head. "Well, never mind. It doesn't mean anything anyway."

"Right." I could tell she didn't believe it, and neither did I. On the other hand, what else could've made those noises?

Derek and Dad returned. "Let's check out your room," Derek said. "Make sure you're safe. Then we'll look around our room before we go downstairs."

"Sounds good," I said.

We all went through both of our rooms, then walked out to scan the entire hallway.

Mom looked at me. "I'm going to do a protection spell."

"Mother," I warned.

"Sweetie," she whispered. "You know I always travel with my supplies. And I brought my new wand with me. I've got rosemary and verbena and my obsidian crystals for protection. And white sage, of course."

"Of course," I murmured. My mother the witch. Whatever was I going to do with her?

She stepped inside her room, opened the top drawer of the dresser, and pulled out a compact leather case that somehow resembled a small version of a doctor's bag. Inside, among the various colored crystals and a deck of tarot cards were several small, tightly wound bundles of white sage. She took one out, handed it to me, and closed the case. "Here you go. It should last all week."

"Mother." Did she really expect me to light the sage and smudge our room every night in order to cleanse and rid it of evil spirits and negative energy? Well, yes, of course she did.

"Please, sweetie. I'll feel better if you take it." She was playing the Mom card. It always worked. "Do it for me. And if nothing else, your room will smell lovely."

That was true enough. I took the fragrant little bundle and watched as she closed her eyes, rolled a purple crystal in her hand, and murmured a few unintelligible phrases. I knew she was chanting a protection spell. After a minute, she stopped and smiled at me. "That ought to do it."

"Okay, good." I wasn't sure why, but I felt better. I slipped the bundle of white sage into my purse, then kissed her cheek. "Thank you."

She smiled but said nothing. That's when I knew she was slowing down. She really needed to get some sleep.

Luckily Derek and Dad walked into the room just then.

"Did you find something?" I asked.

Dad shook his head. "Must've been the cat."

"Not a burglar?" I asked.

Mom grinned. "Maybe a cat burglar."

"Oookay." I glanced at Derek. "We're going."

"Come on, that was funny," she insisted.

I chuckled. "Yes, it was funny. Goodnight, Mom and Dad."

"Goodnight, sweetie," she said. "Goodnight, Derek."

"Sleep well, you two," Dad said.

"And you do the same," Derek said.

Once we were on the stairs, I said, "We both heard those sounds, right?"

"Yes." He stared up at the landing and frowned. "But your father and I looked up and down the hallway and found almost nothing. And we didn't hear anything else after those first bumps and scrapes."

I narrowed my eyes at him. "As though they stopped as soon as you started looking for them?"

He shrugged. "I'm sure it was just a coincidence."

I knew he was trying to calm me down, but Derek didn't believe in coincidences, and therefore neither did I. We headed for the blue parlor.

"Wait," I said, stopping at the bottom of the stairs. "What do you mean, you found *almost* nothing?"

"Wasn't sure you'd catch that," he said.

"It took me a minute, but I definitely caught it. What did you find?"

He slipped his arm through mine and pulled me close, then whispered, "We found what appeared to be blood smeared on a section of the wall panel at the end of our hallway."

The only lights that were turned on in the blue parlor were the ones over the bar. They reflected off the rich dark wood finish and gave that corner a warm, inviting glow. Cameron stood behind the bar, and Claire was perched on one of the barstools. She had a porcelain cup in front of her.

"It looks so cozy in here," I said.

Claire grinned. "We weren't sure you'd make it."

"We had a little incident," I said, then stared at her cup. "What are you drinking?"

"It's hot tea with sugar and a wee drop of Scotch."

I peered more carefully at the liquid in her cup. "It smells wonderful."

"It tastes lovely, too. And it's a nice way to end the evening."

"Would you like one?" Cameron asked.

"I'll try it."

"Derek?"

"I'll have a Scotch."

Cameron held up his glass. "I'm drinking a twelve-year-old Glenmorangie, if that suits you."

Derek chuckled. "It does indeed. Thanks."

When we all had drinks, Derek toasted our host and hostess. "To your health and happiness."

"And to yours," Cameron said, and we all clinked our various mugs and glasses.

"Thank you again for inviting my parents," I said. "I can already tell that they are having a wonderful time."

"I'm so glad they're here." Claire hesitated, then added, "You know, Cameron and I realized early in our relationship that one of the many things we have in common is that both of our fathers are gone. Not necessarily dead," she hastened to add. "Not that we know of anyway. They're just . . . gone."

"I'm so sorry," Derek said. "You still haven't heard from either of them?"

Claire shook her head. "Not a word."

"I thought I would hear from my father over the holiday," Cameron admitted. "He's a sentimental man and he's always loved Christmas. I have so many Christmas memories of him." He chuckled. "I remember one year, I was just a wee lad, maybe six or seven, and I woke up and heard noises. I thought it might be Santa Claus downstairs in the great hall, so I snuck down to see. And there in front of the tree was my father assembling a bicycle. The noises I'd heard were from him, swearing loudly from frustration, I imagine."

"Did he know you were there?" Claire asked.

"Probably, but he didn't turn around or say anything. After a few minutes, I tiptoed back upstairs to bed. Of course, I could barely go back to sleep after getting a look at that gorgeous new bike waiting for me."

"That's a nice memory," I said.

"Aye, 'tis." But he shook his head. "That Christmas came only a few months after my mum had passed on. It had been a bad time for the two of us, Dad and I, living in this gigantic home, both of us lost in our grief."

"Oh no," I whispered, tears springing to my eyes.

"Aye. But still, he tried to give me a good holiday. Christmas morning and there was my bike standing in front of the tree, surrounded by all these games and sporting equipment and everything a young boy could ever want. I was quite blown away. Somehow he made my first Christmas without my mother not just bearable but wonderful. Because of what he did for me."

Claire was sniffling now, too, and she wrapped her arm around his waist.

"I thought I'd hear from him this week," Cameron continued. "At least an e-mail or . . ." He shrugged. "I trust he's enjoying his latest girlfriend, wherever he is these days."

For a long moment, there was silence while we each got lost in our own thoughts. I remembered Claire sharing her turbulent memories of her father and the surprising puzzle he had left for her to solve.

It was good to know that Cameron had some warm memories of his dad, because according to gossip, the former Laird hadn't been as fatherly in recent years. He'd become a spendthrift and a decadent ne'er-do-well. He had walked away a few years ago, and Cameron had finally been forced to take over running the estate. By all accounts, Cameron had done an excellent job of cleaning up the mess left behind and bringing the castle and the land back to its former glory.

It was said that his father was sunning himself on the Riviera with the latest in a string of wealthy widows.

Claire waved her hand as though she could erase our suddenly melancholy moods. "Let me say again that it's simply wonderful to have your parents here with us. They're so full of life and fun."

"They are that, indeed," Derek said.

My laugh was a little soggy as I dabbed the tears away. "They sure are."

"And I believe Aunt Gwyneth will enjoy meeting them, too," Claire added.

"I'm really looking forward to seeing your aunt Gwyneth again."

Claire beamed with pleasure. "I'm expecting her here tomorrow. She'll move in for a few days so she doesn't have to drive back and forth from the village. Not that it's a long drive, but there's a rumor of snow."

"Does it normally snow at this time of year?" Derek asked.

"It's unusual," Cameron said, "but we're looking forward to it."

Everyone was quiet as we sipped our drinks. Then Cameron asked, "What was the little incident you spoke of?"

Derek and I exchanged glances and I said, "When we were upstairs, we heard an odd noise or two."

"It sounded like a heavy chain was dropped," Derek said more bluntly, "and then dragged along the floor."

Cameron and Claire gave each other a look, and I had a feeling they'd heard the noises, too.

"You've heard it," Derek said.

"It just started a few days ago," Cameron admitted.

Claire winced. "We think it might be bats inside the walls."

"Eww." I couldn't help my childish reaction, but seriously. Bats? The thought gave me chills.

"I know it sounds awful," Claire said, "but they're really quite harmless."

I was still grossed out. "But bats wouldn't have made that chain-dropping sound."

Cameron shrugged. "They're liable to make all sorts of sounds when they get stuck inside a wall."

Claire added, "Sometimes they shriek, which could've been the sound you heard."

"But I don't want you to worry," Cameron said. "I'll have Patrick look into it tomorrow morning."

"Patrick," I murmured, wanting to remember the name.

"He's Cameron's new man of all work," Claire said. "And he's really good. He's got a staff of fellows and they can do anything. So I know they'll be able to get rid of the bats."

"I appreciate it," I said. "And I hate to be troublesome, but it did kind of freak us out."

"It's no trouble at all." Cameron smiled. "We would never want to upset you or your parents."

I smiled at him. "Thanks."

"I intend to take care of the problem permanently, but in the meantime, let me reassure you that the bats won't harm you. They're just looking for a warm place to spend the winter. Nevertheless, we don't want them burrowing inside our walls."

"I couldn't agree more," I assured them. "And that reminds me. Is the cat that wanders around our area of the east wing the same cat from before? Is that Robbie?"

"Robbie Burns," Cameron said with a grin, pronouncing it *Rabbie*. "He's a good lad."

"He is," I said. "But isn't Mr. D here, too?"

The name was short for Maxim de Winter, the husband in Daphne du Maurier's classic novel *Rebecca*. Claire had a passionate love for gothic novels.

"Yes, he's here," Claire said. "But he prefers to stay in our suite in the north wing."

Cameron gave Claire's hand a light squeeze. "It's better for all concerned that they keep to their own territories."

We chatted for a few more minutes while we finished our drinks, then Derek and I wished them both a good night. Once we were back inside our room, we stood silently for a long moment while we listened for odd sounds. I rubbed my arms, trying to get rid of the chills I'd had ever since Cameron first mentioned the possibility of bats. I gazed up at Derek. "I don't hear anything, do you?"

"No."

"Maybe they're asleep." I frowned. "Whoever they are."

"Maybe," Derek said, but didn't sound at all convinced.

"Well, I'm exhausted. I'm going to brush my teeth and go to bed. And maybe those bats will do the same."

"Positive thinking. That's just one of the many things I love about you, darling."

Chapter 4

The next morning I woke up to discover that Derek was gone. Checking the clock, I realized it was almost nine.

Almost nine! I never slept that late. But on the bright side, I'd slept like a rock and I felt great. Maybe I'd managed to sleep all of the anxiety out of my system. I hoped so.

On the not-so-bright side, I wondered if I had missed out on breakfast. No way. Mrs. B would never allow it! But that was all the motivation I needed to jump out of bed, wash my face, and brush my teeth. I dressed quickly, then stepped out into the hall, where I came face-to-face—or rather, foot-to-paw—with a beautiful black-and-white tuxedo cat. A very friendly cat who rubbed up against my ankles and purred loudly.

"Hello, there, Robbie," I said, pronouncing it *Rabbie* as Cameron had done. I stroked his back and gave him some scratches behind his ears. That's when I noticed the bright red velvet ribbon around his neck with a shiny silver bell attached. So, even the cats were continuing to celebrate the holiday. "You look very handsome in your red ribbon."

I flicked the little bell and heard the tinkling. The cat stretched his neck and seemed very proud to be wearing the bell.

The lights of the Christmas tree brightened the hall space, and the cat settled onto the thick rug as though he were assigned to guard the tree and our rooms while we were gone.

I walked swiftly downstairs and was relieved to see Derek sitting in the big sunny breakfast room next to the kitchen.

I sat down and leaned over to kiss his cheek. "Good morning, my darling. It appears you slept well."

"I did." He kissed me back. "And you?"

"Like a rock." I closed my eyes and breathed in his masculine scent, along with the savory aroma of bacon and sausages. All of it went a long way toward waking me up. "I'm glad you're still here."

"I wanted to make sure you made it to breakfast."

"It would've been a major disappointment if I didn't."

"My thought exactly. I was willing to go upstairs and drag you out of bed if I had to."

I smiled. "That's very sweet. So, are you on your way out of the house?"

"Yes, just about."

Mrs. B walked into the room. "Good morning, Brooklyn. Can I bring you some coffee?"

"Yes, please," I said.

Seconds later, she handed me a big mug of dark, rich coffee. "Thank you."

"I'll bring another plate for you in just a moment."

She left the coffeepot on the table and returned to the kitchen. I didn't care to have her waiting on me, but a minute later, I was pitifully grateful when she returned with a platter of scrambled eggs with bits of green onion and red pepper.

"Christmas eggs," I said. "They're so festive." There was also bacon, sausages, hash browns, and a basket holding a variety of breakfast rolls and pastries.

"There's cream and sugar on the table, and if you'd like fruit and yogurt or porridge, we have that, too."

"This is perfect," I said. "I love that you're still celebrating Christmas. We left town in the middle of the holiday season, so I appreciate that you're keeping the spirit going for all of us."

"It's my pleasure," she said, with a jaunty bow.

As she left, I snagged a piece of bacon, and Derek reached for the coffeepot to refill his cup. "I'm glad you slept well and didn't hear the bats."

I almost dropped my coffee mug. "You heard bats?"

Suppressing a grin, he took hold of my arm. "No, sweetheart. I was just teasing you. I didn't hear them at all. All I heard were the usual sounds of an old castle settling in the night."

I blew out a relieved breath. "I'm glad I didn't hear anything. I really needed to sleep."

"I agree. That's why I didn't wake you when I got up."

I took another big sip of coffee and began to munch on the bacon. "Thank you again. Although I would've loved to join you for breakfast."

"Me, too." He took a last sip of coffee. "I'm going to hunt down Cameron, and if he hasn't already taken care of it, I'll see about having him send his man Patrick up to fix the problem."

"That would be awesome."

"Indeed. I'd like to have him get rid of the bats before we go through another night of that racket."

"If it really was bats." I whispered the words so as not to disturb the kitchen staff with our talk of bats in the walls. "I don't know a lot about bat behavior, but I doubt they're able to drag chains across the floor."

He shook his head. "Perhaps Patrick can enlighten me on the matter."

"I hope so."

He checked his wristwatch, then stood. "I should be off. I've promised to help Cameron build the bonfire."

"The bonfire." I frowned. "Bitsy mentioned that last night at the pub. It can't be some kind of Scottish wedding ritual, can it?"

"No, it's actually a Scottish New Year's ritual. They celebrate something called Hogmanay, an ancient Scottish tradition."

"I've never heard of it. Have you?"

"I've heard of it, of course. But being English, I haven't yet experienced it. But Cameron enjoys the old traditions, so we're going to be doing everything according to the ancient customs. Obviously a bonfire is part of it."

"Should be fun."

"It'll definitely be different." He grinned. "I assume Patrick will be involved in the building of the bonfire, so if I haven't already tracked him down, I'll broach the subject of bat hunting at that time."

I reached for a cinnamon roll. "Let me know how it goes."

"I shall. Where will you be?"

"I'm going to try the library again, then hunt down Claire. I imagine she'll have some duties for me to perform as her maid of honor."

"It shouldn't be anything too difficult. They both seem quite prepared for their nuptials."

"They really do." I smiled. "As long as she doesn't expect me to fix her hair, I'll be fine."

"But your hair always looks beautiful," he said.

"I love you," I said, and kissed him. "If nothing else is happening, then I'll be upstairs working on Cameron's book."

He grinned. "I'll find you."

"Okay." I pulled off the outer ring of the cinnamon roll as I watched him leave the breakfast room.

I placed a large spoonful of scrambled eggs and a good-sized chunk of hash browns onto my plate. Barely a minute later, my phone beeped with a text notification. I read the message from Derek: P.S. Your parents took a leisurely walk along the shore of the loch.

I texted back: Hope they're having a wonderful time. Thanks for letting me know.

While I ate breakfast, I pulled out my tablet and signed in to my favorite antiquarian book site. I looked up a few of the books on Claire's list. Of the three books I checked, nothing jumped out at me, pricewise, but there were plenty of others on the list that I would research later.

For my own amusement, I looked up *The Merry Muses*, the Robert Burns book that I was repairing for Claire. There were several versions listed, but the one that most closely matched the book I was working on was priced at $504. It was a decent price, and I wondered if Gwyneth had paid even that much for it. Since she owned an antique shop and was savvy in the ways of commerce, I doubted it. It didn't matter, of course. I knew Cameron would love it no matter how much it cost.

Ten minutes later, I took my last sip of coffee, then brought my plate and a few empty platters into the kitchen, where I was greeted by Mrs. B, who gently scolded me.

"Brooklyn, dear." She took the plates from me. "If you bring all of your own plates into the kitchen, our Millie will have nothing to do."

Rather than arguing the point, I said, "I don't think I've met Millie."

"She's busy with the morning dishes, but I'll be happy to introduce you to her."

"Yes, please." From my last visit, Mrs. B was aware that I was always interested in meeting the castle housekeeping staff. It helped to know who was who and what their duties were. Maybe it was a holdover from my years of watching first *Upstairs, Downstairs* and then *Downton Abbey*, but I secretly thought the downstairs crew was more intriguing.

Mrs. B led me through the spacious kitchen to a smaller separate room that was filled with counters and sinks and four built-in dishwashers. I was impressed. I'd been imagining a scene out of *Downton Abbey* with a work-worn scullery maid scouring heavy pots and dishware.

Instead, a perky young woman stood at one of the sinks, scraping plates and placing them in one of the dishwashers.

"Millie?" Mrs. B said.

The woman whipped around. "Yes, ma'am?"

She wasn't as young as I'd first thought. Maybe in her early to mid-thirties.

Mrs. B smiled indulgently. "I'd like to introduce you to Brooklyn Wainwright, a friend of Claire's and one of our guests for the wedding."

"'Tis lovely to meet you, ma'am," Millie said.

"It's nice to meet you, too, Millie. I wanted to thank you for all your hard work."

She looked at Mrs. B with wide eyes. "Och, isna so hard. Truth be told, I'm grateful for the work and the many dear people I spend every day with."

"That's a lovely thing to say, Millie," Mrs. B said.

"'Tis the truth, Mrs. B."

Mrs. B took a few steps toward the door. "We'll let you get back to your work."

"Thanks again," I said.

When we reached the dining room, I turned to Mrs. B. "Thank you for introducing me to Millie. I know you must think I'm some kind of oddball American, but I do like to know the people I'm interacting with."

She gave a wave of her hand. "Now, you mustn't feel odd, Brooklyn. I'll not forget when we were missing our dear Jenny and you found her. And then you found the person who hurt her. We were all grateful to you for that."

"Thank you, Mrs. B." I rubbed away the chills that came up when I thought of poor Jenny.

The kitchen door opened, and a woman stomped into the room wearing a bright pink puffy vest over a dark green thermal Henley and blue jeans. She clapped her gloved hands together, then pulled off her ski cap and shook her curly brown hair loose. "It's chankin out there, Mrs. B. I nearly froze my bahoochie."

"The sun will peek out of the clouds any minute now," Mrs. B said, and winked at me. "Let me introduce you to one of our guests."

"Och." She looked up and saw me standing with Mrs. B. "Lordy, Mrs. B, why'd ye let me blether on like a numpty." She nodded at me. "I'm sorry, miss. Didn't see you there."

I couldn't help but grin at her like a numpty, whatever that meant. She was young, maybe mid-twenties, and very pretty, with short tawny brown hair and big brown eyes.

"Brooklyn," Mrs. B said. "This is our chef, Tamara."

I held out my hand to shake hers. "Hello, Tamara."

Embarrassed, she shook her head again, as if to wake up her

brain, then straightened up and shook my hand. "Lovely to meet you, Brooklyn. I hope you enjoy your visit."

"Thank you. It's good to meet you, too. According to Claire and Cameron, everything you prepare is delicious, so I'm looking forward to dinner tonight."

She glanced at Mrs. B. "Isn't that lovely of them?" To me she said, "I hope you'll find it satisfying."

"I'm sure we will. I just have to ask. What's a numpty? And a bahoochie?"

She covered her face with both hands and moaned. Mrs. B laughed and said, "A bahoochie is your behind." She patted her butt. "And numpty is something like a numbskull."

"Like me," Tamara said, still mortified. "I beg your pardon."

"No, please. I'm fascinated by your words."

She smiled shyly. "You'll hear plenty if you hang out in the kitchen."

"I'll try to do that sometime this week. Right now, I should go find Claire and see what I can do to help her."

"Off you go, then," Mrs. B said. "And please tell Claire to let me know if there's anything she needs from me."

"I will." I started to walk into the dining room but stopped when I heard the kitchen door open and a man's voice greeting the chef.

"Aye, there's a bonnie lass," he said. "You smell as sweet as you look, darlin' Tamara."

"I smell like beef stock, ye bleedin' walloper."

I snuck a peek around the doorjamb and saw Willy sniffing Tamara's neck. She smacked him, but it didn't look like a serious brush-off. In fact, his hand moved down to squeeze her behind—her bahoochie?—and she was still wearing a smile. I had a feeling she wouldn't mind having Willy sniff around her any old time. I couldn't blame her. He was simply adorable, with a smidgen of bad boy thrown in for fun. A girl had to love that about him.

Interesting, I thought, crossing the dining room toward the foyer. The last time we'd visited, I couldn't help noticing that so many of the men in Scotland were ridiculously handsome. Now I realized that the women were equally beautiful.

At the library door, I stopped to check the lock. I spent a few frustrating seconds twisting the knob back and forth, then huffed out a breath of annoyance and moved along down the wide foyer.

It really bugged me that the library was still inaccessible.

I passed the great hall and spied Claire and Sophie seated near the fireplace, having what looked like an intimate conversation.

I took one step into the hall and they both turned.

"Am I interrupting?" I asked. "I can come back."

Claire stood up. "Brooklyn, come in!"

"Yes, come in," Sophie said, standing with her. "How are ye doing today?"

"I'm good, thanks." I grinned. Sophie and I had gotten to know each other pretty well on my first visit. Last night in the pub, she'd had her hair pulled up in a knot, but today her thick dark locks were flowing down her back.

I had to smile. Here was yet another gorgeous Scotswoman.

Sophie gave me a big hug. "Sorry I couldn't get a break and join you last night."

"You were so busy," I said.

"We're getting an influx of people coming to town for Hogmanay."

"Derek's outside helping Cameron build a bonfire," I said. "He tried to explain the festivities to me, but I'm sorry to admit I still have no idea what Hogmanay is."

Sophie laughed. "I occasionally wonder if half of Scotland has any idea what it is. Some of the rituals have changed over the years, but Cameron likes to follow the ancient traditions."

"What does that mean?"

"It would take a while to explain, but for now, I'll just say that it's a celebration to welcome in the New Year. In that regard, it means paying off your debts, cleaning your house, and welcoming neighbors."

"That sounds like a really nice way to bring in the New Year," I said.

"Doesn't it?" Sophie grinned. "It's known as 'First Footing.' But it can get rowdy. Especially the welcoming part. Because frankly some of your neighbors might show up uninvited, and then they just don't want to leave."

"And you mustn't kick them out," Claire added. "It's not considered neighborly."

"Really?" I asked.

"Yes," she said. "It's something akin to bad karma."

"That seems a little . . . odd."

"It's thoroughly odd." Claire laughed. "And I'll admit it's one Scottish tradition I've never taken part in."

Sophie raised an eyebrow. "Don't be surprised if you find a few wandering Scotsmen on your doorstep tonight."

"I'll welcome them with open arms," Claire said.

Sophie laughed. "You won't have a choice, knowing Cameron's views on the subject."

"He does love the old ways," Claire said fondly. She turned to me. "Did you sleep well, Brooklyn?"

"Yes, thanks." I wondered if everyone in the house knew that I'd slept late. "I wanted to let you know that I'm available to help you if you need anything. But if not, I thought I'd go upstairs and work on the book."

Claire's eyes lit up. "Oh, the book. Yes, please!" Then she frowned. "Unless there's something you'd rather do? We can take a walk or go shopping in the village."

I had to laugh, knowing that was the last thing Claire would want to do. "You must know by now that my favorite thing to do is work on books."

"Which makes me a very lucky girl. Thank you, Brooklyn."

"It's my pleasure." I started to leave, then stopped. "By the way, I was hoping to get into the library, but the door's still locked."

Claire gave Sophie a quick glance. "I haven't seen Olivia yet today."

Sophie checked the time on her phone. "Isn't she usually here by now?"

"Yes."

"Maybe she's already in the library," Sophie said.

I frowned. "I didn't knock. I just tried the doorknob and found it was still locked."

"That's strange," Claire murmured.

"Would she be in there with the door locked?" Sophie asked.

"I can't imagine."

"I'll knock a few times on my way back to the stairs," I said. "Maybe she's in there working. But if you see her around, could you let me know? Or just ask her for the library key so I can get in there and check out the books. I'd really like to know exactly what's missing."

Claire looked distressed at the mention of the missing books. "I must be losing my mind. I told you about the missing books and then forgot all about them. We need to introduce you to Olivia so we can work out that mystery."

Sophie grinned. "You've been losing your mind for a while now. I think they call it Bride Brain."

Claire's laugh was rueful. "That makes perfect sense."

"And it's completely understandable," I said. "You've got a lot to think about right now."

She smiled. "Too much, if I'm being honest."

"Why don't we give Olivia a call right now?" Sophie suggested. "Then we'll all know what's going on."

"Yes, I should call her." But Claire didn't pull out her phone.

"I'm sorry if I'm adding to your stress level," I said.

Sophie gazed up at me. "It's not you, Brooklyn. Claire's just not comfortable around Olivia."

"But you hired her to work here."

"Yes, I did," Claire said. "And that's how I found out I . . . well, I'm not at ease around the woman."

I wanted to ask, *In what way? And why?* But I thought it best to save my questions for later.

"It doesn't matter," Claire said quickly. "I have to call her. We need to get that key."

Sophie slipped her arm through Claire's. "I'll stay right here while you talk to her. And then I've got to get to the pub."

Claire grabbed her arm a little desperately. "You're working to-night?"

Sophie laughed. "Easy, girl. I'm just setting up the bar for the onslaught tonight, and then I'll be back here, as promised."

Claire leaned against her friend. "Thanks. I know you think I'm pathetic, but thank you."

"I can stay here with you while Sophie's working," I said.

Claire gave me a look of such gratitude, I didn't know what to say. Was she honestly afraid to talk to Olivia? It didn't make sense, but then maybe I was reading too much into the situation.

Claire straightened her shoulders. "Thank you, Brooklyn. That's very sweet of you, but for goodness' sake, I can handle one silly phone call. You go on up to work on the book and Sophie will stay with me. And when I find out Olivia's schedule, I'll let you know."

"All right." I forced a casual smile onto my face. "I'll be upstairs. And you can text me if you need anything."

Claire gave me a hug. "I will. Thanks."

"You're welcome," I said lightly. "See you both later."

I started to walk away, but Sophie caught my eye and gave me a look that said, *Don't worry, I can handle this.* I hoped that was true, because Claire was clearly upset about the situation with Olivia, and I didn't like to see her like that. She could literally wield any dangerous weapon in the world, but she couldn't handle one little librarian? On the other hand, it was perfectly reasonable that two women might rub each other the wrong way. And since Olivia was in fact a librarian, Claire might be weighing the option of having nobody in charge of the castle library versus simply dealing with a minor personality conflict.

And now I really wondered if Claire suspected Olivia of stealing the books. Or was there something altogether different going on here?

I stopped in front of the library door and couldn't help but grab the doorknob and jiggle it. Still locked up tight, darn it. Then I knocked loudly, but there was no response. What the heck was going on in there?

Halfway up the stairs I stopped to berate myself. I really needed to put an end to all these suspicious thoughts circling around my brain and get to work.

Back in the bedroom, I unrolled my traveling bookbinding kit to reveal all the tools I could possibly need to fix almost any book on the run.

Before starting work, I took a few minutes to study the damage done to the Robert Burns book. The gouges from the broken glass were deep but fixable. Seeing the destruction reminded me that Claire had actually been attacked by someone throwing a glass or bottle of some kind. Derek and I both knew it hadn't been an accident, despite Claire's supposition. And what kind of creep would do that to anyone? I knew I had a suspicious mind, but in this case, I was on the right track. Someone in town was out to hurt Claire.

I had a sudden realization that someone in town must've had a very good throwing arm since they would've hit her square in the face if she hadn't held up the book for protection.

For now, though, I put aside my suspicions, found my favorite glue brush, and placed it in a glass of water to soften the bristles. This would make it easier to get the glue into the odd places it needed to go once I was ready to take off the damaged leather piece.

Opening another of my cases, I sorted through my thin stack of leather pieces and bookcloths until I found a small square of burgundy-colored morocco leather that would match almost exactly the leather on the rest of the Robert Burns book.

Finding the perfect color match wasn't really a matter of good luck. The fact was that when it came to high-quality leather book covers, many bookbinders kept to the classic shades of royal or navy blue, forest green, red, burgundy, brown, and black. Of course, there was always the occasional pink or chartreuse cover, but I wouldn't have to worry about that for this book.

I had put it off long enough; it was time to remove the damaged triangle of leather that covered the corner. I was an experienced bookbinder and knew what I was doing, but I wasn't so vain as to think I couldn't screw it up. In a situation like this one, there was always some possibility of further damage. *But not this time*, I declared silently, and slipped on my magnifying glasses, which would allow me to do close-up work without having to hold a magnifying glass in my hand. Then I carefully slid the blade of my X-Acto knife under the edge of the leather and slowly eased it away from the heavy book board underneath. I used my point-tip tweezers to carefully pull the old leather back from the surface.

When the corner piece was completely removed, I saw that the board underneath had become delaminated, which meant that the stiff cardboard was badly frayed, causing it to split into individual paper-thin layers.

I opened the bottle of polyvinyl acetate, or PVA, that I always carried with me, and poured a few tablespoons into a small ceramic ramekin. PVA was the glue used most by bookbinders because it was pH neutral, which meant that it didn't affect the acidity or alkalinity of the paper. It was also water soluble, but more importantly, it dried clear and remained flexible for a long time. This was vital, because over time, regular glue could become brittle or crack.

I fanned the layers of the frayed corner board even more so I could easily reach between each layer with the glue brush.

I used my fingers to squeeze the layers together. It got a little messy with glue oozing out, but that was okay. I wiped away the excess with a cloth as I pressed and smoothed the corner back into shape.

To prevent the frayed section from delaminating again, I wrapped the corner of the book in a piece of wax paper, then positioned a small square of heavy binder's board on each side of the corner to hold the wax paper in place. Finally, in lieu of a book press or a set of archival weights like the ones I used at home, I took one of my sturdy binder clips from my travel case and clipped the boards and everything in between together. I would leave the clip on for the next hour or until the glue was completely dry and the corner was straightened.

I stood and stretched my arms and circled my shoulders to ease the tension that had built up, then walked to the window to see what was going on outside. I didn't see Derek or Cameron or anything that looked like the beginnings of a bonfire stack. But I saw my parents walking down by the loch on their way back to the castle. They were laughing and chatting and generally enjoying themselves, and the sight made my chest swell with happiness and relief.

I hadn't noticed it before, but out in the middle of the open field next to the two-story garage was an archery range. At the far end of the field, there were two large rounded bales of hay, each wrapped in a big white cloth with a colorful bull's-eye printed on one side. Both of the hay bales rested on two sturdy easels. Closer in was a chalk line, where I assumed a person, the archer, would stand to shoot the arrow.

Two small tables sat back a few yards from the chalk line, and on one of the tables was a large zippered case in the shape of a bow. A smaller cylindrical case leaned against one of the table legs and probably held a quiver filled with arrows.

So, it appeared that archery was another activity at which Claire excelled. I assumed so anyway. She was good at practically anything that had to do with weaponry.

I remembered taking an archery class in high school and really enjoying it. Not that I was that great at hitting the bull's-eye, but it was always fun and challenging. I wouldn't mind giving it a try while we were here.

Since there were two easels with bull's-eyes set up, I imagined Claire and Cameron challenged each other regularly. And I would bet they were both really good at it.

I wondered if Derek was good at archery. He was athletic and good at so many things, so why not archery? I, on the other hand, was good at one thing: bookbinding. Once in a while, that skill came in handy as a weapon, like the time I threw a bone folder—a hand tool used for creasing and folding paper—at a guy who was threatening me. And earlier this year when we were up in the castle tower facing a vicious gun-toting killer, I ended up flinging a children's book at the bad guy. It might've turned into a scene from *The Three Stooges* except that I managed to distract the guy long enough for Claire to throw her knife at him and for Derek to pull out his gun.

Naturally I repaired the children's book when I returned home.

I realized that I had been staring out the window for at least fifteen minutes, so I went back to check the corner of the repaired book and saw, as expected, that the glue wasn't dry yet. It would probably take another half hour at least, so I decided to go downstairs and chat with Mom and Dad for a few minutes. And I wanted to check on Claire. Had she tracked down Olivia? What was the librarian's story? And why in the world was Claire intimidated by her? She could wield a broadsword better than almost any man I knew, and her knife-throwing skills were incredible. Beyond that, she was about to marry the Laird of the castle, which would bring with it a certain amount of power and cachet. Not that Claire would milk it. I knew she wasn't impressed with that sort of thing.

I decided I couldn't wait to meet this librarian to figure out why she had such a hold over my beautiful, talented, powerful friend. And then I would find out how to break it.

Chapter 5

At the bottom of the stairs I ran into Derek.

"You're back," I said, my pleasure at seeing him obvious. He was just shutting the heavy front door, and he looked cold and exhausted.

"Are you all right?"

He smiled. "I'm fine. Half-frozen, but I've had a good day of manly fun."

I laughed. "I'd love more details."

He grabbed my hand. "Come see the bonfire we've built."

"Is it finished?" I sniffed him. "You don't smell like smoke."

He laughed. "I certainly hope not. They won't start burning it until midnight tonight. We've merely built the structure. It's fairly magnificent." He pulled me along.

"Wait. I'll need to go upstairs and get my jacket first."

"Let me show you something." He led me to a door at the edge of the foyer and opened it. Hanging neatly inside were at least a dozen coats, along with hoodies and sweaters and scarves. Lined up on the floor were boots and heavy shoes of every size and style and color. This closet contained everything a guest would need to venture outside in blustery weather.

"That's handy, isn't it?" I murmured. "And smart and thoughtful, too."

"Find something that'll keep you warm, and we can be off."

I hesitated, then began to skim through the various garments and finally found a pretty quilted plaid car coat that fit me perfectly.

"That looks quite smart on you," he said.

"Thank you." It was warm and toasty, too, which made it perfect—except for the glimmer of guilt I felt toward the owner of this cute car coat. But I vowed to take good care of it and return it promptly.

"Let's go."

As we walked out the door, I shivered. "It really is cold." I buttoned the coat up to my neck.

He pulled me closer. "I'll keep you warm, love."

I snuggled up to him. "I tried to look for you from our bedroom window but couldn't see you anywhere. Where did you build the bonfire?"

"Cameron decided to position it closer to the loch," he said. "Remember where we found the hidden entrance to the underground passage?"

"How could I ever forget that spot?"

"Indeed. It's quite near there. The ground is smoother, and there's lots of room to sit or dance or do whatever the locals do around bonfires."

"That's good to know," I said with a grin. "Did you have some help?"

"Cameron's men helped out. They're a good lot. At least ten of them joined us in the effort, and all of them are employed by him."

"That's quite a stable of workers."

"Yes. You've met Angus and Willy. They both helped quite a bit. Good workers, both of them."

"They seem like good guys." I was reminded of my thought earlier, that Willy had a hint of bad boy in him. But apparently he was a good worker and Cameron liked him.

"They are," Derek said. "It's obvious they've known each other their whole lives, because there was a lot of good-natured jostling and winding up between the two of them and several of the younger crew."

"So, they were having fun," I said. "But you got the job done?"

"Absolutely. Cameron made sure of it. All of them respect him and follow his lead in all sorts of ways."

"That's nice to hear. I guess he keeps them busy."

"He does. He's got a permanent construction crew that is refurbishing some of the outer buildings. Others work around the castle dealing with plumbing issues, electrical problems, that sort of thing." He shook his head in wonder. "And Cameron's got skills I wasn't aware of. He trained as an engineer, and he constructed this bonfire as if he were building a home. It was quite an interesting experience."

"I can't wait to see it."

We followed the path through the grass and shrubbery that dotted the front lawn during the colder months of the year. I remembered when we were here in the spring, there was a lovely carpet of green grass surrounded by rows and rows of colorful flowers in full bloom.

We rounded the tree line and found a wide area where the trees had long ago been cleared away. Now the ground was brushed clear of shrubbery and grass, and in the middle of the space was an immense pile constructed of logs and branches and twigs of every size, along with bales of hay and other flammable objects. It had to be eight feet high if not higher.

"Wow." It looked a lot like a great big haystack.

"Look here," Derek said. "Can you see the basic pieces that made up the frame?" He pointed toward the center of the stack.

I knelt down and peered into it. "It looks like you built a tepee first. I can see it."

"Very good, darling."

I smiled at the sound of his praise. "My father was the original Deadhead. We built a lot of bonfires growing up."

"Your father was here to help us," he said. "They were just getting back from their walk, and he joined right in. He had a lot to say about those early days following the Grateful Dead."

"He had a good time back then, especially once my mother joined him."

I studied the stack of wood and other items that made up the bonfire and could tell that Cameron indeed appeared to know what he was doing. Surrounding the central tepee of branches and logs, there was a bottom layer of tinder, small pieces of wood and chunks of hay and old newspaper that would catch fire and burn quickly. Above that was a thick layer of kindling made up of thin branches and smaller pieces of wood that would burn longer and hotter. Finally the top layer consisted of logs and thick chunks of wood that looked like they might've come off a building demo site. This layer would burn for several hours.

Stuffed throughout the structure were dozens of thick clumps of straw that would burn as fast as the hay and newspaper at the bottom.

I glanced at Derek. He looked pleased with the work he'd done. "It looks fantastic. Really solid."

"It is. Cameron knows what he's doing. And of course, your father lent his expertise, too."

"He must've enjoyed himself."

He laughed. "We enjoyed him as well. Got to hear all about the rock 'n' roll bonfires he'd built over the years."

I loved that Derek and my dad could bond over so many things, including, of all things, bonfires. I gazed out over the loch, where the clear midmorning sun was reflected on the calm surface.

"I'm feeling rather lucky to be a part of such a fascinating family," he said, wrapping me in his arms for a long while. Then he kissed me.

After a moment I said, "I feel pretty lucky about that, too."

He touched his forehead to mine. "It's getting colder. We'd better be getting back to the castle."

"I guess we'd better."

"Since you've been upstairs all this time," he said as we started walking back, "I doubt you're aware of the change in schedule."

"I haven't heard anything about a change in schedule."

"According to Cameron, they're expecting half the village to converge on the shore of the loch tonight for dancing and drinking and lighting the bonfire. Cameron said they're planning to set it afire right after midnight."

"Isn't that when they've scheduled the wedding?"

"Yes. So they've wisely changed the wedding to tomorrow morning."

"That makes sense." But I wondered why Claire hadn't said anything.

He must've read my expression because he added, "They just decided a little while ago. Since the temperature's dropping, they decided against having the villagers travel in the freezing cold and darkness."

"That was always an issue for me," I said. "But I'm a bit of a wimp."

"You're nothing like a wimp," he insisted, squeezing my hand in his. "So, this is to be the first of the bonfires, and it'll be set off at midnight tonight. And there will be lots of merriment and drinking and carrying on."

"Won't it be too freezing cold for that, too?"

"It seems the villagers are willing to face the cold if it means they can drink and party and celebrate Hogmanay around a burning hot bonfire."

"Hogmanay. Right." Somehow I'd forgotten all about the actual reason for the bonfires and the celebrations. "I suppose the drinking and partying aspect makes all the difference."

"It most certainly does."

"So, what time exactly will the wedding take place?"

"Approximately eleven o'clock tomorrow morning."

"That sounds much more civilized."

"I agree. It'll be followed by a huge breakfast buffet for all the guests, which essentially includes the entire village."

The morning wedding and breakfast made much more sense than transporting dozens of people to the castle in the middle of the freezing night just before Hogmanay was about to begin. "And I suppose Mrs. B is prepared for everything despite the change of plans?"

"She is. Her staff have already arranged the great hall with dining tables and chairs. She's hopeful that she and her staff might be able to sleep a few hours tonight."

"Good luck with that," I said, picturing the staff working all night to make it happen.

As we walked, I glanced up to admire the west tower. Derek and I had spent some quality time at the very top of that tower, where we ran into a bad guy that wanted to shoot us. Happily he didn't get his way.

But it was a beautiful thin round tower, one of the tallest in the castle, with a roof shaped like a witch's hat. As I stared at the top room, I saw a shadow pass by the window and realized that someone was walking around up there. I stared for another thirty seconds or so, but didn't see the shadow again.

It might just be one of the housekeepers, I thought. But why would a housekeeper be cleaning a tower room in the middle of winter? Nobody was going to be sleeping up there.

"What are you looking at?" Derek asked.

"I saw a shadow pass by that window in the west tower. I haven't seen it again, but I know I saw it. Somebody was up there."

He gazed up at the top of the tower for a few seconds. "I don't see anything, but that doesn't mean you didn't see something. Let's go up and explore sometime, shall we?"

"Yes. How about right now?"

He stared at me thoughtfully. "All right."

We got to the front door and I held out my arm to stop Derek. "I have a better idea. Did you have any plans for the next ten minutes?"

Again, he pressed his forehead to mine. "What did you have in mind, darling?"

I laughed and felt my cheeks heat up. "There's that. But actually, I was wondering if you could help me break into the library."

"You still haven't been able to get in there? And that woman hasn't come by with the key?"

"No. And no." I blew out a frustrated breath. "But I think we can fiddle with the lock and get inside there ourselves."

"Darling, are you asking me to commit the crime of breaking and entering?"

"It's hardly breaking and entering if we're already inside the house. And I'm sort of in charge of some of the books, so I refuse to call it a crime. The only reason we can't get inside the library is because Claire hired this woman who sounds like a flake." I remembered to lower my voice. "I mean, yes, she did organize the library, but that doesn't mean she's altogether trustworthy."

He gave me one of those dark, piercing looks that I had become familiar with from the very first time we met and he accused me of murder. But surprisingly, instead of lecturing me, he leaned over and whispered, "Let's go."

I had to hold in my laughter as we hurried down the empty foyer and made it to the library door.

"I can be your lookout," I said. "You pick the lock."

"You make it sound like I carry burglary tools everywhere I go."

I winced. "Sorry."

"Don't get me wrong, darling," he said, pulling his wallet from his pocket and extracting a credit card. "I do. But I don't like being so predictable."

I stared at the plastic credit card and realized it wasn't a credit card at all. It was the same shape and just as thin as a credit card, but it contained several magnetized slots that held the thin tools that could be inserted into various locks to pick them open.

"That's clever, isn't it?" I said.

"It does the trick, as they say." He fiddled with one of the picks, and barely a minute later, I heard a click.

I stared up at Derek. "It's open already?"

"It is. Now, make sure there's no one coming."

"All right." I stepped past the foyer and stared both ways down the long, wide hall. In one direction I could see the door to the blue parlor. The other way led to the grand staircase that went up to the north wing and Cameron and Claire's suite of rooms. "Nobody's around," I whispered. "We're in the clear."

He slid the card back into his wallet, which he put in his pocket. "Shall we enter?"

"You are amazing." Of course, now that I could walk right in, I was suddenly nervous. It was ridiculous to feel like we were about to break a law. We were perfectly welcome to step inside the library! And if Olivia objected, I would simply refer her to Claire.

"Let's go." I turned the doorknob and pushed it open. The room was dark. I took one step inside and heard an odd sound. A moan? Or humming? Another step inside and I realized it was music. Sort of an airy fairy melody that was hauntingly familiar. Where had I heard it before?

I stepped farther into the room and saw a bevy of lit candles arranged on the floor in a circle.

Two women sat in the center of the circle facing each other, their eyes closed and their hands clasped. They were chanting softly.

I stared in shock. "Mother?"

Her eyes blinked open and she beamed at me. "Hello, sweetie."

"What are you doing?"

"We're conducting a traditional Wiccan cleansing and wellness ritual."

I took a look at the other woman and knew I'd never seen her before. Yet somehow I knew who she was.

"Have you met Olivia?" Mom asked.

"No," I said, leaning over to shake her hand. "Hello, Olivia. I've been looking forward to meeting you."

She stared at me as if she were looking right through me. I supposed I stared back, because she was simply beautiful. Positively angelic. Her face was oval shaped and the only way I could describe her skin was classic peaches and cream. Her lips were full and sexy and her hair was long, thick, and blond. She wore a simple sweater with blue jeans and sneakers, and I wondered for a moment why she wasn't wearing a fairy princess costume, complete with tiara. With her look of adorable innocence, it might suit her better.

All of a sudden, a cat rubbed up against my leg, and I almost jumped out of my skin. "Oh!" After catching my breath, I realized it was one of the black-and-white tuxedo cats. Probably Robbie. Or maybe Mr. D had ventured down from Claire's suite? I would have to learn how to tell the difference between them.

I bent down, picked up the cat, and stroked his soft fur. "Hello, you," I whispered. The cat rubbed its head against my chin in a friendly greeting. After a moment I reluctantly set the cat down and reminded myself that I had things to do.

"Olivia dear," Mom said, "this is my daughter, Brooklyn."

"Oh, Brooklyn!" Olivia's eyes cleared and she extended her hand. "I'm so glad you're here. We have so much to talk about."

"Yes, we do." I glanced back at Derek. "This is my husband, Derek."

"It's good to meet you, Olivia." He gazed down at Mom. "Hello, Rebecca."

Mom winked at him as Olivia looked back and forth between Derek and me. "How did you get in here?"

"We just opened the door," I said lightly.

"I thought I locked it," she muttered to my mother, and started to push herself up from the floor. "I should go."

"No, don't go," Mom said, reaching to grab hold of her hand. "We need to finish our ritual. And then Brooklyn needs to talk to you."

"Yes," I said. "Please stay. We need to talk about the missing books."

Her frown was intense as she continued to glance at the door. "I'm concerned that the locks aren't working."

"They work," Mom said. "It's just that Derek has . . . special skills."

Olivia's eyes widened. "Does he have dragon blood?"

Dragon blood? I stared at the woman. Was that some kind of Scottish reference? Maybe a warrior thing? Or was she just not playing with a full deck?

I glanced at my husband and knew that he was mentally rolling his eyes. I couldn't blame him. But looking around, I could see that the library had been ruthlessly organized and that the shelves were spotlessly clean. And in that moment, I selfishly decided that Olivia's organizational ability was much more important—and impressive—than her sanity.

Still, there was that thorny little problem of twelve missing Christmas books.

I was all set to ask her about the books when I saw my mother's look of concern.

I rarely saw that look, so I took it seriously and shut up.

Clearly Mom didn't want me to interrupt their wellness ritual. Or maybe she was concerned about Olivia's state of mind. I mean really, dragon blood? So I wouldn't speak, not yet. But as soon as she finished the ceremony, I was going to grab Olivia and have a nice chat with her.

"You know, we're going to wait outside until you're finished," I said.

Mom nodded. "I'll let you know."

Derek and I walked out to the foyer and closed the library door behind us.

"Well, that was weird," I said.

"Darling, in your mother's world, 'weird' is as normal as a Tuesday afternoon."

"So, not weird, just wacky. Sorry about that."

"Don't apologize for her." He reached for my hand. "I'm quite fond of your mother and find her to be a warm and loving woman."

"I agree." I squeezed his hand. "Thank you."

"Furthermore, she appears to have become an ally to someone you don't quite trust yet. Perhaps you can use that to your advantage."

Of course I could. I'd already thought it through and come to the same conclusion. My mother could help me find out from Olivia what happened to those books. She might even know who took them and where they could be right now. I would just have to be patient and wait for their ritual to wrap up.

"Is that you?" a voice from the doorway called. "Can it really be? Don Danger?"

Derek whipped around and let out a delighted laugh. "Tanya. Tanya Roma."

"In the flesh, big boy."

I was laughing now, too, as we both walked quickly over to the woman standing at the front door. When we got close enough, I gave her a warm hug. "Gwyneth, hello. It's so good to see you."

"Brooklyn, dear, I'm simply thrilled that you're here." She held my arms for another moment, studying me. "My goodness, you look wonderful."

"Thank you. You look better than ever."

She patted my cheek. "I've always liked you."

We both laughed, and then she turned to Derek. "Come here, you manly hunk." She threw her arms around him and pressed her cheeks to both of his. "Damn it, Danger. You get better looking with every year. I don't like it."

"You look simply marvelous as always," he told her, and squeezed her hands affectionately.

Gwyneth and Derek had worked together at MI6 for ten years and had formed a strong bond of friendship and trust. They had been spies, Derek once explained in confidence to me, so that trust was essential. But their friendship had been an unexpected gift and much more precious because of it. Her senior citizen status notwithstanding, she was a computer genius and also a lovely woman with a wicked sense of humor. She maintained great good health and held an important role in the running of the village. She also owned a charming antique shop on the high street that for many years had operated as a front for her espionage activities.

While working together, Gwyneth and Derek had devised those silly teasing names for each other, and they still occasionally used them. I enjoyed their teasing ways but had once asked why he couldn't simply have been *Derek* Danger.

"Too close to reality," Gwyneth had explained, and that made perfect sense.

We had come to Scotland earlier this year to solve a truly intricate puzzle: to find Claire's missing aunt Gwyneth and bring her to safety. For clues, we had been given an old copy of *Rebecca* by Daphne du Maurier. Certain pages had been marked, spelling out messages in an archaic foreign language.

Among Claire, Cameron, Derek, Gwyneth, and I, there were so many odd connections that I wasn't at all surprised when Claire announced that Cameron had proposed to her. Again, it made perfect sense.

Derek and Gwyneth were still chatting when Mom opened the library door and called to me. "Can you come in, sweetie?"

"Of course." I turned to Derek and Gwyneth. "I'd better take advantage of this invitation while it's available."

"We'll be nearby," Derek murmured, and deliberately kept the door ajar.

I walked into the library and saw Olivia and my mother sitting at the library table in the center of the room. The circle in the floor had disappeared, the candles were snuffed out, and the lights were turned on. That was when I noticed the beautiful Christmas tree standing in the middle of the room. It was decorated with dozens of ornaments and tiny fairy lights that managed to illuminate the room and emphasize the beauty of the rich, dark wood of the wall-to-wall, floor-to-ceiling bookshelves.

On the counter to the right of the Christmas tree stood a stack of at least ten books that I assumed were waiting to be put back in their proper places. I itched to look at the titles, wondering if I might find something new and exciting to read. I supposed it was too much to hope that one or two of the missing Christmas books were sitting in the stack.

The younger woman was clearly in a mellower mood now that their ritual was completed. Before joining them at the table, I took a few seconds to marvel at the beauty of the room beyond the Christmas tree. My favorite features were the high coffered ceilings and the fabulous library ladder suspended from a track that traveled smoothly all the way around the room. You had to love it. The only thing missing from the last time I was here were the layers of dust and the musty odor that had come from the room being closed off for several long years. Olivia had apparently taken care of it, and I was thankful for that.

"I know you want to ask me about the missing books," Olivia said.

"I do." I sat down at the table, and immediately the cat came over and rubbed up against my ankle. He circled a few times and then plopped down right on top of my feet. It made me smile. "So, can you tell me about them?"

She sighed. "The first to go missing was *The Gift of the Magi*. It broke my heart, as it's one of my favorite stories."

"Wait," I said immediately. "You mean the books weren't all stolen together? In one big lump?" I held out my hands to indicate the big lump. It wasn't a very elegant way to describe an armful of books, but Olivia understood.

"No." She shook her head. "The books were taken one at a time."

"How could you tell they were missing?" Mom asked.

Olivia glanced around the room, then gave her a patient smile. "This is a lovely room and the library is impressive, but it's really quite small as libraries go. And since we have people coming in here to browse through the books every day, I make it a practice at the end of each day to survey the shelves. I spend about half an hour methodically scanning each row to ensure everything is tidy. When a book is missing, the gap left behind is noticeable." She frowned. "The books weren't shelved together, so it seemed quite random."

Mom comforted her by softly patting her back. "That's very diligent of you."

As though in answer to the great questions of the universe, she said simply, "I'm a librarian."

"When you finally realized the books were gone, what did you think?" I hated to make it sound like an inquisition, but I was curious and wanted answers. "Did you have a list of the people who came into the library on a regular basis? Was there a particular time of the day that it happened?"

"You ask such smart questions," she said. "But I have no answers. I didn't expect anyone to steal the books. People come in here to read, and the only lists I keep are lists of people who request to take a book home with them. They're booklovers. And they love the castle. I know them. I can't believe they would steal from the Mac-Kinnon."

"So, everyone who comes into the library is someone you know?"

"Yes, of course. They live in the village or nearby. Some even work in the castle or on castle land. They're neighbors and friends. Why would I ever suspect them?"

"Do you think there was more than one person stealing the books?"

"I don't think so," she said hesitantly. "I believe it's just one person. But I'm not sure and I don't want to accuse someone falsely. There are a few people who come in every day on their lunch hour, and they sit and read the whole time."

"And they're friends of yours?"

"Not all of them, but of course I know them. And I wouldn't want to accuse any of them of a crime."

"But you think one of them might've taken the books."

"I can't say who would do it, but it must've been someone with a desperate need."

I couldn't comment on that supposition. Instead I said, "So, you keep a list of the people who take books out."

"Well, of course. That's how it works in a library. They wish to take a book home, so I make a note of the date and their name and the title of the book on cards that I keep in the desk. That way, I'll know when the book should be returned."

She explained it to me as if I were a six-year-old, but I was okay with that. "Can you give me the names of those people you suspect?"

Now she winced. "I don't really suspect them." She emphasized the word *suspect*. "I just think, you know, maybe they were, you know, here on the days the books went missing. I don't wish to bring trouble upon them."

"Of course not," I said gently. "I wouldn't give them any trouble. We just want the books back."

She took a deep breath and slowly exhaled. "Yes. I want that, too."

"I was told that several of the books are so rare as to be irreplaceable, which would make them extremely expensive."

"Aye. But not all of them are so precious and dear. *The Gift of the Magi* isn't an expensive book, nor is the library's copy of *The Velveteen*

Rabbit. So the price shouldn't matter. I want to see them all returned."

"I do, too," I said. "And so does the Laird." I'd deliberately mentioned the Laird, but now I wondered if I'd gone too far, because Olivia began to wring her hands. "Oh dear."

"Now, don't worry, Olivia." Mom reached out and took hold of her hand. "Everyone simply wants the books returned."

Olivia nodded but didn't say anything.

I said, "Maybe you could spread the word around the village that we just want the books. Nobody's going to get in any trouble. Just bring back the books."

She looked at me and nodded eagerly. "I can do that."

"That would be a huge help."

Again, Mom reached out and squeezed her hand. If the younger woman needed reassurance, Mom was here to give it to her.

At that moment the door swung open even wider and Willy walked in grinning. "Olivia me love, are ye open fer business?"

Olivia jumped up. "'Tisn't a good time, Willy."

"Och!" he said. "Sorry about that. I'll come back later."

Mom stood quickly. "No, no, Willy! We were just leaving."

"Yes, we've taken up enough of your time." From where I stood, I could see Derek and Gwyneth lingering outside the door.

"I don't mind," Olivia said, watching Willy's movements as he wandered over to flip through the stack of books on the counter. "It's a pleasure to talk to people who have a love of books."

"I agree," I said, smiling. "By the way, have you ever talked to Claire about getting a computer to help you keep track of the books?"

"Talk to Claire?" She tilted her head, clearly confused. "Uh, no. Cameron and Claire have other things to worry about, so I'm happy to use this system for now."

With the castle's impressive collection of books, it made perfectly good sense to upgrade the system. I would make the suggestion to Claire before I left. Maybe after the wedding when she was more relaxed. I believed I had more of a vested interest in creating a functional library system than anyone else in the castle, even more than Olivia, because . . . books. I was a book fanatic. So I would try to convince Claire and Cameron that a small investment in a computer system would save them time and money in the long run. Especially now, with book thieves cavorting around the countryside. And especially with the kind of beautiful books that Cameron had in his library. In his infinite generosity, he had allowed people to come in and simply take the books they wanted to read. It made it pitifully easy for a thief to walk off with a gem.

"Olivia," Mom asked, suddenly chatty now that we were on our way out. "Are you the only person working in the library?"

"Yes."

"What other tasks do you handle? Besides keeping track in your notebook of the books and the borrowers."

She beamed proudly. "I like to take one day each week to mop and wax the floors. On another day, I polish the furniture and the bookshelves. And I dust the books themselves."

"Aye!" Willy piped up. "She's pure dead brilliant the way she keeps everything spotless clean."

"Ye're oot the window, Willy," Olivia said, but she seemed happy with his praise.

"Do you have a member of the housekeeping staff who can help you with that work?" Mom asked.

"'Tisn't difficult," she said, "and it's important to keep the books free from dust and dirt. Some of the girls don't really understand how vital it is."

I nodded approvingly. "It certainly is."

Over the years I had given highly entertaining lectures and

classes at libraries and bookstores on the subject of maintaining a book collection of any size. And one big problem I had with those books going missing was that they might not be getting the best care—the kind of care they would receive in a library with professional book people watching over them.

For instance, as Olivia had stated, books needed to be dusted regularly. Dust was quite possibly the worst everyday enemy of books. If left to linger, the dust could turn to dirt and grind into the pages and covers.

In the case of a private library inside a private home—or castle—a conscientious librarian would also make regular forays into a given section of the library. There she would pick out one book at a time, hold it by the spine, and use a soft art brush or a clean cloth to wipe away the dust, especially from the top edge. While examining a shelf or a section, she would make sure the books were not crammed together so tightly that it risked warping the spine. For leather books, packing them too close together could cause the leather to sweat, damaging them even further.

It was also important not only to dust the books but to dust the shelves regularly as well. One would want to watch out for sunlight that could cause covers to stain or fade or even burn. Another danger was high humidity, in which books could grow moldy and pages balloon out, and low humidity, which could cause pages and covers to crack. I had personally suffered through each of these horrors and could attest to the pain it caused me.

It would be nice if I could guarantee that a stolen book would fall into the hands of a true booklover, but sadly, someone who peddled in stolen books usually did it for the money alone, not for the love of a book.

"So, you like working in the castle?" Mom asked, disturbing my reverie and bringing me back to the present.

"Oh, aye," Olivia said. "It's a beautiful room, isn't it? And the kitchen staff feeds me a hearty meal every day. I also work one day a week in the village library. It's not quite as fancy, but there are more people coming through, so it's nice to see friendly faces."

"I would think so." Mom gave her a hug. "Would you like to talk tomorrow?"

"Aye, please," she said. "You inspire me. Thank you."

Mom patted her cheek. "You're a good girl."

"Have a good day, ladies," Willy said with a wink as he leaned jauntily against the bookshelf, watching us leave.

He was so darn cute, I had to grin right back. "You, too, Willy."

We were almost at the door when Olivia ran and gave Mom another hug. Whispering, she said, "You're a powerful force, Becky. I would like to learn from you."

"Thank you, dear." Mom turned and slipped her arm through mine and led me out of the library. Once we were farther down the hall, she leaned close and whispered, "Let's go chat in the blue parlor."

"Okay."

We walked down the hall and into the parlor, where I was relieved to find Gwyneth and Derek sitting at the bar, talking quietly. Mom closed the door behind us and turned to me. "That girl is nothing but trouble."

I blinked in shock. "Olivia? I thought you liked her. She seemed nice."

"It's performance art. She's got a dark heart."

I gaped at her. "Wow, Mom. You acted like her new best friend."

"I wanted to keep things calm." Mom began to pace slowly back and forth from the wide picture window to the end of the bar. "She's confused and volatile."

"Well, you really calmed her down. What did you do? Sneak her a Xanax?"

"If I'd had one, I might've."

"Since the door was open," Gwyneth said, "I was able to hear her talking about *The Gift of the Magi*."

"Yes," I said. "She's very fond of that one."

Gwyneth sniffed. "I won that book at the parish auction and gave it to Claire. She put it in the library, and now I find out that it's missing."

"That's not the only one," I said.

"What do you mean?" Gwyneth demanded.

"It seems there are twelve books missing altogether," Derek said.

"Twelve?"

"Yes," I said. "All of them contain Christmas themes."

"Christmas," Gwyneth said, and turned thoughtful. "Well, 'tis the season."

"Indeed," Derek said. "But what are you thinking?"

She met his gaze. "I'll let you know when I've figured it out." She turned and smiled at Mom. "You must be Becky. Derek has said so many lovely things about you."

I squeezed my eyes closed, then sighed. "I'm so sorry, Gwyneth. Please let me introduce you to my mother, Becky Wainwright. Mom, this is Gwyneth Quinn, Claire's aunt."

Gwyneth nodded in greeting. "Delighted to officially meet you."

Mom took Gwyneth's hand in both of hers. "And I'm so happy to meet you, too, Ms. Quinn. Claire is such a treasure to us."

Especially when she was throwing knives at bad guys outside my house, I thought, feeling a chill as I remembered that moment from many months ago.

"She's a treasure to me, as well," Gwyneth said with a soft smile. "I'm so glad she's back home to stay. And please, you're to call me Gwyneth."

"I would like that."

"And speaking of treasure, your Brooklyn is quite the brilliant crime solver."

"Oh, she is that," Mom said, with a somber look at me. "And I think she'll want to hear what I've got to say about this young librarian I just spoke to."

"Okay." I glanced around. "Where's Dad, by the way?"

"He's outside helping the boys sweep up the scattered bits of wood they'll add to the bonfire."

I smiled. "He's probably having a blast."

"Oh, you know it."

"And I should be out there helping," Derek said. "But first, Rebecca, what were you going to say about the librarian?"

"I'll keep it short," Mom said. "First of all, Olivia loves working here. That is, she loves Cameron. But she hates Claire."

I heard the sudden intake of breath from Gwyneth.

I frowned. "She told you she hated Claire?"

"She didn't have to tell me. Every time she mentioned her name, her lip curled up and she rolled her eyes. She said that Claire isn't the angel everyone thinks she is."

"That's positively slanderous!" Gwyneth said. "She is an absolute angel."

"I agree with you absolutely. But Olivia insists that there are other women in town who agree with her."

"Ridiculous," Gwyneth said, her hands turning to fists. "I want the names of those women."

"What's this really about?" I asked. "Is she jealous of Claire? Is this about Cameron?"

"Maybe," Mom said. "But I didn't get a strong vibe in that direction. Mostly, she just dislikes Claire, and I think I know why."

"Why, Mom?"

"Olivia is obsessed with money, and Cameron has it. And now

he's marrying Claire, which means he and his money are no longer up for grabs."

"That's a tacky way to look at it," I said.

"You know it," Mom said. "There's more, sweetie, but you might not want to hear it."

"What?"

Mom took a deep breath and let it out. "She has the strangest aura I've ever seen. I wouldn't call her evil. Just . . . confused. And determined."

Confused and determined? That did not compute.

"But, Mom," I said, "you've seen dark auras before." I spoke as though we talked about auras every day. We didn't. But this was Mom, so I went along with her.

"You know I have," she said. "And this girl's aura definitely hovers toward blackness. But then suddenly I saw it shimmer and grow slightly lighter. Turned a sort of murky gray."

"That's creepy," I said. "Do her personality or her feelings change along with her aura? Is that how it works?"

"Those things can affect changes in aura." She frowned. "Still, this was odd. The gray color turned very dark very quickly. And then it continued to change colors, light to dark, minute to minute." Mom rubbed her arms. "Gave me the shivers."

"You said you thought she was confused," I said. "Sounds like her aura is just as confused as she is."

Mom nodded. "Here's another odd thing. The only time she lightened up was when she talked about her salary."

"So, money makes her happy?" I said. "Nothing wrong with that, I suppose."

"Auras or not," Gwyneth said briskly, "I don't like to hear that Claire is having problems with anyone."

"Yes, I'm concerned for Claire," Mom said. "There's something going on here. I can't quite figure out what it is, but I think she may be in danger."

Gwyneth was obviously alarmed but didn't say a word. She just continued to clench her fists and breathe heavily.

"It might be simple jealousy," I said. "Claire won the Laird, and the rest of the ladies can't handle it."

"Maybe," Mom said slowly.

But now it was my turn to start pacing.

"What is it, love?" Derek asked, tuning into my unease.

"It's just that . . . Claire seems to be afraid of her."

"Afraid of the librarian?" Gwyneth said, then laughed. "My girl is a world-class knife thrower. She can chuck a spear across a soccer field. And she's an archery champion. I have a hard time accepting that she's afraid of this woman."

"I don't get it, either," Mom said. "If she really is afraid of her, why doesn't she fire her? Or have Cameron do it."

"I'll talk to Cameron," Derek said, and picked up his cell phone.

"And I'll talk to Sophie," I said. "She knows Claire the best of all of us, and I think she knows more about Olivia than she's saying."

Mom nodded firmly. "Call her. And let's get this mess cleaned up as soon as possible."

Chapter 6

Derek set down his phone. "Cameron is attending a meeting with his security team. He said to expect him back in about an hour."

"That makes sense," Gwyneth said.

With hundreds of villagers converging on Cameron's land in a few hours, his security team would need to be on high alert.

"I can use the time to finish repairing the book." I checked my wristwatch. "Let's plan to meet here in about ninety minutes."

"I'll walk you upstairs," Derek said, then whispered, "and you can tell me what else occurred in the library."

"Okay." I leaned close to Mom and whispered, "You might want to keep an eye on the library, make sure Olivia stays in there. Or if she comes out, make sure she leaves the castle. I don't want her anywhere near Claire."

Mom saluted smartly. "I'm on the case."

"Do we know where Claire is right now?" I asked.

Gwyneth said, "She walked out with Sophie, who was going to work at the pub for a bit."

"And Claire?" Derek asked.

"She was off to practice her archery."

"How fun," Mom said.

Gwyneth turned to Mom. "Why don't we have a nice chat while the children run off to do their thing."

"There are two chairs outside the great hall," Mom said. "We'll have a perfect view of the library from there."

"Wonderful."

As Derek and I walked out of the parlor, I glanced back at Mom and Gwyneth. "Should we leave those two alone?"

He looked over his shoulder. "Hmm."

"Who knows what mischief they'll concoct while we're gone?"

He chuckled. "We'll simply have to take our chances."

We stepped inside our bedroom suite and Derek closed the door. He surveyed the room, then went into the bathroom and pulled the shower curtain back. He looked in the closet near the door as well as the bedroom closet and reached up to make sure that nothing—or no one—was hiding on any of the shelves. He looked behind the loveseat and under the bed, then pulled the heavy draperies back.

"Just checking," he said mildly.

"I appreciate it."

He leaned against the bedpost. "Your mother isn't one to exaggerate or gossip when it comes to things like this."

"No, she isn't," I assured him. "In fact, she would bend over backward before she would disparage a fellow Wiccan, and when we first saw them in the library, I figured Olivia must be Wiccan." I considered it for a moment. "Maybe Olivia felt it was safe to complain to my mother since she's the super grand muckety-muck of her coven."

"She may not be Wiccan at all, but simply felt comfortable around your mother."

"I don't know what to think now. But until we get more info, I'll go with that theory."

I caught him up on everything Olivia had said to my mother and me. He listened intently, nodding and asking a few questions.

When I wrapped up, he checked his watch. "I'm going to leave you to your work and see you in ninety minutes."

"Okay."

Derek studied me. "Do you have your phone with you?"

"Yes." I pulled it from my pocket to show him. "I'll call you if anything odd occurs up here."

"Be sure you do. And lock the door."

"I will. Do you have your key with you?"

"Of course I do." He pulled me close and kissed me, then left to go downstairs.

As soon as I locked the door, I called Sophie at the pub.

It took three rings for her to answer. I could hear the noise in the background. It was clear that the pub was already crowded with people preparing for New Year's Eve.

"Mackenzie's Pub," she shouted.

"Hi, Sophie. It's Brooklyn."

"Brooklyn," she said cheerfully, then hesitated. "Is everything all right?"

"Yes. Sorry to bother you at work, but I have a quick question for you."

"Of course. What is it?"

"Does the reason that Claire and Olivia don't get along have anything to do with Cameron?"

She gave one quick laugh. "Of course, but not in the way you think."

I chuckled. "Well, that's cryptic enough."

"Sorry. Why do you ask? What's going on over there?"

"This afternoon Olivia had a long talk with my mother, and based on that conversation, we're going to meet with Cameron and Claire and Aunt Gwyneth and my mother to discuss the situation. I thought it would be good if you were here."

"What time?"

I spent a few seconds calculating the time that had passed. "In about an hour."

"Count me in," she said briskly.

"I'm sorry to take you away from your job."

"I was only going to work a few hours today. I'm spending the night at the castle."

"I'm so glad. We'll see you in a little while. We'll be in the blue parlor."

"I'll find you," she said.

We ended the call, and I took another minute to consider the Olivia problem and how to deal with her. It made me wonder if the whole book theft story was a lie. Maybe she had taken the books for herself. And another thought emerged. How could we keep her away from Claire for the next few days?

I was worried about Claire because of my mother's gut feeling that told her Olivia was a possible danger to Claire. I hadn't seen it for myself, and I hadn't caught the same vibe that Mom had. Then again, I didn't read auras.

My family and I had long ago accepted that Mom had an empathic ability to read other people's feelings. But that didn't always mean that we believed her stories or went along with her on every issue. I mean, she also liked to relax at a place called the Laughing

Goat Sweat Lodge, where she enjoyed the earsplitting rhythms of the local shamanic drum circle.

No, I didn't always go along with her schemes and notions. But I loved her and always knew when she was telling the truth.

As far as our meeting later this afternoon, I decided I would leave the strategizing to Derek and Gwyneth, both of whom had spent years dealing with enemies of the state and bad players in general.

Cameron might have some ideas on how to deal with Olivia, as well. And Sophie knew everyone in the village. She was an old friend of Cameron's and she was also fiercely loyal to Claire. She recognized that there was some animosity coming from Olivia. Since she was staying at the castle tonight, I knew she would stay close to Claire.

My mind wrapped around the image of Olivia, the delicately beautiful librarian. It still bugged me that according to my mother, she'd been putting on an act for me.

And that brought up old memories from years ago, when I met and became close to a fellow book arts aficionado. She was another one who looked like a petite angel with long blond hair and big blue eyes. One weekend I invited her to Dharma and introduced her to my family and friends. That afternoon, on the main street in town, another dear friend was shot right in front of me. He almost died. That's when my mother told me that my bookish friend had a gray aura, which indicated that she might be ill, possibly terminally. It later turned out that a gray aura was also indicative of a blackhearted witch who was actually looking to kill my very dear friend.

"Enough," I muttered. I really needed to concentrate on the Robert Burns book. I was determined to finish it in the next hour because I knew that Claire would feel better if she could hold the repaired book in her hands. She was about to be married, and she had a million things to think about and deal with. I wanted to do every-thing I could to help her keep cool and calm. The Olivia situation had clearly affected her, and I didn't want to make it worse, so maybe I would talk to Derek about us tracking down the missing books ourselves.

As long as Sophie and Gwyneth were here, I was certain that Claire would be safe. Gwyneth, especially, would be watching out for her beloved niece like a mama hawk.

So for the next little while, I put those thoughts aside and con-centrated on the book. I removed the binder clip, wax paper, and heavy boards I'd used to keep the corner in line. Now the glue was completely dry, and the corner and sides were straight. It looked pretty darn good, if I did say so myself.

I pulled out my piece of burgundy leather, and the first thing I did was compare the color and texture of the new piece with the old book. It was almost too perfect to be believed, and I breathed a sigh of relief.

Since I was working with leather, I pulled out my left-handed English paring knife and my adorable sharpening stone, which fit perfectly in the palm of my hand, came in its own case, and was small and lightweight enough to take on trips. The knife was made of high-carbon steel and it came with a handle. I mention this because some leather paring knives don't have a handle, and some bookbind-ers prefer it that way, but I just can't deal with that. I'm someone who needs a handle on her knife; otherwise, anything can happen. To put it bluntly, I didn't want to bleed on a pretty book.

The first thing I did with the knife was hone the blade on the stone, bringing it to an extremely sharp finish.

I moved the book out of the way and placed the leather piece on my cutting board. I had already measured the other corners, so I used my metal ruler and my knife to carefully cut a triangle from the larger piece of burgundy leather. I still had enough material left over to cut several more pieces in case I made an error, but I didn't intend to make an error.

I cautiously sliced off one tip of the triangle, and now it resembled an isosceles trapezoid. I had once looked up the definition of an isosceles trapezoid in order to explain it to a bookbinding class, but it was way too complicated for me. The easiest way to describe the revised shape was to draw it. Basically, it was an equilateral triangle with one of the tips sliced off.

I placed the corner piece on the cutting board and began paring the edges. Paring was done along the edges of a piece of leather in order to lessen the thickness so I wouldn't end up with a big clump of leather when I did my turn-in. Properly paring the edge was something that came with practice. You never wanted to cut all the way through the piece; you just wanted to take ultrathin slices off the edges, giving the leather a beveled appearance.

Before I could glue the corner onto the book, I had to pull the pastedown—or endpaper—away from the inside back cover. This was going to be a nerve-racking task for a few reasons. First, because the book was almost two hundred years old and fragile, I didn't want to tear the endpaper while pulling it away from the cover. Second, once it was pulled away, I planned to tuck the leather turn-in under the endpaper in a way that would give no indication that there had ever been a problem. I didn't want to see a tear or a ripple when I finally glued it back and smoothed it down. It was a delicate operation.

Again, I used my X-Acto knife to ease the endpaper up and away from the corner of the book. It was slow going, but I got it done. After that, I was more than ready for my cocktail, but I still had to glue the leather corner to the cover.

Leather is more easily manipulated when wet, so I took a small sponge and wet down the leather corner piece. The moisture was sure to change the color slightly, but I was pretty sure it would be fine. I reached for my soft glue brush and applied it to the backside of the corner piece and then placed it onto the book itself. PVA glue is malleable enough that if I wasn't happy with the placement, I could remove or adjust until it was perfectly even and straight.

I took out my bone folder and began smoothing the leather over the edge of the book and onto the inside of the cover. I used small strokes, carefully flattening the leather against the cover until it was completely smooth. On the edge, I used a rounded movement to smooth the leather down. Inside the cover, I made sure the leather lay flat with no rippling. Then I oh-so-carefully brought the end-paper back over the beveled leather, again using the bone folder to make it as smooth as silk. I used my magnifying glasses to check every inch of that section to make sure there were no folds or ripples or tears. I felt a wave of emotion when I saw that it was simply perfect.

It didn't always work out that way, especially when I was traveling without my best tools. But in this case, it worked. I was happy.

I set the book aside after sliding a thin piece of plastic between the inside cover and the flyleaf. I didn't want any glue transferred onto the book itself.

I wrapped the book in a soft white cloth, then pulled several heavy books from the bookshelf and set them on top of the Robert Burns. This would act as an improvised book press. I would let Claire know the book was ready, but I wanted to press it for a few hours, just to be safe.

As I packed away my tools, I realized that I'd been so nervous about this minuscule but important job that I was now both energized and wiped out. I would've loved to have taken a nap, but that wasn't going to happen. I had a job to do downstairs, a friend to protect, and a meeting to conduct. And then it was New Year's Eve! Good grief. Maybe I would get a cup of coffee before the drinking began. I needed something to help me make it through the night.

I checked my watch and realized I'd spent more than half an hour finishing the book. I stretched my arms out and up, then moved my shoulders back and forth to get rid of the kinks. I had thirty minutes before I had to be downstairs in the blue parlor, so I was about to throw some water on my face and brush my hair when I suddenly heard a piercing, unearthly yowling! It sounded as though it was coming from inside this room!

"What the hell is that?" I raced around the room like a crazed monkey looking for whatever had made that horrible noise. A cat? Maybe, but it didn't sound like any friendly tabby I'd ever heard of.

Were there mountain lions in Scotland?

I stood in the middle of the room looking every which way and wondering if I had manifested that sound myself simply by thinking all those dark thoughts about Olivia.

"Talk about loony," I muttered. "You didn't manifest anything. Something real made that sound."

But what was it? I pulled out my phone, turned on the flashlight app, and checked under the bed. Nothing there. I went through the same motions that Derek had gone through earlier, checking behind the heavy drapes, looking in the bathroom, peeking behind the shower curtain, and searching every one of the closets. I knew I wouldn't find anything. Derek had looked everywhere barely an hour ago, and I'd been in the room ever since.

On a hunch, I ran over to the wide picture window, wondering if there were shrieking cats hanging outside the window. Highly unlikely, but worth a look. Unlatching the window, I pushed it open and looked in every direction but didn't see a thing. Except the beauty of the view. It was a glorious day, so I took a few seconds to soak it in. Then the cold air snapped me back to reality, and I quickly closed the window and locked it.

I'd thought the sound had come from inside the room, but how could that be? There was nothing here! Maybe there was something out in the hall. But since I had effectively freaked myself out, I wasn't too eager to open the door and check it out.

I suddenly recalled what my mother had given me the night before. "No way," I muttered, but I found my purse anyway and dragged that little bundle of white sage out. Taking one of the matches off the mantel, I lit the sage and gently swept it around the room, knowing it wouldn't keep any goblins or monsters away. But as Mom had promised, it was certainly leaving a pleasant scent.

I wondered if anyone downstairs had heard that ungodly sound. And that's when I grabbed the phone again and called Derek.

"Hello, love," he said.

"Did you hear that sound?" I demanded a little too forcefully.

"Hear what?" he asked. "Never mind. I'll be right there."

The phone went dead and I had to catch my breath. Less than thirty seconds later, I heard the key in the lock. The door swung open and Derek rushed inside. He wrapped his arms around me and held on for a long moment. My hero.

I realized I was shaking and felt ridiculous. I took one more deep breath. "I'm okay. I'm fine."

He held me at arm's length, studying my expression. "What did you hear?"

"It sounded like the biggest, angriest cat I've ever heard. It could've been a tiger, even. More like a shriek than a roar. It was loud and it was furious." I blew out a breath and realized I still had no idea what had made that sound. "I don't know. Maybe it was a bat. A really big bat."

"Maybe it was," he said, rubbing my arms to calm me down. He stopped for a moment, sniffed the air, and asked, "What is that interesting fragrance?"

"It's nothing."

"That's funny, because it smells like white sage." He gazed into my eyes. "Darling, if you were driven to the point of burning your mother's white sage, you must've been very frightened indeed. I'm sorry."

"I'm sorry, too. I hope I didn't freak you out too much." I shook my head and dropped down into the chair, realizing that Derek rarely got freaked out. But I did. "I guess I kind of scared myself to death. I'm starting to feel stupid. Maybe that's a good thing."

"Better than being frightened out of your wits."

"I guess so."

"There are cats in this house, darling," he said. He sat on the arm of the chair and was smoothing my hair back. "Maybe some of their friends stopped by to party."

I had to laugh. "That's it. A cat party." With one more deep breath, I stood. "Okay, I'm going to splash water on my face, and then I'll be ready to go."

"Good. Everyone's already waiting in the blue parlor."

"They are?" I checked my watch again. "Give me thirty seconds."

"Are you sure you're all right?"

"Yes," I called from the bathroom. When I emerged, I said, "Thank you for coming to my rescue."

He hugged me and gave me a kiss. "Always."

A few minutes later we walked into the blue parlor and closed the door behind us.

"Oh, sweetie, you look fresh and lovely," my mother said. "Did you take a nap?"

I almost laughed, thinking of the way I'd taken barely a minute to splash water on my face, rub on some moisturizer, apply lip gloss, and brush my hair.

I planted a kiss on her cheek. "No nap, but thank you, Mom."

I noticed a beautiful platter of cheeses and crackers and fruits and veggies and dip had been placed on the coffee table. The fruits and veggies had been arranged in rows to form a Christmas tree.

"Isn't that beautiful?" Mom said. "Tamara cut and parboiled the veggies and then arranged them in this perfect order."

As someone who could barely cook an egg, I was instantly fascinated. Alternate rows featured grapes and cantaloupe bits and chunks of cheddar cheese. Cherry tomatoes acted as ornaments on each end, and carrot sticks were bunched together to make the tree stand. A large piece of cauliflower was cut in the shape of a star and perched on top. It was delightful.

"This is so clever," I said.

"Mrs. B just brought it in," Mom explained. "She gave us the order to eat up and enjoy ourselves."

"I'm happy to follow her orders." I reached for a chunk of cheese, a carrot stick, and a cracker and realized that I was really hungry.

Since Cameron was acting as bartender again, I asked for a glass of red wine. *So much for getting a cup of coffee before the drinking began*, I thought to myself. But that was okay. It turned out being scared half to death was an even better way to stay awake than a cup of coffee would've been.

He pulled a bottle from the wine cabinet under the bar. "We have a stunning 2016 Bordeaux that I think you'll love."

Dad nodded approvingly. "That was one of the best growing seasons France has had in years."

"It sounds wonderful," I said as he poured the ruby red liquid into a tall wineglass.

"I'll have one of those, too, Cameron, if you don't mind," Dad said.

"It's my pleasure." Cameron poured the wine and handed a glass to each of us.

"It's a beautiful color," I said, swirling the wine in the glass.

"Look at those legs," Dad said, staring at the streaks of liquid streaming down inside my glass.

I had learned at a very early age that wine legs generally indicated higher alcohol content, richer texture, and fuller body.

Mom gave us both a look. "Now, don't you two start sounding like wine snobs."

"We're not snobs," Dad said with a wink. "We're just enthusiastic."

Mom, Gwyneth, and Claire were all drinking white wine. Derek and Cameron had Scotch.

When everyone had their drinks, Dad raised his glass to toast Cameron. "Thank you for being an excellent host and a generous man, and I wish you as much love and fun and adventure in your new life together as I've had with my beautiful wife."

We clicked glasses, and I noticed both Mom and Claire were sniffling a little.

"That was a sweet toast, Dad," I said.

"Thanks, honey." He grinned. "I still got it."

Sophie walked in just then, and she turned and locked the door. She walked up to the bar and asked for a glass of water. When Cameron handed her the glass, she took a long sip. Then she looked around and said, "So, what're we going to do about this monster in our midst?"

Cameron looked completely confused. "Are you talking about Nessie now?"

Claire slipped her arm through his. "I doubt we're all here to discuss the Loch Ness Monster." But looking around at our faces, she began to frown. "So, what's going on?" She looked at Sophie, then me.

Sophie took pity on them both. "Your Lairdship, we need to discuss an issue that came up while Becky was in the library talking to Olivia. Her hostility toward Claire has become an issue."

"What?" Cameron took a few seconds to digest that information. "This is a joke, right?"

"It's not," Mom said. "Olivia told me that she and other women in the village would like nothing better than to see you get rid of Claire. There are several issues involved, but for one thing, they're angry that you've chosen to marry an Englishwoman."

"Och," Cameron said, sounding disgusted. "Claire is Scottish! And even if she weren't, 'tisn't anyone's business but mine who I choose to marry." He walked out from behind the bar and began to pace across the length of the room. "Is Olivia still in the library? I'll go talk to her."

"No," Mom said. "She's gone for the day. I walked her to her car and made sure that she left the property. She'll be back tonight, though, because she wants to see the bonfire being lit."

He looked directly at Claire. "We've got to fire her. I'll do it, but not tonight. Next week when she comes back to work, I'll talk to her."

"That won't solve the problem," Claire said.

"No, it won't." Sophie nodded. "There are a number of other ladies in the village who stoke this negativity, and Olivia and others eat it right up. Some of the main voices speaking up against Claire are Olivia's mother and her aunt."

"Her mother and her aunt?" Cameron said. "I know these women. They've always been friendly and kind to me."

"Of course they have," Sophie said. "You're the Laird."

"And Claire will soon be my wife," he declared stoutly.

Dad eased away from the bar. "Are these women jealous of Claire?"

"Well, yes and no," Mom said. "Olivia wouldn't mind marrying the Laird, but only because he's wealthy. She doesn't much care about love or Cameron himself, for that matter. She only cares about getting rich."

Cameron clutched his heart. "I'm devastated."

"No, you're dafty," Sophie said, laughing.

But he was clearly exasperated. "Seriously, I don't understand. What does Olivia want? Why is she angry with Claire?"

"Because Claire snagged the grand prize," Sophie said. "Meaning you. You're it. You're powerful, you have good looks, charm, talent, money, a castle, a boat, a flat in Edinburgh, a dozen cars, and a lovely cat."

We all chuckled at the cat reference, and I marveled that once again Sophie had eased the tension.

Cameron grabbed hold of Claire's hand. "That's why I fell in love with Claire. She came with her own cat."

Sophie's mouth twisted into a smile. "There's a bit more to it than that."

"Well, of course," he said, frowning again. "But maybe you were right the first time, Soph. I'm dafty." He sighed heavily. "I guess I've never really put it all together in words, but the fact is that when I met Claire, she had her own life. I didn't meet her in the village or in school or at the pub or through a friend. She was independent and happy and fulfilled through her own hard work, and she was very successful. She didn't need me, didn't need the job I was offering, didn't need to live in a castle." He shook his head. "I can't tell you what it took to convince her to take the job revamping the great hall. Here she is, the preeminent expert in the world in Scottish weaponry, and I was offering her this incredible position in her chosen field. I thought she'd fall all over herself to take the job. But she turned me down."

"I think we're getting a bit off topic," Claire said, her cheeks turning pink.

Cameron reached out, smoothed her hair back, and kissed her. "Perhaps so," he admitted, and turned to Mom. "I think you had more to tell us, Becky."

"I did," Mom said. "I spent quite a bit of time with Olivia this afternoon, and I'll just say it. That girl's got some problems."

I studied her for a moment. "You're not saying she's evil or anything. Right?"

"No, of course not. She's . . . misguided. And yet, she's quite determined. Frankly, I don't think she can be trusted."

Derek's gaze met mine, then he looked at Mom. "What happened in there, Rebecca? What did she say to you?"

Mom took a breath. "To explain what happened, I first need to give you a thirty-second primer on Wicca."

"I'd love to hear it, Becky," Claire said.

"This is going to be good," Dad said, rubbing his hands together.

Mom settled herself. "I won't speak for all Wiccans, but for myself, I believe in the divinity of nature. I celebrate it. I love the rain and the wind and the sun. I joined a Wiccan community a few years ago because I enjoy the celebratory rituals and the magic. I enjoy the company of like-minded women. I believe in magic, and frankly I'm as capable as the next person of making magic happen."

"That's my girl," Dad said, tugging her close and kissing her cheek. Mom beamed at him.

"So, how did you approach Olivia?" I asked.

"It was mainly timing."

Dad nodded. "Isn't everything?"

"Yes." Mom smiled. "I went for a walk early this morning, and as I was coming back, I met Olivia at the front door. It seems she likes to arrive early before anyone is awake and then lock herself away in the library. So I said hello and complimented her hair, and she invited me into the library. I told her I needed to meet my husband for breakfast and I would be back afterward. When I returned to the library, she needed to take care of something at her desk, so I wandered around, looking at books. And that's when I saw a stack of books on the counter. And guess what? On top of the stack was a book called *Financial Planning for Wiccans*. So that opened things up for me."

Financial Planning for Wiccans. I had to laugh. "If that book hadn't been there, you'd have found another way to get her talking."

"Of course." She smiled. "I'm a people person."

"But seriously? *Financial Planning for Wiccans*? Does it contain spells and rituals to make money happen?"

"Why not?" Mom said with a little shrug.

"Is Olivia a Wiccan?" Claire asked.

"She dabbles," Mom said without judgment. "So we talked about Wicca and money and finances and how she's determined to get rich. Her main interest in life is money, so she's willing to try anything that might unlock the key to making her fortune. Even Wicca. Every other book in that stack was about getting rich. The girl is a bit obsessed."

"Obsessed with money," Cameron said, "not with me." He blew out a breath. "Good. That's good to hear."

"But you have a lot to do with it," Sophie said.

"Okay, there's just one thing I want to know." He turned to Claire. "Is Olivia rude to you?"

"Yes," she said simply.

He frowned at her. "Why didn't you tell me?"

She straightened her spine and shook her hair back. "Several reasons. First, I can fight my own battles."

"You tell him, Claire," Mom said.

"And second," Claire continued, "to be honest, I consider her attitude to be the price I'll have to pay to be with you."

Cameron looked appalled. "The price you'd have to pay? What does that even mean?"

She smiled patiently. "You know what I mean. You're so popular, and so many people want your attention, I knew I'd have to get used to that. You're a good man and you help everyone in town. I love you, so if I have to pay this price, it's worth it."

"Come on, Claire," he murmured.

"I'm serious. Most of the time, people are very polite and friendly, and I appreciate that." She sighed. "But there have been moments. Some folks are incredibly jealous. And then there's Olivia. Sophie can tell you about some of her worst attacks. I really don't want to talk about the bad ones."

"The bad ones?" Cameron took her hand in his. "What the hell? This is a mess. I'm so sorry."

"It's not your fault."

"Tell me what Olivia did."

"I don't . . ."

"I'll tell him," Sophie said. "There are too many instances, so I'll keep it to the highlights. Olivia is smart and she's subtle, but when she's talking to Claire, there's always a rude comment or a direct cut."

"Direct cut?" he asked.

"You really need to read more romance novels," Sophie said with a sigh. "In Regency England it was called 'the cut direct.' Let me demonstrate." She walked toward him and stared right at him but didn't say a word, didn't acknowledge him. Just stared right through him and kept walking. "You simply ignore the other person," Sophie explained. "It's the height of rudeness."

"That was quite odd," Cameron admitted.

"And very rude," Sophie concluded.

"Yes," Cameron agreed.

"She talks behind my back," Claire said. "And it doesn't help that her mother is headmistress at Atherton Academy."

"Atherton?" Cameron said, smiling now. "That's where I went to school. It's a wonderful place."

"Yes, I know," Claire said. "I love hearing you talk about growing up in your village with all of your mates and how you all went to that wonderful school with its activities and sports teams and the academic excellence."

"It was quite the best place to go," he said softly.

"Yes," Claire said, smiling. "And I want our children to go there, too."

He nodded. "I'd like that."

"But I recently received a pamphlet from the academy," Claire said. "And somehow it ended up in the library. Olivia made a point of assuring me that our children would never be allowed to attend Atherton." She shook her head angrily. "She's such a cow."

"Yes, she is," Sophie said. "And I much prefer to see you angry than to see you wallow. It's a much better look on you."

"Agreed," Claire said.

"But Claire, darling," Cameron said. "It doesn't matter what Olivia thinks. Or, for that matter, where our children go to school. That's something we'll decide when the time comes. It only matters that they're loved and cherished. If it comes to that, we'll teach them at home."

"Cameron, it does matter, and there is no way we're going to homeschool our children." She had to exhale and walk over to the bar for a glass of water. She glanced around at the room in general. "Sorry, everyone. You probably didn't care to have a front-row seat for this conversation."

"We're loving it," Dad said.

Claire laughed. "Thank you, Jim." She looked at Cameron. "You've always talked about how wonderful your childhood was and how much you loved going to the academy. I want our children to experience that same wonderful childhood. As you know, my own childhood left much to be desired, so this is important to me. I want our children to be happy, and I don't want anyone in the village spreading rude rumors about their mother. Namely, me."

He pulled her into his arms and rubbed her back. "I don't want that, either. So, what are these rude rumors you're speaking of?"

"I can answer that one," Sophie said, wearing a silly grin.

He grimaced, then glanced at Claire. "I suppose if Claire can take it, so can I."

"You can take it," Sophie said. She seemed to enjoy giving Cameron grief. He usually appeared to appreciate her slight digs, though, and that made me like him even more.

"And so can I," Claire muttered.

"Okay," Sophie said. "It's mainly to do with Olivia talking behind Claire's back. And her audience is primarily the women of the OWC."

He frowned. "The Oddlochen Women's Club?"

"That's right. Within the club there's a small group of powerful women who've decided that Claire doesn't belong here."

"What?" The word was like an explosion. "I'll shut them down."

"You can try," Sophie said. "But if you think the men in this town are powerful, the women have them beat by a mile."

"I'm aware of that," he said, practically snarling. "But it's going to change."

"That's good to hear," Sophie said. "Because you'll remember how we mentioned that Olivia's mother is headmistress of Atherton Academy?"

"Aye. I'm hearing you." Cameron's expression turned thunderous now.

"I really need to share one more story with you," Sophie continued.

"I'd rather not hear it."

"I know." She patted his shoulder. "But you're a part of this one."

"Then let's get on with it."

"One day Claire discovered that her new white Stella McCartney blazer had been dredged through the mud and left in a dirty puddle over by the garage. A few days later, Olivia was spreading rumors all over the village that Claire had been arrested for shoplifting the blazer."

"That's impossible," Cameron said, shaking his head.

Sophie folded her arms across her chest. "You'll like this part, Cameron. According to the gossip, you're the one who bailed her out, and you paid the cops to keep it quiet."

"What?" He almost whispered it. "That's ridiculous."

"Hasn't anyone confronted her about these lies?" Derek asked.

"Oh, all the time," Sophie said. "She completely denies she's lying and gets very upset when anyone accuses her. And she has the women of the OWC backing her up."

Dad asked, "Why do they have this kind of power?"

"It's her mother who has the power. She's the owner and headmistress of Atherton Academy. And her aunts are powerful, too. One is the president of the OWC. And her aunt's husband is the mayor. The other aunt's husband ran the village bank until he died recently."

"Oh, jeez," Dad said. "Triple whammy."

"This won't continue," Cameron said through clenched teeth. "The mayor is a good friend of mine, and I'm on the board of trustees of the bank. I have a few tricks up my sleeve. But first I'll talk to Olivia. And then I'll fire her."

Chapter 7

As Derek and I walked upstairs to change into warmer clothing, we talked about Olivia. She would be away from the castle for a while longer, so we could relax for a bit. Maybe I was being naive, though. Maybe she'd walked with my mom out to her car, driven away, and as soon as Mom went back inside, came right back onto the castle grounds. She probably knew plenty of places to hide her car. Maybe she had set some kind of trap.

And maybe I should rethink my mother's story about Olivia.

"And maybe I'm giving myself chills," I said as we reached the landing. I took a quick sip of wine, glad we'd decided to pour ourselves another drink before coming upstairs.

"You're giving me chills as well," Derek groused.

I laughed, knowing that Derek didn't get chills. He enjoyed walking in the cold evening air of San Francisco and up in Sonoma all year long. But I so appreciated him claiming to have chills. We unlocked our bedroom suite, and I hurried inside as Derek locked the door behind us.

"Why am I laughing?" I said.

"Because you're having to step into the mind of what might be a twisted personality," he muttered. "And it's all rather awful to contemplate. So we laugh."

"Does that make us sound wacky? Because we're also putting all of our trust in my mother's belief that this woman is some kind of a diabolical monster. And . . ."

"And what?"

I scowled. "I don't know. Olivia just didn't come across that way to me."

"Do you think your mother is wrong?" he asked.

I didn't have to think about it. "My mother can be kooky and odd, but I also absolutely know for certain that Olivia told her exactly what Mom reported to us. Mom is inherently honest, so she wouldn't lie or exaggerate about something like that. So, yes, I believe that Olivia thinks that Cameron should get rid of Claire."

He nodded and walked over to the window. The sky was beginning to darken, and it wouldn't be long before people across the country would light bonfires and open their doors to their neighbors to honor the tradition of First Footing. I knew Derek was considering the situation as he took a minute to close the drapes.

"So? What do you think?" I asked.

He gazed at me. "I think that even if your mother were a complete fruitcake, which she most definitely is not, we would still have the statements of Claire and Sophie to go by. I believe both of them, and I'm convinced that if Olivia were pushed into a corner, she could be dangerous. So we should trust your mother and do everything we can to protect Claire tonight."

I nodded. "Should we call the police?"

He sipped his Scotch and took a moment to ruminate. "You probably recall from our last visit here that Gwyneth does not have a lot of confidence in the members of the local constabulary. I'm quite certain she'll suggest that we'd be better off depending on the defense skills of Cameron and his security team."

"And yours," I added. "And Claire's knife skills."

"Indeed." He set down his glass. "I have no doubt that Gwyneth vetted all of Cameron's men, knowing that they would be guarding Claire at some point."

"You'd be right about that," I said. "Claire is as precious to Gwyneth as she is to Cameron."

We sipped our drinks for a few minutes, and then it was time to get dressed for the bonfire. I changed into silk long underwear and heavy denim jeans, plus sturdy boots and thick socks. I wore a turtleneck sweater under a thick fisherman's sweater and topped it off with a down jacket, gloves, and a ski cap.

Derek wore faded jeans and a thick sweater under a down vest. His boots were old and rugged, and at my insistence, he brought a ski cap with him.

I went next door to see if my parents were ready. The door opened immediately, and I could see that they were good to go as well.

"You kids look ready to rock 'n' roll," Dad said.

"We are," I said, although the thought of staying inside and curling up by the fire was starting to sound pretty darn good. But it was New Year's Eve, and we were here in Scotland with my mom and dad and our dear friends, and there was lots of fun to be had out there, so I soldiered on and led the way downstairs, where Mrs. B welcomed us into the dining room. That was where we saw the beautiful spread of pre-bonfire goodies she'd laid out for us.

"This looks wonderful," I said.

"It really does," Mom said. "After eating like this for a week, we'll be waddling home."

There were thick slices of yummy-looking pizza, popcorn shrimp, mini-quiches, little hot dogs in puff pastry, bacon-wrapped sausages, and several other hearty treats, along with a variety of gorgeous-looking desserts.

To celebrate the impending nuptials, she had also included several bottles of champagne chilling in buckets.

"Mrs. B, you're a treasure," Derek said.

"I've never seen anything so beautiful," my mother said. "Don't tell me all of this was cooked right here in the kitchen."

"Tamara is a truly gifted chef," Mrs. B said, "and she has several equally talented assistants to help."

I shook my head in disbelief. "How can you do all this when you're also planning a wedding breakfast for the entire village?"

She beamed. "Would you believe me if I said we have an army of elves to lend a hand?"

I laughed. "I do believe it."

"There's no other way you could do all of this." Dad popped a mini-quiche into his mouth. "It must be elves. Mm, it's not only beautiful to look at; it's simply delicious."

"You are too kind," she said, but I could tell she thrived on our compliments. "It's what we love to do. And you're all such delightful guests, and Claire and Cameron are so sweet and so lovely and always so appreciative, you all make our jobs worth doing well."

We were soon joined by Cameron and Claire and then Sophie and Gwyneth. There were lots more oohs and aahs from them, as well, and shortly after that, we all settled down to eat the hearty appetizers before venturing out into the frigid night air.

Cameron stood and walked over to the door leading to the foyer. He closed and locked it, then locked the other door, as well. That one led to the kitchen, and there was some good-natured teasing about cutting off our food supply.

"I don't want anyone to overhear us," he said, explaining the locked doors. "Just want to take a minute to remind everyone that we need to be vigilant out there tonight. I don't mean to make it sound like we're going into battle, but after hearing what Claire has had to endure from some of our townspeople, I'll be keeping a close watch on things."

Claire spoke up. "I don't believe I'm in any danger, Cameron. But regardless, I'd like you to remember that I can take care of myself." She pulled a small dagger from a hidden pocket of her sleeve and held it up.

The exquisitely bejeweled dagger had to be a few hundred years old. It was encrusted with several dozen good-sized diamonds and three massive emeralds at the top of the dagger handle. At the very tip was another emerald that hinged open to reveal a gold and onyx watch. A watch! Because one would need to be checking the time when one was about to slice someone's neck open.

"That's gorgeous," I said. "It's like a piece of jewelry."

"Wow," Dad said. "I wouldn't want to tangle with you."

She slipped the knife back into its safe hiding place. "I have three more daggers stashed in various places on my person. Like I said, I can take care of myself."

"Only three more, love?" Cameron said as he leaned in to kiss her.

Claire gazed at all of us. "But I'm still very grateful to know that you all have my back."

"We certainly do," Mom said, whipping out her new cherry-wood wand and giving it a whirl.

"Oh, Becky," Claire said, laughing. "I love you."

"And I love you, sweet girl," Mom said, and wrapped Claire up in a warm hug.

Because I am who I am, my eyes filled with sentimental tears. "Nothing's going to happen to you. We won't let it."

"Thank you." Claire slipped her knife back into its pocket. "And tonight I'll have another secret weapon with me. A large bag of Mrs. B's famous sweet biscuits that I'll be handing out to everyone in the crowd."

"It'll be tough fighting off the cookie fanatics," Dad said.

"But we'll manage," Derek said. "We'll keep a sharp eye out for danger of any kind."

"Thank you, Derek."

Claire caught up to me as we headed for the front door. "I don't intend to use this dagger tonight, but I'll carry it with me. I've always appreciated the sense of security it gives me."

I grabbed her gently in a hug, being careful to avoid any of her hidden knives. "You're my hero."

"Och now, I've seen you throw a book with as much panache as I can throw this dagger. We each have our gifts."

"I'd rather not throw a book at anyone tonight," I said. "But if I were to do it, I'd aim for her head."

She laughed, and soon after that, we were heading out to torch a bonfire.

"My security men are scattered throughout the area," Cameron said. "Please be vigilant, but also enjoy yourselves and try not to worry too much about anyone interfering with our good time."

"Thanks for letting us know about the security guys," Dad said.

"By the way," Cameron said, "before it gets too crowded and crazy, and since we were talking about it a while ago, I wanted to let you know that I actually received an e-mail from my father."

"That's wonderful," I said. "Is he all right? Healthy?"

"As far as I know." He pulled a piece of paper from his pocket and unfolded it to read. "Basically he wishes me a happy holiday with my beautiful fiancée, and that's it. No news about him." He shrugged. "That's the way it goes."

"So, he's met Claire?" I asked.

He frowned. "No."

"Oh, but he knows you're getting married."

He blew out a breath of frustration. "He didn't hear it from me."

"Oh, well, it's still wonderful that you heard from him. It must be a relief to know that he's alive and well and keeping in touch."

"Such as it is." He snorted. He waved the e-mail and said, "I might as well toss this into the bonfire for what it's worth." But for now, he shoved it back into his pocket.

As soon as we arrived at the site of the bonfire, I realized that there were a lot more people here than simply Cameron's village. There had to be five or six hundred people scattered across the property, as well as thirty or forty boats out on the loch.

"It's a good crowd," Dad said.

"More than I thought would be here," Cameron admitted, then held out his arms. "Claire."

She waved at him from a mere twenty feet away, and he nodded.

Gwyneth followed her and stood nearby. I was willing to bet she could handle a jewel-encrusted dagger as well as her niece could, if not better. I glanced up at Derek. "Can you throw a dagger and hit what you want to hit?"

"I used to be able to do it quite well, but I haven't done much practicing in the last few years."

"We should practice."

He smiled down at me. "You want to learn to throw a dagger."

"I do. It's like throwing an axe. It's fun."

"Actually, darling, it's nothing like throwing an axe. The center of gravity is completely different. But I'll gladly show you how to do it."

"I would love that. Thank you."

"Because there are so many occasions when you need to throw a dagger."

I gazed up at him. "You never know."

He laughed, then moved to stand behind me and wrap his arms around me. I was able to lean back and enjoy seeing all the people as they arrived to watch the bonfire and party. Many of them had brought picnic baskets, which appeared to contain mainly beer, wine, and other types of liquor.

I figured it would help keep them warm, if not necessarily sober. But then, maybe they'd all had a hearty meal before they left their homes.

"Thank you for holding on to me," I said, straining to look up and back at Derek. "I feel warm and cozy."

"It's my pleasure," he murmured.

The crowd began to chant, "Fire, fire."

Derek said, "It's almost time."

Then someone belted out the lyrics of an old Doors song: "Come on, baby, light my fire."

And the crowd cheered them on. They were getting louder and rowdier, and the fire hadn't even been started yet. I caught a glimpse of Mom and Dad dancing on the sandy shore of the loch about thirty feet away. It looked as though they would be safe over there, but I would try to keep an eye on them. After a few more minutes I realized it was going to be impossible when the fire was lit and much of the crowd began jumping and shouting and dancing.

I looked around for Claire and saw her standing barely ten feet off to my left. She held the large bag of biscuits—cookies—in front of her, and the crowd seemed to surge forward to grab one of the treats. But I watched as several women in the crowd turned away when they realized it was Claire handing out the biscuits. The men seemed to have no problem and happily grabbed them from her and popped them into their mouths.

I shook my head in disgust. Something would have to be done about this weird attitude from these women.

I forgot all about it as Cameron and Derek strode forward, each holding one of the unlit fire batons.

I recognized Silas Abernathy, Cameron's head of security, as he approached Cameron holding a fire lighter that he aimed at the baton. The crowd was too loud for me to hear the clicking sound of the lighter before the first baton burst into flame. Cameron held the flame out to Derek and he lit the baton he was holding. It erupted in fire. Cameron handed one baton to Silas, who moved around the bonfire setting alight the clumps of hay that were stuffed here and there along the bottom of the structure.

Derek heaved his baton into the inferno as the entire stack slowly began to catch fire. It was amazing to watch as well as listen to. The sound it made when the fire finally swept through it was like a thunderous roar.

The crowd roared back as the excitement built.

"It's beautiful!" Claire shouted.

As Cameron supervised the fire, Gwyneth kept an eagle eye on her niece. I did, too, as well as I could. Occasionally some dancing fool would step in front of me, and I'd lose sight of her. But I knew that one of the others in our group would keep her in sight.

"Can you see Claire?" I shouted to Derek.

"Yes. She's fine."

"Good."

I was starting to get really warm and thought about moving away from the bonfire and closer to the shore with Mom and Dad. I caught sight of them again, waving their arms in the air and dancing in the sand like the Deadheads of yesteryear. I smiled. It had been a long day, and I'd had a few more glasses of wine, so I decided to stay right where I was in Derek's arms. I closed my eyes for just a moment because the fire was so bright.

I saw Gwyneth smiling and knew she had her eyes on Claire. I gazed around at the crowd and noticed that Claire had stooped down next to a child who was staring at the fire and clapping with so much joy, it was mesmerizing. Claire was laughing and talking with her, but of course I couldn't hear her words.

I relaxed again, knowing Gwyneth was watching her.

I scanned the crowd, and my eyes were drawn to the far side of the area, where I noticed Willy and Angus were standing. I was surprised there were no women nearby, because both of them were so attractive, they had to be popular among the local girls.

Right then they appeared to be shouting at each other, trying to be heard above the roaring fire and the noise of the crowd.

Then without warning, Angus shoved Willy. Willy came rushing at Angus and shoved him back harder. The crowd around them took notice, and the two young men stopped their shoving match but continued to yell at each other. Then Willy stormed off and Angus watched him go, his expression furious. A few seconds later, Angus disappeared into the crowd.

Now, what was that all about?

I turned to ask Derek if he'd seen the fight, but he had walked over to help Cameron with the fire.

I looked the other way to make sure Claire was safe, but I didn't see her. I stared down at the spot where the little girl had been standing and didn't see her, either.

Claire was gone.

"Claire!" I shouted, but nobody could hear me. "Don't panic," I whispered.

Someone tapped my shoulder and I whipped around.

It was Gwyneth, pointing toward the shore. "She's over there by your parents," I heard her shout.

I let go a heavy sigh of relief and mouthed the words *Thank you.*

She grinned and gave my arm a quick rub, then made her own way through the crowd.

People were having a blast. There was laughter and screaming and dancing and silliness everywhere. Many in the crowd carried a bottle of beer or a big plastic quart-sized container that held liquor or a cocktail of some kind. I wondered where those had come from.

In a much better mood, I turned and gazed at the crowd that had gathered farther away from the shoreline. This view showed more dancing and frivolity, and I wondered if it would go on all night long. I smiled at the sight of a group of girls dancing in a circle and laughing. I walked that way to get a closer look and saw that they all had flowers woven in their hair. If they hadn't been swathed in bulky jackets and boots, I would've thought they were celebrating May Day.

It was fun wandering through the different crowds of people. There were the hardcore beer drinkers who were playing screaming headbanger music on what looked like an iPhone. It was amazing how loud it was, even over the screams and shouts of the crowd.

There was a group of young families gathered around a table on which several picnic baskets were laid out. Three of the women carried babies in backpacks, and two of the men were tossing a Frisbee back and forth. Two others were hunkered down in front of a cribbage board. Now that was weird.

I walked on. And suddenly through the crowd, I saw a woman wearing a black ski mask, winding her way toward the castle. Her face was covered, but she couldn't disguise the long blond hair that flowed out from under the mask.

"Olivia!"

She couldn't hear me, of course, since she was at least eighty or a hundred feet away. She didn't seem to be in a hurry, but I still had to wonder if she was here to cause trouble or just enjoy the bonfire.

I ran as well as I could, weaving my way in and out and around the hundreds of people who were dancing and singing and shouting and simply enjoying the night.

I turned back to scan the area around the bonfire and find my group, but I didn't see anyone familiar. It was no wonder, since the crowd was growing larger by the minute. I made my way toward the bonfire while trying to keep an eye on Olivia, but in the brief moment I had turned away, she had disappeared into the crowd.

"Damn it," I muttered. I was the world's worst security guard. The one thing I could be thankful for was that Olivia was by herself. She wasn't dragging Claire away to be tormented. Not that she'd be able to since Claire would have that dagger out and pressed against her carotid artery in a heartbeat. But still, I was glad Olivia didn't seem to be anywhere near Claire.

I scanned the crowd again, looking for Derek. He was so tall, I figured he would stand out. And when I turned around again, he was standing five feet away from me.

"I found you!" I shouted, and wrapped my arms around him.

"I believe it was I who found you," he said loudly, with humor in his voice.

"Claire?" I asked.

"She's with Cameron. They're all over on the shore with your parents."

I nodded, and together we pushed through the crowd and made it to the shore. And there they were, my group, my mini-tribe, my people. Claire, Gwyneth, Cameron, Sophie, and Mom and Dad were all dancing and frolicking and laughing like loons. I was lightheaded with relief. I'd only been separated from everyone for fifteen or twenty minutes, but it felt like hours.

. . .

*A*n hour later we were safely ensconced back in the castle, where we all decided to convene in the blue parlor to consider what the plan was for tomorrow.

"We're having a wedding, after all," Claire said. "But I'm beginning to think we should postpone it to the afternoon, at least. Or even push it back another day. There's just so much going on."

"I hate the thought of postponing it one more hour," Cameron said, running his hands through his hair in frustration. "But it has been a long night, and I'm afraid we'll be dealing with hangovers and worse tomorrow."

"Hangovers might be the least of it," I said, scowling. "Did anyone besides me see Olivia at the bonfire?"

Claire's mouth fell open in shock. "No!"

"Damn it!" Cameron shook his head. "Pardon my language, but no, I didn't see her. I should've."

"You were involved in the burning," Claire said. "And we knew she might show up."

"And there were hundreds of people out there," Derek said. "She hasn't been fired yet, so why wouldn't she come to the Hogmanay bonfire with everyone else in town?"

"Indeed," Cameron said. "Why wouldn't she?"

"She was heading toward the castle," I said, and frowned. "Not sure that means anything."

"Well, she didn't cause any trouble tonight," Claire reasoned, "so I think we're safe for now."

"At least until I fire her," Cameron said. "Then we may indeed see some trouble."

"Speaking of Olivia," I said, "with everything that's been going on, we've never really discussed all the missing books."

"Do you have a theory, sweetie?" Mom asked.

"I have a couple," I said with a smile. "I can't help but think Olivia took them herself and sold them. She is fond of money, after all."

Mom heaved a sigh. "I thought the same thing after I spoke with her."

I took a sip of my tea and Scotch. I had never been a Scotch fan, but I was beginning to enjoy the flavor and wondered if I would continue drinking it once we got back home. Probably not. I rarely indulged in a nightcap, but when in Scotland . . .

"I'm still bothered by her," I said. "Even if she didn't steal the books herself, she managed to lose twelve important books from your collection. The fact that they're all Christmas books is particularly upsetting. But I was also surprised to hear that they were taken one at a time. It makes me think we should check the castle rooms. Maybe someone took a book to one of the rooms to read and left it there. You never know. We might find one or two, and we can return them to the shelves."

"It's all about the books with my girl," Dad said jovially.

"Thank you, Brooklyn," Cameron said. "If you can find even one of the missing books, I'll be grateful."

I remembered the shadow I saw in the tower window and knew I had to climb up there tomorrow. What if the book thief had left one of the books up there? What if they'd left more? I would try to get Derek to come with me.

Suddenly there was a loud hammering at the front door.

"Now what?" Dad said.

"That's someone at the door," Cameron said, then looked abashed. "I suppose I'm stating the obvious."

Every one of us followed him out to the foyer as he headed for the door.

Gwyneth's shoulders sagged. "We certainly didn't need any more excitement tonight."

"It's barely half past midnight," Cameron said, giving her a quick hug. "Early for Hogmanay."

"Hogmanay," I whispered to Derek. "Do you think this is part of that First Footing thing?"

"No doubt," he said.

"Perhaps some of the mischief makers from the bonfire have decided to stop by to wish us well," Sophie guessed.

"Or," Dad said, "they're coming to storm the castle."

Cameron chuckled at that. "They wouldn't be the firsts." He walked to the door and was about to open it when, all of a sudden, the door banged open so hard that it crashed against the back wall. A woman strolled into the house and stood with her hands on her hips.

"What in the—?" Cameron said. "Bitsy?"

The rest of us stood speechless at the far end of the front foyer.

"What do you suppose she wants?" Mom wondered under her breath.

"I doubt she's here to scrub the kitchen sink," Gwyneth muttered.

"Definitely overdressed," Mom agreed, and Gwyneth snorted.

Bitsy was looking very fancy in a short, slinky gold lamé dress with a high collar and long sleeves that hugged every single inch of her. Her stiletto heels were gold, as well, and strappy. And very sexy.

"She must've been freezing out there," I murmured.

"Is it really Bitsy?" Dad asked quietly. "The girl from the pub?"

"Yes, it's Bitsy Kerr," Sophie said.

"Well, you might as well come in," Cameron said, always the gentleman and cognizant of his Hogmanay First Footing duty.

"She doesn't look the same as the girl in the pub," Dad said.

Sophie snorted. "She's tarted herself up so her own mother wouldna recognize her."

"Can't believe she'd wear that outfit to the pub," I murmured. "It would be impossible to get the ketchup stains out of it."

Sophie laughed out loud, then she strolled to the door to give Cameron some reinforcement. "Bitsy, what're you doing here dressed like a damn roaster? Have ye gone aff yer heid?"

I wasn't sure about *roaster*, but I didn't need any translating on the rest of it.

"Shut yer puss, Sophie Mackenzie," Bitsy shouted angrily.

Again, no translation needed.

Mrs. B came out from the kitchen wrapped in a thick bathrobe. "What is all the shouting about?"

"It's Bitsy," Sophie said. "Here to celebrate Hogmanay and cause trouble, no doubt."

Mrs. B looked at Cameron. "I suppose she'll need a room."

"She can sleep in the green parlor," Cameron said decisively. "She'll have her pick of the couches, or she can always claim the hearth."

Bitsy gave him the coldest, dirtiest look I'd seen on anyone in a long time. Maybe she didn't care for the color green. Either way, we'd have to watch out for Cameron's safety this time around.

"I believe Cameron has reached the end of his patience," Mom murmured in my ear.

I nodded. "He may be rethinking this whole First Footing tradition after tonight."

"I'll take care of this one," Mrs. B said quietly. "I know the girl. She's not the brightest bulb, but she isn't much trouble normally."

"No?" I was doubtful. She seemed willing to make plenty of trouble.

Mrs. B shrugged. "I'm afraid she's got a burr in her britches for the Laird."

"Sounds uncomfortable," I whispered, and was gratified to see both Claire and Sophie suppress a laugh.

"And she's not the first one to show up with a burr tonight," Gwyneth said to Mrs. B.

I supposed she was referring to Olivia showing up at the bonfire. I could only hope Olivia was tucked safely in her own bed in her own home by now.

"Oh dear," the housekeeper said. "But our Cameron was always popular with the ladies."

"Just so you're aware," Gwyneth added, "if that first lady shows up at the castle, you're to notify Cameron or Derek or me immediately."

"Who is that?" Mrs. B asked.

"Olivia, the librarian."

Her eyes widened in horror. "Good heavens." She turned and glared at Bitsy. "You'll watch yourself in this home, Bitsy Kerr."

With a sneer for Mrs. B, Bitsy tossed her hair back and strutted down the hall to face Cameron. "I know you respect and abide by the old ways of Hogmanay, Cameron MacKinnon."

"Aye, I do," Cameron said, giving her a suspicious look.

"So know this," she said loudly, as though she were making a proclamation. "I won't be leaving here until I'm good and ready. I trust you to keep your promises and welcome me into your home— for as long as I wish to stay—and share your abundance with me."

"That's ballsy," Dad muttered to the rest of us as we watched from the far end of the foyer.

Sophie leaned in close. "Not sure I'd have the audacity to pull it off."

"Seeing this girl here," Mom said softly, "it occurs to me that Cameron must've thought he'd died and went to heaven when he met Claire."

"Aye," Sophie said. "She's surely the best thing that ever happened to him."

Mom sighed. "I certainly hope this girl Bitsy isn't rude to her like Olivia was."

"I wouldn't bet on it," I murmured.

"Come along, Bitsy," Mrs. B said. "I'll show you where you can sleep."

"I'd like something to eat before I tuck into bed," Bitsy said, as though she ruled the place. "And don't lie to me, Mrs. B. I know you have plenty of food, because you're about to feed several hundred people tomorrow morning. You'll surely have a sandwich and some biscuits for me to eat."

Mrs. B took hold of her arm and pulled her into the dining room. "This is no way to ingratiate yourself to His Lairdship."

The rest of us scurried down the hall like a bunch of kids and gathered close to the open doorway to hear the conversation.

"Why would I care to ingratiate myself to him?" Bitsy said.

"What other reason would bring you here in the middle of the night all tarted up as you are?" Mrs. B asked.

Bitsy shook her hair back in defiance. "Maybe my car broke down and I needed a place to stay for the night."

"Did your car break down?"

"Nae," she admitted grumpily. "But it could've."

"It's Hogmanay, so we'll give ye the benefit. And you'll be leaving in the morning, then?"

Bitsy opened her mouth to speak but was momentarily struck dumb. Apparently she hadn't practiced her lines this far into her invasion strategy. Which made me think she somehow planned to stay for as long as possible.

But why?

Bitsy harrumphed, followed by more hair tossing. "I'm absolutely not leaving in the morning. I'm attending the wedding tomorrow."

"Och, what a choob she is," Sophie whispered. "I'll take Olivia the librarian and her witchy oddness over this entitled blibbity-blob any day of the week."

"I hear that, girlfriend," Mom murmured.

I stared at Sophie. "Is blibbity-blob a Scottish thing?"

"Nae." She chuckled. "It's just me trying to avoid saying the B-word."

Claire had reached the end of her patience. She pulled Cameron away from the dining room doorway, and the two of them walked around to the blue parlor. We all followed, of course. Dad was the last one in and he closed the door.

Claire reached for Cameron's arms and whispered, "How would you feel about postponing the wedding?"

He answered instantly, "I would've said there's nothing that will keep me from marrying you, but I've come to realize that's not quite accurate."

Claire laughed. "I feel the same way. I don't want to be married while Bitsy Kerr's ugly energy is darkening our home."

Cameron touched her cheek. "I'll gladly postpone our nuptials if it'll get rid of that infernal woman. I pray she'll be gone by tomorrow."

"I'd like to postpone it for three days," Claire said. "That should take care of the current situation."

"Meaning Bitsy," Cameron said, rolling his eyes.

"Yes, and I'll talk to Mrs. B. Most of the food should keep for a few days, but for anything that might go bad, we can take it to the church for them to distribute."

"Aye." Cameron nodded. "And we can order more."

"Then it's done." She glanced around. "Sophie, can you help us make the calls?"

"Of course." She leaned against the bar and checked her wristwatch. "I'll text my phone tree people right now. For the older folks who don't text, and there are plenty, we'll have to telephone. And we oughtn't start until—hmm, I'd say, half six in the morning. That gives us four and a half hours to alert everyone in the village and beyond." She smiled. "We can do that."

Claire grabbed Sophie in a grateful hug. "Thank you."

"It's a pleasure." She patted Claire's back but then scowled. "We both know that idiotic, mean-spirited choob is only here to disrupt your wedding, so we'll turn it around, disrupt her malicious plan, and ruin her day." She paused, then shook her head, and gave us all a repentant look. "Och, I'm sorry. These witchy cows are turning me angry and mean."

"Me, too," I said, then frowned. "By the way, what's a choob?"

Sophie smirked. "A stupid person."

"Okay. That fits." I was starting to notice there were quite a lot of Scottish slang words to describe a stupid or annoying person. I might have to make a list.

Cameron sat down in the big blue chair and pulled Claire down next to him. She gazed at him for a few quiet seconds, then said, "Are you sure you don't mind waiting a few more days?"

"Och nae, love." He kissed her. "As far as I'm concerned, we're already married in our hearts. They can't take that away from us, as hard as they may try."

Sophie reached over and punched him lightly in the arm. "I trust ye haven't any more women waiting in the wings, Cameron Mac-Kinnon."

"Och." He leaned over and buried his head in his hands. "If another shows up, you have my permission to shoot me."

Chapter 8

Since there wouldn't be a wedding tomorrow—or rather today—and it was well past midnight, Gwyneth suggested that in the early afternoon, the ladies of our group visit the tearoom on the high street. There was unanimous consent, and I couldn't wait to get a taste of the local coronation chicken she and Claire had been raving about.

The men finally decided that Cameron would take Dad and Derek for a lively tour out on the loch and would no doubt stop for a wee dram at a pub along the shore. I would've insisted on joining them, except that it was going to be freezing out there on the water. I was happy to pass that up for a nice warm lunch in a pretty tearoom.

It was almost three o'clock in the morning when Derek and I finally walked into our room and bid my parents good night. Derek was about to close the door when the friendly black-and-white cat came rushing inside our room.

"I believe we have company, darling."

"I'm okay with that," I said, and hunched down to pet Robbie and scratch his soft ears. "Hello, little guy."

When we finally climbed under the covers, Robbie jumped up, and after circling the spot three times, he made himself at home at the foot of the bed.

"He's so sweet," I said. "Makes me miss Charlie."

"I know." Derek pulled me close and we were asleep in minutes.

We'd been so distracted by everything that had happened that evening, we completely forgot to listen for the noises. I didn't know if the creatures behind the walls were still back there or sneaking along the hallways, but we never heard a sound. Maybe they had fallen asleep as well.

It was blissful to wake the next morning knowing we didn't have to jump out of bed and prepare for the wedding. Not that I wasn't looking forward to the happy celebration. I was. But it was lovely to spend a few extra hours sleeping off the craziness of the night before.

Today wouldn't be a free day, though. We still had Bitsy to deal with. I doubted we would be lucky enough to go downstairs and find her gone. No, I had a feeling she was lingering down there somewhere, waiting to annoy Cameron some more. She'd probably want to get in some digs at Claire as well. Along with anyone else who came face-to-face with her. I just hoped she would leave my mother and father alone, because nobody was allowed to treat my parents badly. If it happened, I would have to hurt her. I didn't know how, because despite all my talk about knives and such, I was pretty much a pacifist. Unless someone went after a loved one. Then I'd find a way.

Maybe I would suggest to Mom and Dad that they take advantage of our free day and visit the Clava Cairns. When I saw Cameron downstairs, I would ask him if Timothy was available to drive them if they wanted to go. If they left early enough, they would both be back in time for the ladies' trip to the tearoom and the fellows' tour of the loch.

I turned to find Derek with his eyes open, staring at me.

"How long have you been awake?" I asked.

"About five minutes." He smiled and stroked my hair back from my face, then stretched and yawned. Sitting up, he said, "I think we should get up and go downstairs as soon as possible in case Claire and Cameron need us to run interference for them."

I sighed. "It would be too much to ask for Bitsy to simply be gone."

He chuckled dryly as he stood and ran his hands through his hair. "She appears to be the type who's determined to do as much damage as she can get away with before someone comes along and kicks her out."

"Who will be the one to kick her out? Cameron? Claire?"

"I don't think so. She's got some sort of agenda with regard to those two, and I think she'll stay to see it through. I'm afraid the only way she'll walk out of here is if her parents or someone else in authority shows up and forces her to go home."

"I've never met her mother, but I wouldn't be surprised to find out that she's the one who convinced Bitsy to come here."

"You could be right."

"So, we're stuck with her," I concluded.

"That's most likely true."

I washed my face and brushed my teeth while Derek dressed for the day. Since we had no firm plans for the morning, I went for a casual look with black jeans; a long, thick, cozy turtleneck sweater; and black booties. I grabbed my puffy vest in case we decided to walk outside.

Derek's thin black wool sweater was one of my favorites, especially when he wore it under a heavy charcoal gray windowpane-weave shirt and blue jeans. He looked like a rich sexy cowboy. A rich sexy English cowboy.

It was a good look on him. He added a lightweight bomber jacket, no doubt to hide the shoulder holster he was strapping on. Things were starting to get real.

When we got downstairs, we were met by Mrs. B, who suggested we take a seat in the breakfast room and help ourselves to coffee.

I sat down at the table while Derek poured two cups of coffee and handed one to me before sitting down.

Mrs. B brought in a platter of croissants and pastries. *As an appetizer*, I thought, and got ready to eat too much, as usual.

"I've seen Claire and Cameron this morning," she said. "They've left the castle to take a drive and plan to be back in just a few hours."

"I'm glad to hear it." I took a long sip of the excellent coffee.

"Yes," she said. "I'd like them to enjoy some peace and quiet for a few days before the thundering hordes descend."

Derek laughed. "By that you mean, their friends and neighbors?"

She chuckled softly. "That's what I meant to say."

We both sipped our coffee as Mrs. B walked out of the room. Two minutes later, she came back and set down a platter of fried eggs, ham, sausage, grilled tomatoes, mushrooms, and baked beans. In the center of the platter was a sweet little Christmas tree—an actual live tree!—with ornaments and lights.

"That's adorable," I said.

"Mrs. B, you are an artist," Derek said.

She laughed. "Go on with yourself."

"I mean it."

"Thank you, dear. I'll be right back with more coffee. Is there anything else you'd like? Yogurt? Granola?"

"Good lord, no," I said, holding my stomach.

She laughed again. "You're good eaters. I like that."

Less than a minute later, she returned with a full pot of coffee and more cream.

"Please enjoy."

"We will, thank you."

"Mrs. B," I said, leaning closer to her. "Is everything going all right for you this morning?"

She looked both ways, then whispered, "Before you arrived for breakfast, I was getting Bitsy taken care of and settled in the yellow parlor."

"Not the green parlor?" I said.

"She's sleeping in the green parlor but doesn't want her sitting room to be the same as her bedroom."

"So, the yellow parlor is her sitting room?"

"That's right, and she's taking her meals in there. It's smaller, but it's got a nice view of the loch."

"Will she be coming out to say hello?" I asked.

Mrs. B waved that thought away. "I'm going to presume that she isn't interested in mingling with the Laird's friends." She rolled her eyes.

I noticed that Derek had tuned out of our conversation while he sent a text.

"I've been wondering," I said, "how many sitting rooms do you have here?"

"There are six rooms on the ground floor that are used for conversations and get-togethers. The blue parlor is the largest."

"It's lovely," I said, and sipped my coffee. "So, do you think she'll stay long?"

She bit her lip. "She's threatening to stay for several weeks."

My mouth dropped open. "You must be joking."

"She says she'll stay until she gets the job done."

"What does that mean?"

Derek looked up at Mrs. B. "I'm sorry, I had to take care of that message." He turned to me. "What were you talking about?"

"Mrs. B was saying that Bitsy is threatening to stay for several weeks. Until she gets the job done, she says."

Derek sucked in a breath and thought for a moment. "I doubt she poses a credible threat to Claire or Cameron, but we'll keep an eye out." He gazed up at the housekeeper with sympathy. "You are a saint, Mrs. B. If you need our help with anything, please let us know."

She touched both of our shoulders. "You are two angels. Thank you. My staff and I will be fine." She let out a heavy sigh. "I know Bitsy wants to make trouble, but it comes from having a troubled heart. And that's why I know that in the end, we'll all abide."

"Yes, of course we will," Derek said.

"Have you seen my parents?" I asked.

Mrs. B said, "They just left for the Clava Cairns."

I smiled at Derek. "Great minds."

"Yes," he said. "They texted me to let us know they're off on an adventure. I believe Timothy is driving them."

"Yes, Timothy," Mrs. B confirmed. "He works with Mr. Abernathy quite often and occasionally drives for Cameron."

"I'm glad to hear that." If Timothy worked with Silas Abernathy, then my parents were in safe hands. "Thank you. They'll enjoy that."

"They seemed quite excited to go," Mrs. B said.

"Oh, the Clava Cairns are right up my mother's alley." I frowned. "I'm sorry. Does that phrase make sense to you?"

"It does, yes. We use that phrase in Scotland, as well. Similarly, we might say, it's just her cup of tea. Or it's not. Either way."

"Oh yes." I smiled in relief. "Very similar. I'm glad it made sense."

"Unlike some of the words you heard last night?" She chuckled. "We do have some odd ones."

"Yes, and I love them," I said. "They're so colorful."

"Indeed." She raised an eyebrow. "Although some are quite *off* color."

We all laughed and I asked, "Were you able to take care of all the wedding food?"

"Yes, Vicar James was happy to handle the distribution to the various agencies in the area."

"That was nice of him."

"He's a good man," she said. "Now, I understand that your parents will return from their outing to Clava Cairns in time for your mother to join you at the tearoom and for your father to join Cameron and the Commander for the tour of the loch."

"Oh, that's good to know," I said. "Thank you, Mrs. B. You really are a marvel."

She waved away my praise. "Not really. I just take good notes." She headed for the door. "Enjoy your breakfast."

A minute later we heard footsteps approach and exchanged glances. Now what?

A young man walked into the breakfast room holding a paper cup and reached for the coffeepot. "Good morning."

"Angus," I said. "Good morning. How did you enjoy the bonfire?" I wasn't about to tell him I'd seen him arguing with Willy.

"It was a beautiful burn."

"Darling," Derek said, "I think I told you that Angus actually helped with the building of the bonfire."

"I remember." I smiled up at him. "You did a fabulous job. Everyone did."

"I stuck around to make sure it lit up just fine, then I hustled out onto the loch and watched it with a few of me mates. One of them has a tour boat he uses for Nessie fans. We had a grand time."

"Sounds like great fun. Doesn't Willy's family have a boat? Does he ever take it out for this sort of thing?"

He poured cream into his coffee and pressed a plastic cover over the top of his cup. "No, it's strictly a fishing boat." He grinned. "You wouldn't want to hang out on his boat and have a party, if you know what I mean."

"Yes, I guess I do."

"Speaking of Willy," Angus said. "Have you seen him around today?"

I glanced at Derek, then we both shook our heads. "Haven't seen him," Derek said. "Sorry, mate."

Angus shrugged. "He might well be sozzled after the party last night."

I grinned. I could guess what *sozzled* meant.

"Maybe so," Derek said. "If he does stop by, where shall we tell him to find you?"

"I'd appreciate it if you'd tell him to find me in the upper garden, where I'll be helping the gardeners work the soil."

"That's fascinating," I said. "What do you do for the soil when it's this cold?"

"We've already added a bit of compost, and today we're layering straw over that to prevent the soil from eroding."

"Well, try to stay warm," I said.

"Och, it's gonnae be Baltic," he said, but gave us a cheerful wave as he left the room.

I looked at Derek. "I'm going to guess that *Baltic* means it's cold out there."

"It's *very* cold out there," Derek amended.

. . .

*A*fter breakfast we walked back to our room to relax for a few minutes and decide what to do with all of our sudden free time.

"We could explore the tower," he said.

I smiled at him. "I'd love to. And I'd especially love to find a book up there."

"Let's give it a go."

"Let me change my shoes first. Then I'll be ready to go."

Having walked that narrow spiral staircase more than once on our last visit, I exchanged my cute booties for sturdy walking shoes.

"I'm not taking anything but my phone," I said. "What about you?"

"That's good," he said. "Travel light. Let's go."

He said it all so casually that I immediately figured he must be taking his gun and maybe a knife and whatever else one brought when one was traveling light. But since he didn't say anything more, I let him have his secrets. Until it became important. Like, if someone jumped out from a closet holding a knife to my throat, I would want to know that Derek had his gun with him.

We held hands as we left our room and walked down the hall, past the stairway, and into the west wing of the castle. Passing two closed doors, Derek reached for the third and turned the handle. It opened easily and we stared up at the narrow spiral staircase that led to the west tower.

He smiled. "Funny how it all comes back to you."

"It was a memorable time," I said.

After walking slowly up the stairs for a few minutes, Derek asked, "Are you experiencing any déjà vu?"

"I hate to admit it, but yes, I am. Are you?"

"I am," he grumbled, "and I don't like it." He had lowered his voice because the stairwell caused our voices to echo.

I wondered if he was concerned because he thought we were in danger, so I asked, "Do you think we're safe?"

"I think so." He said it cautiously, and then he pulled out his gun.

"Oookay. I'll stay behind you."

"Yes, you will."

As we ascended the tower, it grew more difficult because each step was higher and steeper and narrower than the one before.

When we finally reached the landing and stared at the doorway leading to the small room at the top of the tower, Derek said, "Stay close behind me."

"Watch your head," I whispered, recalling how low the ceiling was in this room.

"I will."

Suddenly a light flashed and he shouted, "Come out of there!"

I might've screamed a little. My heart was pounding, and I was pretty sure it wasn't the caffeine rush that was making me shiver.

"It's all right, sweetheart," Derek said, slipping his gun back in his shoulder holster. "Nobody's up here but us."

"You scared me to death!"

"I'm sorry. I knew if someone was hiding up here, they would hear us coming, so I decided to give them a shock. Clearly it wasn't necessary."

"But you didn't know that till you got here."

"Exactly." He took a step toward the room, then turned and showed me his phone with the flashlight attachment turned on. "That's where the flash came from."

"Good to know," I muttered.

He pointed to the window. "It's a bit too small to light the room, so why don't you turn on your own flashlight app? I'd like to search for some evidence that someone was up here. You did see a shadow, right?"

"That's right." I imagined my heart rate was just starting to creep back down to normal, so after another couple of slow breaths, I turned on my flashlight. It helped calm my nerves, although I realized I was still kind of scared, even with Derek standing ten feet away. It didn't help that I was shivering from the cold, and I lamented not bringing my puffy vest.

Of course, after climbing all those steps, I would've been sweating by now if I'd worn it.

I mentally rolled my eyes at my fashion dilemmas and concentrated on searching the room. It was a familiar space, of course, because we had searched it completely the last time we were here. We'd even taken up a few floorboards in our search. I didn't think that would be necessary today.

Derek aimed his flashlight along the far side, away from the door, so I walked along the wall closest to the door.

The one window on the north wall allowed enough light in to see the basic features of the room. But the flashlight app was really helpful, especially in the corners.

And that was where I found the book.

*B*ack in our room, I sat down on the loveseat to finally get a good look at the book.

We hadn't found anything else in the tower room, but I was thrilled with what we'd discovered. We'd taken the book and left, slowly descending the stairs. Happily we hadn't run into anyone on our way back.

Derek pulled over one of the chairs from the table and set it right next to me so he could look over my shoulder.

"It's *A Child's Christmas in Wales*," I said.

"Dylan Thomas," he said, sounding pleased. "We had this book in our house while growing up. Mum used to read it every Christmas."

"Did it look like this?" I held up the dust jacket cover for him to examine.

He stared at the cover. "I definitely remember the red lettering." He opened the book. "Pretty certain this one is exactly like the book we had at home." He laughed. "Look, it's even got the price written on the dust jacket. One pound."

"Pretty good deal." I opened the book to the title page. "Hey, there's no copyright date." I paged through the book, checking the gutters of some of the pages and finding them clean. The spine was intact and the endpapers were pristine. "It's in really good shape for being shoved into a corner of the tower."

"Perhaps you should check the back outside cover," Derek said, frowning. "I recall seeing some printing back there."

"Really?" I carefully removed the fragile dust jacket, and sure enough, the back cover not only showed the publisher's name but the copyright date and even the address of the New York publisher. "Well, that's different. I've rarely seen this sort of information put on the back cover before. I'm amazed you remembered that."

"My mother read it to us every Christmas for years, and she always let each of us read a page or two."

"That's a nice memory." I smiled at him. "I'm surprised the book survived with five rowdy boys in the house."

"She had it covered in that archival plastic wrap you use for all your books."

"Did she? That's awfully smart of her."

"Yes. Even back then, she knew how to guard against the ravages of the five."

I laughed. "The five. Is that what you called yourselves?"

He pumped up his arms like a weight lifter. "We were a force to be reckoned with."

"You still are."

He snickered. "Except for Dalton."

I laughed at the typical brotherly insult and punched his arm in Dalton's defense. Dalton was the youngest, and he was as tall and broad shouldered and handsome as the rest of them. He lived in Dharma with my sister Savannah and had worked as a cryptographer for MI6 when I first met him. The other brothers all worked in high places for various branches of the government.

"It was copyrighted in 1954," I said, returning to the book. "Probably a first edition. And it appears to be in fine condition." I looked inside the front cover. "Text and endpapers are clean and unmarked. Even the dust jacket is clean with no tears and no fading. They could probably sell it for four or five hundred pounds."

"You think someone took it and hid it in the tower in order to sell it?"

"What do you think?"

He thought for a moment. "Perhaps someone who works in the castle is taking books out of the library simply to read. The tower room is quiet and peaceful, and no one will bother you up there."

"Maybe so. But I can't help being suspicious, because this is one of the Christmas books that went missing."

"This book is on the list that Claire gave you?"

"Yes."

He shrugged. "Well, then that makes sense. And so does your theory that there could be other books hiding in quiet places around the castle. We just have to figure out why."

"Now that we've found this one, I can't decide if some of the books were taken out of the library by a voracious reader with a sentimental urge for a Christmas story or if they deliberately left the books in obscure places and plan to go back for them."

"And sell them, I presume?" he said.

"Yes. And in either case, we should definitely start looking for them ourselves." I studied the book for another moment. "Did Olivia take it up there to hide it? Maybe she didn't think she could get it out of the castle right away, so she hid it until it was safe to move it out."

His expression was dubious. "That's a long, uncomfortable walk up those stairs. There are probably a lot of safe places down here that would be easier to get to."

"True. And maybe it's not Olivia. Maybe someone completely different is taking these books. She did claim she was innocent."

Derek tapped his fingers lightly on the book cover. "You're saying, just because she's obsessed with money, it doesn't mean she's a book thief."

I had to laugh. "Exactly. And, you know, I keep thinking about how much respect she showed for the books in her charge. How could she turn around and sell them? But then again, if money's her thing, she could've gotten a lot for some of them."

"Indeed she could've."

"Well, no matter who's taking the books and hiding them, I think we need to be the ones who find them."

Since we weren't on familiar territory at the castle, we came up with a simple plan. First, we strolled out to the shore of the loch. Angus was right when he said it was Baltic cold. But this time I had my puffy vest and I felt pretty toasty. We walked along the shore until we found the perfect spot. From here, we could see most of the length of the castle, along with all the main towers and turrets.

"I think this will do," Derek said, and held his phone up to take a few pictures of the castle.

Then we walked back and came in through the kitchen door. Mrs. B was talking to the chef who stood by the large stove.

"Oh, Commander, this is Tamara, our very clever chef," Mrs. B said. "Brooklyn, I know you and Tamara have already met."

"Hello," she said, sounding a bit shy.

"Lovely to meet you, Tamara," Derek said. "You are a truly talented chef."

"Thank you, sir."

"It's great to see you again, Tamara," I said. "And thank you for your brilliant work. Everything's been delicious."

Tamara blushed at the praise. "Thank you, both. It's always a pleasure." She glanced at the stove and appeared anxious to start working. Or maybe she just wanted to escape the overly enthusiastic visitors.

Either way, Mrs. B took pity on the chef and walked with us out of the kitchen. "I'm afraid we won't have her much longer. Her work is simply outstanding, so I fear she'll be moving on to some fancy restaurant in Edinburgh or even London one of these days."

"What a shame," Derek said. "We'll have to enjoy her food while we have the chance."

"Indeed."

"Mrs. B," I began, "we'd like to ask you about some spots inside the castle."

She looked a bit mystified. "All right."

"Where would someone go to find some peace and quiet and hide away from everyone?"

She thought for a few seconds. "Well now, the towers are probably the best spot, although most of them are a bit difficult to get to."

Derek said, "We took a picture and were hoping you could point out the best ways to get to the different towers." He showed her the photo he'd taken from the shore.

"Aren't you clever?" Her smile was broad. "You're looking for the books, aren't you?" She gazed at both of us. "Am I right?"

"You're absolutely right," Derek said.

"We actually found a book in the west wing tower," I explained, "so now we're hoping to find some others."

"You found one!" She thought for a moment. "So, they might not be stolen after all."

"That's what we're hoping."

"Well, if anyone can find them, it'll be you two. You're like a detective duo on the telly."

We all chuckled at that, then we walked into the breakfast room, and Mrs. B pulled a small notepad from her pocket. She sat down with Derek's photo.

"It's a lovely sight, isn't it?" she said softly, staring at the photo.

"It's beautiful," I said.

Then she got down to business, pointing at the towers and giving us the best routes to get to them. I counted seven different towers, each designed in a completely different style, either in shape or height or width or rooftop. The original Laird in charge of building the castle must've surely had a whimsical streak.

"This is very helpful," Derek said.

I nodded enthusiastically. "Yes, thank you so much for your time and for all this information."

"I hope you find what you're looking for," she said.

"Thank you."

We had realized out on the shore that it would soon be time to leave for our respective outings, so we put the book hunt on hold and climbed the stairs to our rooms. I needed to freshen up for the girls' lunch at the tearoom and Derek wanted to change into warmer clothes for the cruise on Loch Ness. Then, later this afternoon we would meet back here and go hunting for another book.

"I'm surprised we haven't seen Bitsy around all afternoon," Derek said as he pulled on his fisherman's sweater.

"I keep forgetting that she's even here. I wonder what she's been doing all day."

"It would be too much to hope that she's gone home."

I snickered. "Fat chance. I imagine she's hunkered down with her phone and her favorite social media app. Or maybe she's reading a book in her private sitting room."

"You're probably right. If she leaves, she forfeits the First Footing prize."

"There isn't really a prize, is there?"

"No," he said dryly. "Just the adoration of your peers."

I laughed. "Well, no doubt she'll emerge to torment us when we all come back from our outings. And that should be interesting."

I pulled on a sweater and then brushed my hair. "She's so angry and I have no idea why. It can't simply be about the wedding. There's something else going on here."

"I'm just glad there'll be a bunch of us around to witness her bad behavior, so maybe she'll calm down a bit."

"We can only hope."

I took a quick look around the room to make sure things were in order. Then I saw the newly repaired Robert Burns book on the table, still wrapped in the simple white cloth. I grabbed it and slipped it into my bag. "I'm going to give this to Claire. Maybe it'll cheer her up a little."

"Very nice, love."

As we left the room, I said, "I hope you'll be careful out there on the water. Look out for the monster."

He squeezed my hand. "And you be careful, too. You never know what monsters may lie in wait inside those tearooms."

"All those scary little teapots," I said with a laugh. "Anything might pop out."

Derek met Dad and Cameron at the bottom of the stairs, and they took off for the small marina a half mile away. The marina was on MacKinnon land but far enough away that Cameron preferred to drive. He had mentioned that he kept several boats at the small private marina. He also allowed the tour boats to dock briefly for picture taking and refueling.

Then Claire, Gwyneth, Mom, Sophie, and I climbed into Claire's SUV, and we drove into the village. Claire found a parking spot one door down from the tearoom, and as we stepped out of the car, I slipped the book into Claire's hands.

"What's this?" she asked, then realized what she was holding. "You finished."

"Yes, and I think it looks wonderful."

She unwrapped the cloth right there on the sidewalk. "Oh, Brooklyn." She hugged me. "Thank you so much. It's beautiful." She examined the book, front and back, then pressed it to her heart. "You'd never know anything had happened."

"I hope he loves it."

"I know he will. Thank you." She put the book inside her purse. "Now, let's get out of the cold."

"Yes, please," I said with a laugh.

Within a minute we were stepping inside the elegant tearoom. White lace curtains were pulled back to give patrons a view of the high street. The tables were covered in white cloths and set with gold-rimmed dishware and Baroque-style sterling silver utensils. The salt and pepper shakers were of the same design. Under each plate was a lace doily, and the napkins were pure linen.

"This is lovely," Mom said, glancing around.

"Isn't it pretty?" Gwyneth agreed. "And you may be surprised by the quality of the food. It's quite excellent."

"That's always good to hear."

The hostess, a young fresh-faced girl of about twenty, led us through the main room of twelve tables and into an alcove that contained one table that would seat all five of us. There were curtained windows on three walls, so we all had lovely views of the village and the loch beyond.

"Oh, there's Gregory," Claire said, and waved to the man sitting by a window in the main room.

I had to think for a second who Gregory was. "Oh, the vicar."

She stopped to say hello while I took a moment to take in the room, with its historical paintings and the dish rail filled with vintage tea saucers. "This is so nice."

"It's charming," Mom said as Claire joined us. "I'm glad you thought of this, Claire."

Sophie winked at her friend. "It's the next best thing to getting married."

Claire rolled her eyes, but she was smiling. "I'm just glad you're staying for a few more days, Becky. I'm not sure I could face another Bitsy confrontation without you."

The sound of high heels clomping across the main room's wood floor brought us all to attention. Our table in the alcove was blocked from a view of the main room, so we couldn't see who was making all that noise. But we heard the clomping stop, and a woman shouted, "I demand that you give it back!"

"B-but, Matilda, I don't—"

"I need it now. You track it down, or I won't be responsible for what happens to you."

Then her clomping heels took off in the opposite direction. The front door opened, and the woman in heels stormed out of the tea-room. The door slammed shut, and we were left staring at each other.

"Oh my God," Mom whispered. "I wonder what she wants to get back."

"Perhaps her youth," Gwyneth suggested.

Claire burst out laughing and I was right there with her. "Oh, Gwyneth. That's priceless."

Just then, a well-dressed woman walked into our alcove. "I beg your pardon, ladies."

"Don't you look pretty today, Mrs. Cardon," Claire said, smiling up at her.

It was true. The woman was quite lovely, with bright red hair worn in a neat bob tucked behind her ears. She wore a tartan skirt with a navy blue sweater and navy flats. I assumed she was the manager or possibly the owner of the tearoom.

"Hello, Helen, dear," Gwyneth said cordially. "We don't have menus yet."

"Hmm, uh, no." The woman looked sick to her stomach. "I . . . I'm sorry, ladies, but I must ask you to leave."

"What's wrong, Helen?" Gwyneth pushed her chair back and stood. "You look a bit queasy, dear. Can I get you a glass of water?"

"No. I'm fine. You . . . you've got to go now."

I met Sophie's gaze and got a raised eyebrow from her. Then she looked at Claire. Mom and Gwyneth exchanged wary glances.

"Why is that?" Mom asked.

"Yes, what is the problem, Helen?" Gwyneth said, her voice calm but edging toward fury.

Then Claire stood. "Let's go, ladies." And she walked out of the tearoom.

Each of us stood slowly. I watched Gwyneth's expression warn of reprisal. "Yer aff yer heid, Helen."

My mother hissed loudly, "What kind of a place is this?"

I personally gave Mrs. Cardon my best *You'll be sorry* glare as I passed in front of her.

I heard Sophie say, "We'll take our business to the pub. Food's better anyway."

Out on the sidewalk, I caught up to Claire, who was walking very quickly back to the car. I grabbed her arm. "What was that all about?" Although I had a sneaking suspicion.

"We'll talk in the car," she said.

Once we were all inside the car, Claire said, "I'm sorry."

"Don't you dare apologize," Gwyneth snapped. "Who does she think she is, throwing you out of her piddling little tea shop? And look at all the business you were bringing her today. Five ladies ready to spend lavish amounts of money in her shop. She should count her lucky stars that you're her customer."

"You mean, I *was* her customer," Claire muttered.

"She looked as frightened as a little rabbit," Mom murmured.

I asked, "Is that one of the women Olivia is hooked into?"

"Yes." Claire started the engine but didn't drive off yet. Instead, she turned and faced us. "Olivia has told certain people that I was spreading a rumor that Mrs. Cardon watered down the tea and that she didn't really bake her own scones. According to my anonymous sources, who happen to be Mrs. B, Tamara, Sophie, and Sally, the upstairs housekeeper in the north wing, rumor has it that I've been going around telling people that Mrs. Cardon buys her scones at a discount bakery in Inverness."

"That would cut deep," Sophie said. "Mrs. Cardon is very proud of her scones. She bakes them daily and she's won prizes for them."

"I know," Claire cried. "I love her scones. I didn't spread the rumor. But someone did. They're slandering me."

"That tears it," Gwyneth said. "We need a battle plan."

*I*nstead of going to the pub, where Sophie would no doubt be pressed into service, we decided to walk upstairs to Gwyneth's lovely apartment above her antique shop just a block away. She had sweetened the deal by telling us about the beautiful cheese, leek, and onion quiche in the freezer that she could heat up in an instant, along with everything we'd need to make a very strong pot of tea.

"I've even got biscuits," she said.

"That nails it," Mom said. "Let's go."

Now we were ensconced in her light and airy second-story apartment with its view of the loch as well as a sweeping view of the high street and the hills that rose above it.

"This quiche is wonderful, Gwyneth," Mom said.

"Better than anything," I agreed, then muttered, "Stupid tearoom lady."

"Helen Cardon is a lovely woman," Gwyneth said as she poured tea into her cup. "But she's got absolutely no imagination and no spine."

"She looked scared to death as we were walking out," I said. "Almost as though someone were watching her every move and reporting what she did to the thought police."

"That's a skeerie reference," Sophie said with an involuntary shiver. "But if you know anything about the OWC, it fits."

"The Oddlochen Women's Club," Claire elucidated for us.

"It's not really that bad, is it?" I asked, assuming the term *skeerie* meant "scary."

"You all heard the woman who was yelling at the vicar, didn't you?" Sophie asked.

"Yes," Mom said. "Who was that?"

Sophie's wide grin dripped with irony. "That was Bitsy Kerr's mother."

"Oh, ouch." Mom winced. "That can't be good."

"There's more to this twisted tale," Sophie said, and she sounded like she was enjoying it. "Bitsy's mother is the sister of Olivia's mother, who's also the headmistress of the Atherton Academy."

"Wait." I did the math. "Olivia and Bitsy are cousins? So Bitsy's mother is married to the mayor?"

Sophie smiled. "No, that's the third sister. Bitsy's father died a few months ago."

"Doesn't that just make all sorts of sense?" Gwyneth asked.

I frowned. "Unfortunately, yes."

"It's a small town," Claire said, as if that explained everything. In a way, it did.

"This is beginning to sound like the plot of a twisted horror movie I saw when I was young." Mom took a quick sip of tea. "It took place in an English village, and all the children were born with white hair and strange eyes. Turns out they were mutants. They could stare at someone and that person died. There was a lot going on with the military and scientists, but I can't remember if there were aliens involved."

I laughed. "There are always aliens."

"I remember that film," Gwyneth said brightly. "I came home from the theater and stood staring at my mother, but nothing happened."

Claire laughed. "You're all doing a bang-up job of cheering me up. Thank you."

Sophie frowned. "What's so cheery about aliens and mutants?"

Claire was still laughing as she gave Sophie a light smack on the shoulder, then hugged her. "I love ye."

"Back to ye, girlie," Sophie said.

"Look, my girl," Gwyneth said. "It's not like you're going to move away from Oddlochen."

"Of course not," Claire said. "First, because they can go to Hades before I'll be the one to move away. And second, Cameron and his people are tied to this place by hundreds of years of family tradition. And third, I love Oddlochen, too. This is my home. I'm too strong to give in to stupidity, and I'll not be defeated by this silly club—or whatever it is—or any of the crap they try to throw at me in the future."

Mom and I immediately stood up and applauded. "You go, girl!" Mom cried.

Sophie stood and joined us, and finally Gwyneth pushed up from her comfy chair. "Crikey, it's like *Les Misérables* around here," she said, and made us all laugh.

The doorbell rang and Gwyneth shrugged. "Good thing I'm already standing up. I'd better see who that is."

The stairs leading down were in the back of the building, not facing the street. She wasn't gone thirty seconds when we heard her footsteps leading back upstairs. And there was another set of footsteps following, as well.

"Look who's here," Gwyneth said, and ushered the vicar into her living room.

"Gregory," Claire said, and stood up to give him a light hug.

"Hello, Vicar," Sophie said, saluting him from across the room.

"Hello, all," he said, taking off his heavy coat.

"Would you like a cup of tea?" Gwyneth asked.

"That would be excellent," he said.

"I suppose you saw us being tossed out of the tearoom," Sophie said.

"On our proverbial arses," Gwyneth added.

"I did, and I'm sorry for it." His frown was intense. "I intend to speak to Cameron, er, His Lairdship, as well as the town council when they next meet. That cannot be tolerated."

"We would very much appreciate anything you can do," Gwyneth said, handing him his tea in a lovely vintage cup and saucer.

"It's gone too far," he murmured, shaking his head.

I wasn't about to ask questions right now, but the vicar clearly knew more about the situation than some of us did.

"Sit down here, Vicar," Gwyneth said, pointing to the comfortable chair that she had abandoned.

"Thank you." He took another sip of his tea, then set it on the coffee table in front of him. Glancing over his shoulder at Gwyneth, he said, "I've come to ask for your help."

"Of course," she said. "Whatever I can do."

"I wonder if you could give back the book you won at the church auction."

Gwyneth flashed a look of pure suspicion, and coming from someone with a lifetime of experience in espionage, that look could be lethal. "What do you mean, give it back?"

The vicar sighed. "It seems that Fluff Kerr found the book in her family's bookshelf and brought it to me for the auction. Without her mother's permission, obviously."

"I was in charge of the auction," Gwyneth said. "Why wouldn't she bring it to me?"

He had the good grace to look embarrassed. "I believe she has, er, um, a bit of a schoolgirl crush on me and wanted to impress me by appearing to be helpful. Or . . . something."

"She's hardly a schoolgirl," Gwyneth muttered, rolling her eyes. "But do go on."

"This donated book was something that her mother cherished," he said. "It was one of the last gifts her husband gave her before he died."

"Oh dear." Gwyneth patted her chest. "Why would the girl ever donate it to the church auction?"

"I suppose she didn't realize how important it was to her mother."

"What's the book?" I asked.

He was startled by my question, almost as though he'd forgotten there was anyone else in the room. "The title of the book is *The Gift of the Magi*."

Gwyneth and I stared at each other.

"And this book belonged to the Kerr family?" Claire asked.

"That's right," he said. "Needless to say, Matilda is furious with Fluff. Just this morning, she finally got the truth out of her daughter. Shortly after that, she stormed into the tearoom and demanded that I get the book back from whoever bought it."

"Did you tell her who won the book?" I asked.

"I didn't know who won until I returned to the church and checked our records. When I saw that it was you, I was quite relieved."

"Why is that, Vicar?" Mom asked.

He lifted both hands as though he were about to bless us all. "Why, because Gwyneth is the soul of reasonableness."

"She absolutely is," Claire said, and gave her aunt a quick hug.

Gwyneth nodded. "If this book belongs to Matilda, I will return it immediately."

"Yes, of course," Claire said. "Although I must admit, the book was not in the best condition when we received it."

"I agree," Gwyneth said. "I thought it might've been scuffed up during the auction."

"I'm sure she won't mind," the vicar said. "She's quite anxious to get it back."

I glanced at Gwyneth and then Claire and knew we were in agreement. It was almost guaranteed that Bitsy's mother would whine and moan about the state of the book no matter how quickly she got it back. But that was only if we could find it and get it back to her. Maybe we could bargain with her. We'd give her the book if she would take her daughter home with her. I was half kidding since I knew that wasn't quite ethical. The book did belong to her, after all. Still, maybe we could work out a deal. I mean, her daughter belonged to her, too.

I chuckled at my goofy thoughts.

"Besides the scuff marks, Vicar," I said aloud, "there's just one tiny problem with the book."

"What's that?" he asked.

"It's been stolen," Gwyneth said flatly.

Chapter 9

It was midafternoon when we returned to the castle. Mom and I had stopped at a darling little shop on the high street to find holiday presents for Charlotte and Ginny. We found an adorable, huggable stuffed kitten wearing a tartan sweater for Charlotte and an elegant Scottish-themed deck of tarot cards for Ginny. I could've spent all day in there and picked up gifts for everyone I knew, but we wanted to get back to the castle.

Derek, Dad, and Cameron had been back for an hour already and were conducting an impromptu Scotch tasting in the blue parlor.

I pulled Derek aside. "Do you feel sober enough to check out another tower this afternoon?"

"Darling, I've barely had a sip, sad to say."

I rubbed his arm in a consoling way. "That is really sad. But I was thinking we still have time to search at least one or two towers before the sun sets."

"What has brought on this fervor to hunt more books?" he asked.

"I'm always in the mood to hunt for books, but I do have a specific interest right now." I explained about the vicar's visit and the need to find *The Gift of the Magi* as soon as possible.

He grabbed my hand. "Let's go."

After an hour, we had searched two more towers and only found a bedroll, which basically consisted of a threadbare sleeping bag with a blanket rolled up inside. It had been shoved under an old oak table in one of the towers. It was dusty, and Derek surmised that it hadn't been used in a while.

But I did have a question about anyone sneaking up here with their ratty bedroll to sleep. I decided I'd bring the matter up to Cameron when I had the chance.

"So, you don't think the bedroll belongs to our nighttime noisemakers?" I asked.

"No. Judging by that layer of dust, it's been at least six or eight months."

That was the bad news. But the good news was that we also found another book.

"I'm so psyched!" I said. "I can't believe we found another book."

Derek had been going through the bedroll, but now he looked up. "Tell me about it."

I stared at the cover. "I'm a little embarrassed to admit that I'd never heard of this book before I saw it on Claire's list. And I'm a little ashamed of myself because I simply assumed that, with that title, it was a Christmas book. I didn't even look it up."

"We were a little rushed at the time, darling."

"Thank you for giving me an out, but I'm still going to wallow in self-blame for another minute or two." I sighed. "Anyway, it's called *The Greatest Gift*. Is it a British story?"

"I have no idea," he confessed. "I've never heard of it, either."

"Well, at least I'm not the only one." I pulled my phone out of my pocket. "I'll look it up."

"There you go."

Through the browser on my phone, I got to my favorite book site and called up the title. I read through the search results for another minute, then stared at Derek. "This book was the basis for the film *It's A Wonderful Life*."

"Very definitely a Christmas book," Derek said.

"Yes. The author of the book self-published it in 1943, and it was published traditionally in 1944." I held up the book, which was only in fair condition, with bent corners and a smudge on the cover. "A similar book to this one is currently on sale for three thousand dollars."

"You're joking. It can't be more than thirty pages long."

"I'm not joking. And it's sixty-four pages long."

"I shouldn't be shocked at that price since I live with a book expert who comes up with outlandish numbers like that all the time."

I smiled. "And this number isn't even as much as I usually come up with."

"Right. This is only, what? A paltry three thousand?"

I smiled. "Pretty good for a book neither of us has ever heard of before."

Fifteen minutes later, we were on the steps that led to the next tower, which I had taken to calling the fat tower since the stairs were wider and the tower itself was shorter. The pointed roof was taller, though, than many of the others.

"This tower room is much larger than the one in the west wing." Derek strolled to the door on the other wall. "It's even got an extra room."

"The west wing tower was tall and skinny," I said, then stared at the closed door. "Maybe it's a bathroom. Or a closet."

"Maybe there are more books in there," he said, reaching for the doorknob.

"I hope so."

He looked inside. "It's a closet."

"Any books in there?"

"I can't see much." He pulled out his phone and used the flashlight app. "Oh no." His voice had turned somber.

"What is it?" I stepped closer to get a look inside.

He held his arm out to stop me. "Don't look, darling."

We didn't find any more books. But we did find a dead body.

*T*here was no easy way to convey the horrifying news over a speakerphone or in a text, so Derek called Cameron and told him we needed to see him immediately. On the way to the stairs leading to the north wing I detoured into the great hall to see if anything had been disturbed. Everything looked perfectly normal, no glass was broken, and the displays were locked up tight. The only problem I saw was that one of the daggers was missing.

As we climbed the stairs to the north wing, I had a fleeting thought that we'd made it through the foyer and up the stairs without running into Bitsy. I wondered if she might be sick or something. The thought faded when Cameron opened the door almost immediately.

And Derek and I prepared to break their hearts.

"Hello, you two. Come in."

We walked into their very elegant living room, and I took a moment to check it out. Two dark red velvet couches faced each other separated by a heavy-footed antique coffee table. Two green-and-gold brocade chairs sat at either end of the couches. The artwork on the walls was a pleasing mix of old world and modern, and I would bet that everything was original. Most of one wall was glass and it looked out over the loch.

"Wow," I said. "This is just beautiful."

"Have you never been up here before?" Claire asked.

"No," I said. "And that's okay. You both deserve to have a special place to get away from the world."

"I think so, too," Claire said. "But that doesn't include good friends. This space is mostly for Cameron to get away. He deals with a lot of problems every day, and this is a refuge for him."

"Well, once you go downstairs," I warned, "there will be no more refuge."

"True," Cameron said, grinning. "I was there for a few minutes to taste the new Scotch I purchased but then decided to come up here for a brief respite with my wife-to-be."

"We truly hate to ruin your day," I began.

"Something's wrong," Cameron said.

"What is it?" Claire demanded. "What happened?"

I reached for Derek's hand and held on tight. "Say it fast," I murmured.

He nodded. "We were looking for books up in one of the towers. And we found a body."

"What?" Claire cried.

"What in the world?" Cameron demanded. "Who is it?"

"You should sit down," I said. "Please."

Without another word, they sat down.

"I'm so sorry," Derek said. "It's Willy."

"Willy?" Cameron said sharply. "Willy Smith?"

"Angus's friend Willy?" Claire asked.

"Yes," I said.

She gasped. "Oh God. No. No." Then she began to sob.

"I'm so sorry," I whispered, and felt my own eyes filling up. I thought I had managed to stop crying before we climbed the stairs to their suite, but seeing and hearing Claire's sobs, I couldn't help myself.

"How?" Cameron asked, trying to keep to the facts. "Which tower?"

"The short one," I said. "Near that pink sitting room."

"And you found him right there in the tower room?"

"We found him in the closet."

Cameron muttered a string of Gaelic words we couldn't understand. He stood again, needing to move. Finally he said, "Och, hell." His voice was filled with sorrow. "Why would anyone hurt that poor kid?"

"We've got to call the police," Claire said.

"Before you do," Derek said, "there's something else you should know."

"Good God. What else?" Cameron asked, and sat down next to his fiancée. He grasped her hand, clearly not sure he could take any more bad news.

I put my hand on Claire's shoulder. "We saw a jeweled dagger sticking out of Willy's neck."

As the others took care of alerting the police, I thought about the awful sight I'd seen in the tower closet. I had recognized Willy right away from his distinctive black wool peacoat he'd been wearing at the bonfire. The coat was unbuttoned now, and I could clearly see the dagger in his throat. And the blood. I shivered at the memory, actually surprised that I hadn't passed out at the sight.

In the closet, Willy had apparently tried to write something in the thick dust covering the floor. His finger was matted with dust as well, which made it clear that he had been attempting to leave a message. Derek and I had taken a minute to try and work out what he'd been trying to convey.

"It looks like the numbers zero and one," I'd said, staring at the figures.

"Or the letters *O* and *I*," Derek had said.

"Not a lot of help," I'd murmured.

"But it must mean something," Derek had decided. "We'll think about it. For now, we'd best get out of here and go alert the authorities."

We had closed the closet door and descended the circular stairs to find Cameron and tell him the news.

Cameron asked his security man Silas Abernathy to come to his suite, and when the man arrived, Cameron and Derek told him what had happened. Silas suggested that he himself call the Inverness police to report the murder since he knew a lot of the members of the department. "They'll send the MIT," Silas said after he hung up. "And of course they'll want to talk to you, Commander, and you, Brooklyn."

We'd been on a first-name basis with Silas since our last visit to Oddlochen.

"What's the MIT?" I asked.

"Major Investigations Team," Silas said. "They handle murders and other major crimes."

"Got it."

Silas checked his wristwatch. "They'll be here within a half hour. I gave them the bare details, and they assured me they'd rush."

"Good," Cameron said. "Thank you, Silas. I'm glad you're here."

"Thank you, sir," he said. "I'll wait for them downstairs. If you need anything, I've got my cell."

Cameron wrapped his arm around Claire. "We'll stay up here."

When Silas left, Derek said, "We'll go, too."

"No," Claire said. "Please stay. Sit down. And tell me about the dagger you saw."

"All right." We sat down on the couch across from them, and I began. "It's that rich blue lapis lazuli with diamonds and those fleur-de-lis cutouts. I've seen it on display in the great hall."

Cameron reached for Claire's hand. "For a moment, I thought it might be your emerald dagger."

Claire blinked. "Oh, I keep that one with me." Then she reached down and pulled up her pant leg to reveal the thin ankle holster. She pulled out the emerald dagger and showed it to Cameron. "I'm still wearing it."

"That holster is cool," I said, then felt foolish. But it really was cool.

Cameron shook his head, then leaned over and kissed her. "Good thinking."

"So, someone must've stolen the lapis knife from the glass display cabinet in the great hall." She looked at me. "It's from our collection. It's worth a fortune."

"I remember seeing it there," I said. "It's beautiful." I winced inwardly, thinking of the thing being thrust into Willy's neck. "I checked the great hall on the way up here. Nothing is damaged. No glass was broken. So whoever stole the dagger must've had a key to the display cabinet."

"Which means he's a stupid thief," Cameron said harshly. "Instead of selling it for thousands, he used it to kill that innocent young man."

"*He?*" I said.

Cameron gazed at me. "You think it's a woman?"

"I don't see why not. When we first met Willy, Claire told us how he and Angus liked to go into the library to flirt with Olivia. Maybe they had a disagreement."

"It's possible," Claire said. "But I don't think Olivia has any skill with a knife."

I shrugged. "If you're up close to someone, it doesn't take much skill. Just a lot of determination. And some strength, of course." I looked up and saw them all staring at me. "Not that I have any personal experience with the whole killing-with-a-knife thing. But, you know, I read books."

Our mood was somber, but Derek managed a half laugh. "Yes, you do."

"But why would she kill him?" Claire asked. "They're friendly."

I shook my head. "I'm just throwing out possibilities."

"Keep doing that," Derek said, brushing my arm. "Because someone killed him, and we might as well start listing possibilities."

"I have another one," I said, wincing. "But you're not going to like it."

Claire had stood up, but now she pounced. "Who?"

"The night of the bonfire, I saw Willy and Angus arguing."

"Willy and Angus?" Claire said. "But they're best mates."

"Tell us what you saw," Cameron said.

"Well, it started with them yelling at each other, but then they began shoving. I mean, really hard."

"How did it end?" Derek asked.

"Willy stormed off and Angus watched him go. He looked angry. No, he looked infuriated, but he didn't follow him. A few seconds later, though, he faded into the crowd, going in the same direction as Willy."

They were quiet for a moment, and Cameron reached for Claire's hand.

"Today at breakfast," I continued, "Angus said he watched the bonfire from a boat on the loch. The boat belongs to a friend, he said. Now, timingwise, it's a little tight, but it's possible that he had the fight with Willy, then ran off to join his friends on the boat."

"Also at breakfast this morning," Derek added, "Angus said he was looking for Willy."

"I just don't want to believe that Angus and Willy were at odds," Claire said, shaking her head slowly. "But Brooklyn knows what she saw."

Cameron nodded. "Even though we work with Willy and Angus and the others every day, it seems we don't really know them."

"Oh, love," Claire said. She couldn't seem to come up with any other words of consolation.

I waited for a moment while they hugged each other, then sighed. "Hate to bring up the possibility that Olivia might've had something to do with Willy's death, but she was here for the bonfire. And looking at the timing, Willy could've been killed around the same time."

"She may be completely innocent," Claire said.

"True," I said, and left it at that.

"What was he doing up in the tower?" Claire wondered.

"If he was up there with a woman," Derek began, "which, sorry to say, is the most likely scenario, they wanted complete privacy to do whatever they had in mind to do."

"Oh God," Claire said. "Do you think she lured him up there?"

"It's possible," Derek said.

"What if he was killed by a man?" I asked, and couldn't help thinking of Angus. "Why would they go all the way up to the tower?"

"No matter how angry Angus might've been," Cameron said, "I can't see him actually killing Willy. They were best mates."

"And whoever did it would've had to stop to steal the dagger,"

Claire reasoned, "which would make his actions premeditated. And as far as Angus is concerned, I can't see that happening, ever."

We were all silent for a moment, then Claire took a deep breath. "Maybe we should postpone the wedding indefinitely."

"Don't do that," I said immediately. "You might wait a few days, maybe even a week out of respect for Willy. But you and Cameron and all of your people deserve to celebrate your wedding. You're going to need a happy, life-affirming occasion like a wedding for everyone to get past this tragedy."

"Brooklyn's right," Derek said, taking hold of my hand.

"And besides, you two have been through a lot. You deserve to be married and happy." I rested my head against Derek's shoulder.

Claire leaned forward, her elbows resting on her knees. "Thank you. I appreciate your advice. And I think you're right."

"So do I," Cameron said. "No matter what happens, I want to be married to you within the next three days."

Claire gave a firm nod. "Then we'll make it so."

"There's a good thought," Derek said.

"Now tell us about the books you've found," Claire said, very obviously needing to change the subject.

"We have a few theories," I said. "But to keep it simple, I thought someone might've just wanted to read for a while. They might've sneaked a book out of the library and looked around for a quiet place to spend an hour or so reading. And then they just left the book right there."

Derek continued, "And the quietest places to hide away inside the castle are up in the towers."

I nodded. "Also, when Derek and I were walking outside yesterday at about midday, I saw someone up in the west wing tower."

"So we climbed up there," Derek said, "and sure enough, we found a book."

"We found *A Child's Christmas in Wales*," I said.

"Oh, I love that book," Claire said.

"I do, too," Cameron said. "My father read it to me at Christmas when I was a young lad."

"In our family, it was Mum," Derek said with a smile. "So, once we found that book, we decided to keep looking. And we found one more. We have more searching to do, and we hope to find a few more."

"That's amazing," Claire said. "I was sure the books had been stolen."

"It's still possible that some were taken. But some of the books are hardly worth anything, so why would they be stolen? As Brooklyn said, maybe someone just wanted to read for a while, and when they were finished with the book, they just left it there."

"It seems that the library is open to anyone from the village," Derek said. "That may attract some folks who simply want to read in a warm place for a while and then take a nap."

Claire shook her head. "I suppose some people might enjoy that."

I shrugged. "Obviously I haven't thought the theory all the way through, but since we found the two books, we'll keep looking."

"By the way," Derek said. "We went to Mrs. B to get directions to all the towers."

Claire smiled. "Very smart."

"Right?" I said. "And it's a good thing we did, because that's how we found Willy."

"Poor Willy," Claire murmured. "He was harmless."

I glanced at Derek. "Maybe he saw something he shouldn't have seen."

"Always a possibility," he said.

"By the way, Claire," I asked, hoping to keep her on point instead of watching her dissolve into more heartbreaking tears. "Do you keep your display cabinets locked?"

"Of course," Claire said. "But whoever got in there and stole the knife must've known where we keep the keys."

"Did Olivia ever see where you keep them?" Derek asked.

Claire and Cameron stared at each other for a long moment. Finally Claire admitted, "She might've."

"Yes, it's possible." Cameron checked his watch one more time. "But let's continue this conversation later. Right now, we'd better go downstairs and meet the MIT. I don't want to keep them waiting."

I'm Assistant Chief Constable Rory Logan, and this is Assistant Chief Constable Tom Johnson. We're with the Major Investigations Team, and both of us will be available to answer any questions or handle any problems you have."

Assistant Chief Constable Rory Logan was a petite blond woman with a ready smile who had probably fooled a lot of crooks into thinking she was a lightweight. She clearly was not. Assistant Chief Constable Tom Johnson was a tall, thin, balding man who couldn't hide his smile and bright blue eyes. Despite that happy face of his, he was no lightweight. They were both kind and treated all of us with respect and care.

Cameron introduced himself and Claire, then turned to me and Derek. "Commander Derek Stone is a decorated officer who worked for MI6 for many years, achieving his current rank. He now runs his own security company with offices in London and San Francisco."

"Commander," Rory Logan said with a nod. "Always good to know who we're dealing with."

"Indeed," Derek said, and turned to me. "My wife, Brooklyn Wainwright, is a rare book restoration expert."

"Rare books," Logan said. "Fascinating."

"It is," Derek said. "I mention her profession because we found the body of the young man while we were up in one of the towers searching for lost books."

"Searching for books and instead you found a body," Rory Logan said.

"We found some books, too," I said.

"Well, there's something good," she said.

Silas Abernathy joined the group at that moment, and Cameron started to introduce him. Both Rory Logan and Tom Johnson held up their hands. "We know Silas." They all shook hands and Rory Logan said, "Good to see you."

It was decided that Derek and I would show the two assistant chief constables, Logan and Johnson, where we found the body. Cameron and Claire would give Logan's assistant, Constable Murphy, all the relevant information about the guests staying in the castle.

Before we headed up to the tower, we were both asked to wear cloth booties and thin rubber gloves to avoid contaminating the crime scene.

"We were already up there looking for books," I said, "so we might've contaminated the scene."

"Understood," Logan said. "We'll just try to minimize that from here on."

We led the way, going slowly up the spiral staircase. I prayed I wouldn't slip and fall in the flimsy cotton booties, and my prayers were answered when we reached the landing at the top.

"He's over here," Derek said.

"Please wait," Logan said, and signaled Johnson to lay down a long, wide sheet of thin plastic for us to walk on.

Then Derek walked to the closet and opened the door. "Here he is."

He backed away so the police could observe the body and begin to do the work of investigating the crime.

"That's quite a knife," Logan said.

"It's an antique dagger," I said. "Worth over one hundred thousand pounds. From the collection in the great hall. Claire can show it to you later and give you more information."

"So, instead of stealing it and making some money, they used it as a weapon." She shook her head.

"Exactly." I could see she was having the same reaction we'd had earlier.

Derek and I stayed in the tower room for another ten minutes. I was pleased when Logan mentioned the dust on Willy's forefinger and had a feeling they were really good at their jobs. Then Logan told us we could go downstairs. Assistant Chief Constable Johnson followed us down, and while he reconnoitered with Constable Murphy and two of his fellow constables who were interviewing staff members, we escaped the police presence and ran to the blue parlor, where we found Cameron and Claire.

I was giddy with relief to see them.

"We probably shouldn't think about having a drink while the police are on the premises," Claire said. "But my nerves are completely frazzled."

"Let me pour you something, darling," Cameron said. "Red wine?"

"Yes, please."

"Brooklyn?"

"I'll have the same."

"Derek? Scotch?"

"No. I believe I'll have a glass of red wine as well."

"Coming right up." He poured the wine and delivered our glasses, and the four of us toasted. "We'll drink to Willy."

"Thank you," Claire whispered.

We had a brief moment of silence while we all sipped our wine. Thinking of that nice young man, helping build a bonfire and working in the fields. And fishing with his father. I thought of the way he had touched Tamara's bahoochie without her objection and then how he'd breezed into the library, calling Olivia his love. Innocent flirtation, or was he dating both women at once? And if so, did they know? He had grown up in Oddlochen and everyone seemed to like him. We only knew a few facts about his life. But we knew he didn't deserve to die so young or in such a brutal way.

"Good lord," Cameron said. "Weren't we just toasting to our upcoming nuptials a day ago?"

"It feels like a month ago," Claire said.

"Hey," I said, "maybe having the police roaming the castle will be the impetus for Bitsy to leave."

"Oh," Claire said. "From your lips."

"Let's toast to that possibility." I raised my glass.

"Hear, hear," Cameron said, and we all clinked glasses and took a hearty sip of the excellent Bordeaux.

"Let's talk of mundane things," Claire suggested.

"All right, I have a question," I said.

"What is it?" Claire asked.

"If we happen to have a day to spend doing whatever we want, what would you suggest we do?"

Cameron said, "I would drive up to Tain and visit Glenmorangie."

"The Scotch distillery?" Derek asked. "That's a brilliant destination."

I smiled at him but then gave Claire a beseeching look. "I like

Scotch, too. But are there other things to do in Tain besides visit the distillery?"

"Yes," Claire said. "It's a pretty little town, and they have a beautiful glass and pottery shop nearby. Or you could think about stopping at Dunrobin."

"Aye," Cameron said. "'Tis a right imposing castle on the coast, just a few miles north of Tain."

"I think you would love it," Claire said. "The rooms are quite elegant and they have a wonderful library. Oh, Brooklyn, you would love the library. And there's a gift shop and a tea room and the most glorious gardens."

"Sounds wonderful," I said.

"And for a more manly activity," she said, biting back a smile as she gazed at Derek, "they have falconry."

Derek's eyes grew wide. "You're joking."

"She's not joking," Cameron said. "It's quite spectacular."

"I adore watching the birds," Claire said.

"How have we never heard of this place?"

Claire smiled. "We do have a plethora of fantastic places to see and things to do."

"It sounds fabulous," I said, and wondered if we might venture up to that area while we were still here.

"By the way, love," Claire said. "I texted Aunt Gwyneth to let her know about Willy and asked her to let the others know, as well."

"They've probably seen the constables, so they must know something's amiss."

I frowned. "Also, we haven't seen Bitsy at all today."

"I told the police they should speak to her," Cameron said, "so I know she's still here."

"Come to think of it, she was essentially alone for part of the day. I wonder if she saw Willy."

"Or Willy's killer," Derek said.

Claire and Cameron suddenly looked gobsmacked.

"I never even considered that," Cameron said.

"Why would you?" I said. "I'm afraid we've had enough run-ins with bad people that our brains are always going in that direction."

"It's highly unlikely, however," Derek said. "You do have a full staff of people working here."

"Yes, of course," Cameron said. "And the police interviewed each of them."

"I'm sure Bitsy remained tucked up in her sanctuary all day," I said, trying to calm their worries.

"But now you've got me thinking," Cameron mused, his brow furrowed in concern.

"I suppose," Claire said. "Whenever she shows herself, we'll deal with it."

"And we'll be right behind you," I said.

She gave me a pleading gaze. "Perhaps you could be in front of us?"

We all managed a laugh, and I patted her shoulder. "I can be wherever you need me to be."

Claire's text notification interrupted us. "Well, here's good news. Sophie's back."

"I didn't know she'd left," I said.

Claire nodded. "She had to check in with her bar manager and her waitstaff."

"I'm glad she's back," I said. "And I think when we're all ready, we should get Bitsy out of her room to join us."

"Really?" Derek said.

I laughed weakly. "Yes. The sooner we show that we're not afraid of her, the sooner she'll leave."

Claire wasn't looking too excited about the idea. "Do you think so?"

Cameron nodded. "She's right. Eventually Bitsy will have to come out and join the party."

"Yes. Otherwise, why is she here?"

Why indeed? I wondered, although I was pretty sure I knew the answer. But after dealing with a body in the tower and the police interrogating everyone in the castle, I didn't think Cameron and Claire deserved more aggravation from someone like Bitsy Kerr. It wasn't fair, especially to Claire and also to Cameron. But it would be best if we dragged her out of her cave and shined a light on her, so to speak.

Cameron had made it very clear that he'd rarely dated anyone from the village. He had known Bitsy for years, but as Claire had said, they'd never done anything more than act as the other's plus-one on a few occasions. It had never grown into anything serious. Naturally they had attended events with groups of friends, but he insisted they had never been boyfriend and girlfriend. Her showing up at the castle didn't make sense, which was why I had to wonder what was actually going on here.

And there was still Olivia to consider. I hadn't thought of Bitsy and Olivia as two of a kind, but they were cousins, after all, and their mothers were both powerful women in a small town. It made a mean kind of sense that Claire was getting hurt by both of their actions. And not only Claire but Cameron, as well. And by extension, their friends and wedding guests and indeed the whole village.

This had not been a good day for Claire. She had been humiliated and thrown out of the local tearoom, then we had informed her of the murder of a good friend right inside the castle. It was going to be a challenging evening, to say the least, and Claire wasn't going to be the only one facing the formidable wrath of Bitsy Kerr.

Chapter 10

Sophie arrived in time to be greeted by Assistant Chief Constable Logan walking out the door. As Sophie explained to us later, she had known Rory Logan and the others for years and had spent many an evening in the pub supplying the local constabulary with the best offerings, usually at a discount price. "They're public servants," Sophie said as we watched the police caravan drive off. "They deserve to be given a break."

We walked with Sophie down the hall as she explained, "They've still got one team of three collecting evidence in the tower above the pink parlor. They'll be another hour at the most."

We walked into the blue parlor, where Mom and Dad and Gwyneth had already settled in with beverages and snacks provided by Mrs. B. This time there were homemade tortilla chips with red and green salsa—more Christmas colors—courtesy of Tamara and the kitchen crew. Mrs. B joined the rest of us for a few minutes to discuss having a wake for Willy.

"We'll have a dinner tomorrow night and invite his friends, if that suits you and your staff, Mrs. B," Cameron said. "I spoke to Willy's parents earlier, and they're planning the funeral and wake for next week. I asked if they'd mind if we held a small wake for his friends here at the castle, and they were quite pleased that we would think to do so. So the dinner tomorrow night will serve as a wake for Willy."

"I think that's very thoughtful," Mrs. B said. "We'll get right on it." And she left to inform her people.

Now that we were all settled in the blue parlor, we discussed the best way to deal with Bitsy and decided to take it one step at a time. Mom and I would be the first step. And that was how the two of us found ourselves knocking on the yellow sitting room door to officially introduce ourselves.

"We're about to confront an angry woman," I whispered to Mom.

"Good times," she said.

I almost laughed, but then the yellow door opened, and Bitsy said, "What do you want?"

Mom wore a big bright smile. "Hello, Bitsy! I'm Becky Wainwright and this is my daughter Brooklyn. We met at the pub the other night in case you don't remember us."

I hurriedly added, "We're about to have cocktails and hors d'oeuvres in the blue parlor. We'd love to have you join us."

Bitsy's eyes narrowed in suspicion and I couldn't blame her. After all, this was enemy territory as far as she was concerned. And Mom's smile radiated almost too much joy, which was instantly suspect. But the ball was now in Bitsy's court. She would have to decide if she was going to hide away like a recluse or join the party.

"All right," she said. "I'll need to freshen up first. I'll be there in five minutes."

"Wonderful," I said, way too cheerfully. "See you in five."

Mom and I walked away, and when we turned the corner of the

hallway, we ran like giggling schoolgirls all the way to the blue parlor. Once inside, we closed the door and Mom said, "She'll be here in five minutes."

"After she freshens up," I added. Which was ridiculous, of course, because Bitsy looked like she had just stepped out of a day spa with perfect hair, nails, and makeup professionally applied. She had probably spent all day primping, just waiting for someone in the house, preferably Cameron, to knock on her door.

"Good job, ladies," Gwyneth said, and lifted her glass in a toast to us.

"What's her vibe?" Dad asked.

I looked at Mom. "I'd say she's in a major snit."

Mom nodded. "That's a good word for it. We obviously took her by surprise, though, so she didn't have a chance to turn volatile. But give her time."

Cameron managed a chuckle. "Thank you for lightening the mood, Becky. At least for another minute or two."

Mrs. B and one of her servers opened the door and walked in with two large beautiful platters of hearty hors d'oeuvres. Skewered slices of beef tenderloin with a tangy port wine sauce, meatballs in a rich tomato sauce, puff pastry balls filled with cheese and bits of sausage, something delectable wrapped in bacon, and several other savory goodies were spread out on the trays. They set one down on the bar and the other on the coffee table between the two blue sofas. The server quietly left the room.

"Thank you so much, Mrs. B," Claire said. "This looks absolutely scrumptious."

"The salsa was delicious, by the way," I said.

"Tamara's specialty," she said. "I'll let her know you enjoyed it."

Claire walked over and hugged the older woman. "I know you and your staff are mourning the loss of Willy as much as we are."

"Aye," she said. "And poor Angus is crushed. He's lost his best mate."

"I know. I'm so sorry."

"But we will carry on," she said, "because we must."

Cameron joined them and gave her another big hug. "Thank you for all that you do, Mrs. B."

"You make it a pleasure, sir." She cleared her throat, but I could still hear the emotional pain she was suffering as she announced, "If you don't mind, this will serve as your dinner tonight, as I'm letting some of the staff go a little early."

"This looks perfect," Claire said, and with a glance at Cameron added, "We'll go with you to the kitchen. We'd like to offer our condolences for their loss."

"That's very kind of you, Claire," she said.

The door opened just then, and the same server entered carrying another tray filled with slices of pie and cake and brownies, along with bowls of whipped cream, a brandy sauce, and hot fudge.

The hot fudge did it for me. I almost slid right off the couch.

"Wow," Sophie said.

"Ditto," Dad said.

Claire smiled. "This is lovely."

"Thank you, Mrs. B," Cameron said.

She nodded to all of us and walked out of the room, followed by Cameron and Claire.

We began to help ourselves to the goodies, and a few minutes later, they returned, accompanied by Mrs. B. She had apparently appointed herself the referee for the moment, because Bitsy followed right behind her and walked inside. I was close enough to the door to hear Mrs. B whisper, "Behave yourself, lassie," and then leave.

Bitsy gave her a look of utter contempt, and she huffed and puffed her way over to the bar.

"I want a martini," she demanded of nobody in particular.

I wondered if Mrs. B's words had inadvertently stoked the shrew's fire.

Derek strolled over to the bar in place of Cameron. "Vodka or gin?"

She sneered at him. "A vodka martini. Extra dry. Three olives."

I knew Derek had stepped up to save Cameron from the rage that was about to erupt.

"How is your mother, Bitsy?" Gwyneth asked. "I haven't seen her lately. Is she well?"

"She's busy," Bitsy said, and didn't elaborate.

"Isn't that nice?" Gwyneth said, and it sounded as if sugar would melt in her mouth.

Mom coughed in order to suppress a laugh.

"Oh, Bitsy," I said in an attempt to make conversation and also cover up Mom's attempt to choke down a laugh. "I don't know if you have any interest in books—"

"What d'ye mean by that?" she said with a snarl.

She wasn't making it easy, but I powered on. "Just that the library looks beautiful with the Christmas tree and all the lights shimmering. I'd be happy to show you around, and maybe you'd like to take a book back to your room to read later."

She huffed in answer and reached for one of the olives in her cocktail.

"I'll take that as a no," I whispered to Derek, who patted my knee in commiseration.

Claire stood, and I could see she was trying for a happy and carefree look. "Since you're all here, I was going to wait for our wedding day, but who knows when that'll happen?" She laughed and the rest us joined her in solidarity.

"I have a gift for my fiancé that I'd like to present to him now."

She told the brief story of finding the book and then using it to shield herself from the flying object. Then she mentioned my part in repairing it. Then she handed it to Cameron. "It's had its ups and downs as we have, so I hope you'll love it always."

"How could I not love it?" he said. He stared at the book, turned it over and opened it to the title page. "Robert Burns. Of course I'll love it." He leaned over and kissed her. "And I love you."

"I love you, too."

The rest of us applauded.

"Well done, Claire," Gwyneth cried.

Bitsy rolled her eyes. "Who cares about an old book written by a dead guy? I can't see what the big deal is about."

Nobody said a word in response to that comment, so Bitsy flounced down on the couch and stared into her martini. She took a tiny taste and I saw her make a sour face. I guessed she didn't drink martinis on a regular basis. She was probably more of a Long Island iced tea girl. That is, if they even served that drink in Scottish bars. I'd have to do the research on that one.

Cameron walked over and sat down next to me, still holding the book in his hand. "I can tell you did a beautiful job of repairing the damage. It looks brand-new. Thank you. I know you brought some relief to Claire's heart by taking on the task."

"I'm glad I could help." I lowered my voice. "Did she give you any more details about the attack that day?"

"No, just what you heard her say a minute ago."

"Derek and I took a brief walk by the place on the high street where the flying object came out of. We can both investigate further if you'd like."

"I'd like that. We can talk after . . ." He glanced at Bitsy. "When we're alone."

"Good." I patted his arm. "Enjoy the book in good health and love."

He kissed my cheek. "Thank you."

As I stood, I stole a peek at Bitsy and saw her continuing to stew. I wondered if she was annoyed with having to talk to any of us specifically or just annoyed with the world in general. I wasn't going to ask.

Claire noticed the same thing and ostentatiously turned to my mother. "Becky, how was your visit to the Clava Cairns?"

I realized I hadn't even asked Mom about her trip, which made me the current worst daughter in the world.

"Incredible," Mom said. "I enjoyed it so much, and I believe I made contact with two spirits."

"Two spirits, Mom?" I asked.

"Yes, sweetie. They came to see me at the behest of Ramlar."

"Ramlar?" Claire said.

"Ramlar X, my astral travel spirit guide." Mom's laugh was filled with joy. "We've had our adventures, let me tell you."

Claire glanced at me, and all I could do was smile and nod.

I turned to Dad. "Did you see any spirits while you were there?"

"You know, I did," Dad said. "One of them recommended a great local pub, and believe me, I was ready for a cold one by the time we left that place."

"Oh, I believe you, Dad."

He winked at me. "Right?"

"I could've stayed all day, but we wanted to get back for our little adventures. The tearoom was such fun. It's a shame we couldn't stay." Mom winked at me, and I realized she'd said that for Bitsy's benefit. I fully expected the woman to get on the phone to her mommy and whine about the fact that the tearoom owner didn't obey her edict to shun Claire.

At least I hoped so.

"I'd like to go back to the Clava Cairns again later in the day to see the exact moment when the cairn is aligned with the sun. It's supposed to be quite an astronomical feat."

"I've seen that," Gwyneth said. "It's remarkable that people living four thousand years ago could figure out how to arrange their burial site at such an angle that the winter sunset would shine down the central passage, filling the interior cavern with sunlight."

Dad nodded. "That idea blows my mind."

As I listened to the others, I went back to studying the Robert Burns book still in Cameron's hand. The burgundy leather corners were so pretty. Cameron noticed my interest and handed me the book. "Thank you." I opened the front cover and took a closer look at the endpapers. They were a soft blur of plaid in green, navy, and red, giving the pattern a Scottish feel.

"Do you like it?" Cameron asked.

I ran my fingers over the endpapers. "I love this. I think every decision this bookbinder made was smart. I'm truly impressed." I smiled up at him. "And then there's the fabulous words of Robert Burns."

"Aye. It's quite special." He glanced at his fiancée. "And so is Claire."

"Oh God! I'm sick of hearing you whinge on about a stupid book!" Bitsy stood and rushed over to grab the book from my hands.

I whipped it away just in time and managed to push the grasping woman back. "What is wrong with you?" I shouted.

She burst into tears and screamed at me, "You're no book expert! You don't know anything!"

"Bitsy, stop it now!" Cameron shouted.

Bitsy turned and shook her finger at Cameron. "You're a liar!"

There was a moment of horrified silence while everyone stared at the woman. She stared back and seemed unsure of her next move.

"And you're out of control," I said as calmly as I could manage. "Just sit down."

I realized I was out of breath and had to think for a minute. What was wrong with this girl? She didn't seem to know how to act in civilized society. I was happy she hadn't gotten hold of the book, because she probably would've torn it apart cover to cover. Why?

"Come sit down," Sophie said, and urged Bitsy over to one of the big blue chairs. "Where's your drink?"

"I don't like it." She sounded like a five-year-old.

Now I had even more reason to detest her, not only for what she was doing to Claire and Cameron, but for attempting to grab that book and do something awful with it.

Claire leaned over and whispered in my ear, "I want to kill her." She was upset enough that her whisper was shared with more ears than just my own.

And that was when Mrs. B walked in followed by two women. "We have more guests." Instantly she realized something was wrong and looked at Cameron. "What is it? Can I help?"

"No, Mrs. B," he said, touching her shoulder. "But thank you." Then he got a good look at the women standing behind her just outside the door and muttered, "Och, what next?"

"Mummy!" Bitsy cried, and ran to the older woman.

The woman grabbed her daughter in a fierce hug and glared at Cameron. "What did you do to her?"

"Matilda," Gwyneth said in her most drippingly polite tone. "So nice to see you."

The other woman—Matilda—scowled. "I've a bone to pick with you, Gwyneth Quinn."

"How charming," Gwyneth murmured. "But I'm afraid Cameron

did absolutely nothing to hurt your daughter. It's Bitsy that seems to be causing the chaos around here. Would you know anything about that?"

Matilda sniffed contemptuously. "I don't know what you're talking about."

"Of course you don't, dear." Gwyneth's polite tone oozed sarcasm, and I loved her for it.

So, this is Matilda Kerr, I thought. The woman who had demanded the book from the vicar in the tearoom earlier today. Was she here to collect her daughter and take her home, or was she here to try to get us to turn *The Gift of the Magi* over to her? The book that was lost.

This might get ugly.

"Mummy," the younger woman said just a bit too loudly, "who are all these people?"

It was something a young girl would ask. *But this girl is in her early twenties, too old to talk like a baby,* I thought.

Gwyneth rushed forward with a flourish to usher Matilda and her loud daughter into the room. "Allow me to introduce Matilda Kerr and her younger daughter Fleur."

"Everybody calls me Fluff," Fleur said. She had a squeaky little girl voice that would've been adorable if she were, in fact, a little girl instead of a twenty-five-year-old woman.

"Why do they call you that?" Mom asked.

She made big circles with her hands. "Because I'm, you know, fluffy."

"Of course you are," Mom said kindly. "It's a charming name."

"Thank you." Fluff gave a little curtsy. "And what's your name?"

"I'm Rebecca Wainwright and people call me Becky. This is my husband Jim. We're from Northern California, the wine country."

Mom moved around the room, touching our shoulders as she said our names. "This is my daughter Brooklyn. She's a bookbinder, married to Derek Stone."

Gwyneth took on the final leg of the introductions. "The Kerr family have lived in Oddlochen for several generations. Isn't that right, Matilda?"

"My husband was a very influential banker"—Matilda pressed a handkerchief to her mouth and sniffed—"before he passed on."

"I'm so sorry for your loss," Mom said.

"It was quite recent, wasn't it?" Gwyneth said.

Matilda's eyes narrowed in on Gwyneth, and I felt chills trickle down my spine.

Matilda finally answered Gwyneth's query. "It was four months ago."

"Oh dear," I said. "That's very recent. I'm so sorry."

Mom spoke up. "I find that children are such a comfort in one's hour of sadness."

I almost spewed red wine at that one. Mom gave me a quelling look.

"Well," Matilda said grudgingly, "that's true, I suppose."

I didn't believe her, because we had just met her children. I couldn't see any comfort coming from those two.

I glanced around the room. Everyone had stopped talking. It was an uncomfortable moment, sitting with these three strange women who didn't seem at all happy to be here. Why didn't they just go home?

Maybe after they departed for the evening—hopefully taking Bitsy with them—we would get the whole story from Gwyneth.

That is, *if* they ever actually departed. The odds were fifty-fifty at this point.

. . .

*T*hey weren't leaving.

Cameron began taking orders for a second round of drinks. He looked at Bitsy and said, "Another martini?"

She tossed her hair back. "I'll have a grasshopper."

It had been obvious from the first sip that the martini had been a little too real for her. But a grasshopper?

"A grasshopper," Cameron repeated through clenched teeth. I knew he would never throw a drink in someone's face, but he looked like he wanted to.

Derek strolled over to the bar. "I can handle this one if you've got crème de menthe and crème de cacao."

"I have those," Cameron said, his relief visible. "What else do you need?"

"Cream. And ice."

"I'll get cream from the kitchen," Gwyneth said quickly, and walked out of the room.

"And I'll get the ice," Sophie said, opening the back cabinet refrigerator and pulling out a bucket filled with ice.

When all the ingredients were poured into a shaker, Derek added the ice and then shook it briskly. He used a strainer to pour the liquid into a fancy martini glass and handed it to Bitsy.

"Ooh, it's so pretty," Fluff said. "Can I have a taste?"

"No." And Bitsy began to sip the silly concoction. "Mm, delish."

Fluff gave her a dirty look and then batted her eyes at Derek. "May I have the same, please?"

Derek repeated the recipe and delivered the cocktail to Fluff. Then he walked away from the bar and signaled Gwyneth, who followed him out of the room.

I watched them leave and wondered if they had a plan to get rid of the three Kerr women. I hoped so.

I was sitting on the couch sipping my red wine when Claire and Cameron sat down on either side of me. They looked upset.

"What's wrong?" I asked.

"We wanted to thank you for rescuing the Robert Burns book from that ham-handed dingbat," Claire whispered.

I grinned. "You're quite welcome. And she is. I don't know how you can put up with any of this."

"We'll be fine," Claire said.

"That's right," Cameron agreed, taking her hand. "I still love you and you love me. We're still alive, and things will get better. And we'll be married. Nothing will change that."

"I love you, too, but . . ." She bared her teeth. "That woman. Trying to grab that book. Who behaves that way?"

"She's a barbarian," I said more forcefully than I intended. "She should never be allowed to get near a book again."

Claire managed to suppress a laugh. "Thank you, Brooklyn."

"What did I say?"

Cameron grinned. "You brought it back to the book."

"Oh." I winced. "Right. I tend to do that." I took another sip of wine. "I know she was out to hurt you both, but she didn't succeed. She didn't even damage the book." I smiled. "So I call that a win-win-win."

Cameron excused himself to go check on Mrs. B and the kitchen staff. He was gone for almost twenty minutes, and when he returned he explained quietly, "I found Mrs. B fixing a special platter for the police, who are still working in the tower. I took it to them myself and let them know they're welcome to take a break in the pink parlor."

"She literally thinks of everything," Claire said.

"After they have a bite to eat," Cameron continued, "they'll have another hour or so of evidence collection. Then they'll head out. Luckily they've already transported the body back to their headquarters in Inverness."

"Wow, this has been intense," Dad said.

"It certainly has been." Cameron glanced around, noticed that the Kerr women were sitting at the opposite corner of the room whispering intently. Cameron shook his head and lowered his voice. "And here's this group of unhappy women who think the world owes them something special. It's quite a contrast."

"I suppose we'll all be dining together tomorrow night," Sophie said.

"We can do this," Claire said. "We're all young and strong and smart."

"That's right," Dad said, then added, "some of us are younger than others, of course."

"I'm not sure how," I said. "But we'll get through it for you and Cameron." As I stood and poured myself another half glass of wine, I had a brilliant idea. "Why don't we shoot bows and arrows tomorrow? I've seen your archery setup, and I know you, Claire, so you must be an excellent archer."

"My Bitsy was a champion archer at Atherton Academy," Matilda crowed. "She puts the best archers in the village to shame. The local judges wanted her to try out for the Olympics, but it didn't work out."

I wanted to roll my eyes, but instead I went for perky. "That's fabulous. Bitsy, you and Claire should have a competition! Won't that be fun?"

"Fine," Bitsy said. "I'll play."

"Wonderful!" Claire said. "I doubt I could come up to Bitsy's archery standards, but I'm not too bad for an amateur. Shall we say, ten o'clock tomorrow morning? The winter light is best at that time of day."

"Anytime is good for Bitsy," Matilda insisted. "She knows how to rise to any occasion."

I happened to get a look at Fluff and saw her eyes narrowed and her lips pressed together in a serious scowl. Maybe she was simply tired of her mother constantly bragging about her big sister. I couldn't blame her for that.

My mother looked at me as if I'd just lost the rest of my brain, but then she joined in. "Sounds like fun! Brooklyn, didn't you play bows and arrows in school?"

"Bows and arrows?" Bitsy's words were saturated in pure contempt. "It's known as archery."

"Archery smarchery," Mom muttered, but pasted on a brilliant smile. "Can't wait!"

"Won't this be fun?" Matilda said. "We can all watch." Then she turned to our host. "Cameron, do you play?"

"I do." He glanced at Derek. "What about you, Derek? Are you up for a match?"

Derek gave me a sideways glance. "I haven't shot an arrow in years, but I'm willing to give it a go."

"We'll have a betting pool," Matilda decided. "I'll be taking bets. I should warn you, though. Bitsy is known to win against all comers. Did I mention she was her class champion four years in a row?"

"So was I, Mother," Fluff muttered, but Matilda ignored her. Fluff flashed her mother and sister a dirty look and flounced off to the ladies room. *It isn't always easy being the younger daughter*, I thought.

Once Fluff returned, the three Kerr women announced that they were retiring for the night. "We'll see you bright and early at the archery field," Matilda said. It sounded like a threat coming from her, but we all smiled and wished them a good night's sleep.

And like magic, Mrs. B showed up at the door to usher the women off to the green parlor for the evening.

As soon as the door was closed, Cameron walked straight to Claire and wrapped his arms around her. "Everything good?"

She gave him a tentative smile. "Couldn't be better."

His laugh was rueful. "It seems we're having an archery competition tomorrow."

"I suppose it's better than sitting around and staring at them while they think venomous thoughts about us."

"Watching you kick her butt at archery will be fun," Mom said.

"But didn't you hear?" I said. "Bitsy was the class champion at Atherton Academy."

"My money's on you, Claire," Derek said.

She gave a swift curtsy. "Thank you, kind sir."

"So is mine," I said. "I've seen you wield knives and swords and . . . what do you call that thing? That Lochaber axe of yours? Right. I'm sure your skills extend to archery as well."

"They do," Cameron said. "Believe me. And her Lochaber axe is hanging on the wall of the great hall whenever you'd like a demonstration."

"That would be fun," I said. "Maybe after you've said your wedding vows."

He laughed out loud and it was good to hear it. After a few more minutes of chatting and laughing, we all said good night.

Once we were in bed, Derek said, "Those women are quite awful."

He rarely criticized people like that, so I stared at him. "I agree, of course, but I didn't expect to hear you say it."

"I'm concerned for Claire tomorrow," he said.

"I think she'll be fine. I expect her to win, but it doesn't matter. Either way, Bitsy will pitch some kind of fit."

"Unfortunately, I think you're right."

We changed the subject, thankfully. Derek talked about their cruise on the loch and the ruins of Castle Urquhart on the opposite shore. The ruins were fascinating, he said, because they clearly showed how the people had lived there back in the thirteenth century.

I told him what happened at the tearoom that afternoon, and he was righteously aggravated. "We really have to back Cameron in this fight to stop this women's group from trying to destroy Claire."

"Oh, we'll stop them all right," I insisted. "They won't know what hit 'em."

"We'll work out our strategy tomorrow," he whispered. "Now go to sleep, love."

But I was already there.

I had no idea what time it was when the chains began clanking. Derek leaped out of bed, swung the door open, and went running down the hall.

"What?" I had to rub my eyes to focus and take a few deep breaths to wake myself up. I grabbed my puffer vest and ran after him, spotting him at the end of the hall. I slipped my vest on and joined him. "Did you see anything?" I asked.

"Nothing," he said, practically snarling. "Let's go back to bed."

I knew it would take a long time before we'd be able to sleep after being awakened so suddenly.

The next morning we woke early and dressed warmly for the archery tournament. Despite our rude awakening in the middle of the night, we both got a few good hours of sleep.

"Should we set a trap?" I asked as we walked downstairs.

"I'm thinking about it," he said. "Once Claire's archery competition is finished, we'll talk to the others and get some ideas."

"I'm not sure anyone else heard that racket," I said. "And it wasn't bats."

Derek grinned. "No, I don't think bats drag chains around."

We met Cameron and Claire in the breakfast room, and Claire poured each of us a cup of coffee.

A minute later, Mrs. B scurried in with her usual platter of fabulous breakfast goodies. "Good morning," she said cheerfully.

"Good morning, Mrs. B," Derek said.

"Everything looks scrumptious, as always," I said.

"Thank you, dear. Enjoy." And she bustled out of the room.

Derek immediately fixed me a plate, then served himself. Cameron did the same for Claire.

"Okay, what's going on?" I asked, when everyone had food in front of them. "Why do you look so unhappy?"

"The police just called me," Cameron said.

"Did they have news about Willy?"

"No," he muttered. "They called to tell me they found no fingerprints on the glass display case."

"Oh, crumbs," I said.

"I probably shouldn't have said anything more to them," Cameron said, "but I went ahead and mentioned that someone saw Angus fighting with Willy at the bonfire."

"Oh dear. What did he say to that?"

"He reasoned that folks tend to get a little wound up during Hogmanay and will occasionally misbehave. They might drink to excess or make a little too much noise. And with everyone else behaving foolishly, they can get caught up in the silliness. It doesn't mean that they're bad people."

"That's probably a good thing," Claire whispered. "I would hate to see Angus dragged off to jail."

"You're right." And hearing her whisper reminded me that Angus was Mrs. B's nephew. She would be heartbroken if he was accused of murder.

I plucked a cinnamon roll from the platter and began to unwind it. And for some reason, I had a sudden memory of Mom and Olivia in the library surrounded by candles. And then later, watching Willy swagger in to flirt with Olivia? It made me want to cry. But instead, I had an idea. "We should search the library for books."

"Why do you say that?" Derek said. "I mean to say, that's a fine idea, but why did you come up with it just now?"

"Too many word associations to mention, but I was just thinking of that stack of finance books that Olivia had on the counter. Maybe there are others in there. It couldn't hurt to look."

"We'll do it right after breakfast, before the archery tournament," he said.

"Okay, great." I turned to Claire. "I can help you set up the archery range if you need help."

"I'd be very grateful if you could help," she said. "Cameron has a conference call with the MacKinnons in a few minutes."

"That's intriguing," I said, tearing off another piece of the roll and munching it.

"Aye," he said. "We're discussing our annual gathering, and for the first time, we'll be holding it here."

"How exciting for you."

"It'll definitely be a first," Claire said with a strangled laugh. "Can't wait."

"Maybe you could have an archery competition," I said.

Claire pointedly ignored that idea. "More coffee?"

Cameron and Derek were both laughing as she poured another cup for each of us.

"Are you ready for some archery?" Cameron asked us.

"Oh yeah." I pulled off another piece of the cinnamon roll, stuck it in my mouth, and savored the amazing flavors. "Actually, I'm really excited to watch. And maybe we'll all be friends by the end of the competition."

Claire's eyebrows shot up. "You're kidding, right?"

"Yes, I'm kidding. The thought of mingling with those over-bearing she-devils makes my skin crawl. But I'm trying to change my attitude."

Claire smiled. "I can see you're trying really hard."

"I can't promise anything," I said, enjoying the last of the cinnamon roll and reaching for the bacon. "I'm just hoping I don't go nuclear."

*A*t nine o'clock Claire and I walked over to the archery range to make sure everything was in order. We wiped the morning dew off the tables and chairs where the scorers would sit, and we set up some folding chairs since we'd probably have an audience. We moved the bull's-eye easels to the regulation distance of fifty meters. Claire pulled out her tape measure just to make sure and recorded the distance on her notepad.

"I know whatever measurement I set it at, Bitsy will object. But that's too bad."

"What distance do you set it at?" I asked.

"For future reference, the official MacKinnon Castle regulation distance is fifty meters."

"That sounds pretty far. How far do the professionals shoot?"

"They can go up to seventy meters and more."

"Wow. But they've got those high-powered crossbows and things."

"Aye. Their equipment is quite sophisticated."

From her satchel, she pulled out notepads and pens for recording the scores and set them on the tables.

"Each team will have a scorekeeper. They'll sit at these tables."

"Do you have extra equipment I can borrow?"

"You mean, you didn't travel with your archery gear?"

I smiled. "For some reason, I forgot everything. Sorry."

She grinned. "We have plenty. I'll get it all out so you'll be ready if anyone else wants to play."

She walked into the garage and opened a cabinet. "I use a twenty-five-pound recurve bow. You're taller than me, but you haven't done this in a while, so we'll set you up with a fifteen-pounder. I'll string it for you. You'll need an arm guard and a finger tab, a quiver, arrows, and a bow stand. Anything else?"

"Maybe a little green Robin Hood outfit with the hat and all?"

She laughed. "The competition might protest. You'd be a distraction for the other players."

I laughed. "In that case, I think you've got it covered. Thanks."

She packed everything into a handy equipment bag made for that purpose. Hers was already packed and ready to go.

Once we had our gear, we walked out of the garage and over to the deserted range.

"Does anyone ever walk back here?" I asked.

"Nobody walks around back here, but we still can't take the chance, so when we're shooting, we turn on the warning lights. They're along the garage wall, and a few are along the parking area."

"Oh, that's smart."

"I'd like to go inside and get a cup of coffee and see if Cameron's finished with his phone call."

"I'll go with you and check on Derek."

Inside the front door, we both checked our phones for the time and agreed to meet back at the range by nine forty-five.

"I'm sure Bitsy will be out there by then, but that'll still give me enough time to take a few practice shots, just to get my muscles working."

"Sounds good," I said. "See you then."

*A*t nine thirty, Derek and I walked out to the archery range. He wanted to arrive a few minutes early to make sure there were no nasty surprises waiting for us. We held hands as we crossed the parking area on our way to the garage. And as he often did when we were out walking, he looked around in every direction. Because you just never knew.

"Claire and I were just out here a little while ago setting everything up, so I doubt we'll find anything amiss."

We heard loud female voices as we reached the garage. "Sounds like Bitsy and her people are already here."

I turned and saw Claire and Cameron coming out through the front door. "There's the Laird and his Lady," I said in as good a Scottish accent as I could manage.

Derek smiled, then we turned and waited for them to catch up.

Claire was rubbing her arms. "It's still cold."

"We're sort of getting used to it," I said. "That's a lie, of course. I'm freezing my bahoochie out here."

Claire and Cameron both laughed, then Cameron asked, "Who have you been talking to?"

"Tamara. She's a delight. She taught me a few new words."

"I can guess what your bahoochie is," Derek said suggestively, making me laugh.

"It's a good word to have," Claire said. "I use it regularly."

We were still laughing when we got to the garage and began to walk over the grass to the tables and chairs Claire and I had set up earlier. The Kerr ladies were gathered around one of the tables, and Bitsy's equipment was scattered all around in no particular order. She did not appear to be the most meticulous archer in the land.

Even Fluff seemed to disapprove of the less-than-professional way in which her sister presented herself.

"It's about time," Matilda said, checking her wristwatch.

"We still have time," Claire said easily. "I'm going to take a few practice shots. You're free to do the same, Bitsy."

"I'm ready," she said, tossing her ponytail back and forth.

Claire checked her watch. "We'll start in ten minutes." She unzipped her bow and strung it quickly, then strapped on her bracer—or armguard—to protect her inner forearm against whiplash from the bowstring. Finally she slipped on her finger tab, which would protect her finger from being cut by the bowstring. She stood with her bow in hand and pulled the string back a few times. Then she set her quiver nearby and pulled out an arrow. Holding it by the fletching—or feathers—she slid the nocking—or the slotted end tip—onto the string and lifted the arrow until it pointed right at the bull's-eye. She expertly pulled the string back to her chin, then let it go.

And I let go of the breath I was holding.

The arrow hit the center ring.

I'd schooled myself to rein in my enthusiasm, but I couldn't help it. "Yay!" I said.

"Nice shot," Derek said.

Claire smiled. "Thanks."

Matilda gave us a withering glance. "It was just practice, for God's sake."

Her two girls didn't say a word, but they didn't look happy. But since Bitsy was the school champion, I was sure she'd be just as good once she was standing on the line.

"Wait for us!"

I turned and saw Mom and Dad and Gwyneth walking quickly toward the chalk line.

"Don't worry, you have three minutes," I said, and jogged over to meet them. I whispered, "You should've seen Claire's practice shot. Total bull's-eye."

"All right, Claire," Mom said.

"How's the competition?" Gwyneth asked.

"I haven't seen Bitsy take a shot yet, but so far, they're their usual snooty selves."

"Should be fun for everyone," Dad said.

We moved a few chairs over to sit behind Claire, and when we were settled, Claire said to Bitsy, "Are you ready to start?"

"I hope they're not going to make all sorts of noises to distract me."

"Of course not," Claire said. "That wouldn't be sporting."

"They're so insulting," Gwyneth whispered.

"Without even trying," Mom said.

"Bitsy, we always shoot six arrows each, so I hope that's agreeable to you. I'd also like to point out that the distance from the chalk line to the bull's-eye is fifty meters. If you'd like to measure it before you start, you're welcome to do so."

"It's fine," she said, tossing her ponytail.

I wasn't sure why everything she said sounded so condescending, but there it was. She was not a happy girl.

"Since you're the visitor," Claire said, "you're free to go first. Or we can toss a coin if you'd rather."

"I'll go first."

"Okay. Good luck." Claire stepped back behind the chalk line and sat down between Cameron and me.

Bitsy stepped up to the chalk line, nocked her arrow, then aimed and shot.

I couldn't tell exactly where it hit, but it wasn't a bull's-eye.

She pulled another arrow out and went through the same routine. She did that until she had shot all six of her arrows.

With each shot, her sister Fluff grew more and more angry. By the end of her run, Fluff was red-faced and steaming mad. Had she bet money on the match? Her sister had obviously let her down, but her reaction felt way off base.

"Are you going to shoot now, or should I retrieve my arrows first?" Bitsy demanded to know.

Claire smiled pleasantly. "I'm going to shoot now, using the second target. Then when I'm finished with my six arrows, we both approach the targets along with our scorekeepers. Then we walk back to the chalk line, and you take your second round."

"How many rounds?" Bitsy asked.

"We usually go five rounds, but we're happy to do whatever you want."

"Well, aren't you just a happy clappy bunch."

Claire gazed at her, not smiling. "Aren't we just."

Bitsy rolled her eyes but still didn't answer.

"So, I'll ask you again. How many rounds would you like to play, Bitsy?" Claire asked, and I wondered why Bitsy didn't spontaneously combust from the fire shooting out of Claire's eyes.

"Five, I guess."

Claire simply nodded and picked up her bow. Bitsy sauntered back to sit with her mom and sis. None of them looked happy, but their bunch wasn't the happy clappy type.

After Claire's first six arrows landed in the center ring, it was clear that Bitsy was outclassed and doomed to fail this little competition.

Forty-five grueling minutes later, Bitsy and her crew walked off the range without a handshake or a "thanks for the game" or anything.

I watched them walk away and noticed when Fluff stuck her foot out and caused Bitsy to trip.

"Hey!" Bitsy cried out.

"Oops," the younger girl muttered.

Matilda flashed Fluff a look of warning so threatening that my brothers and sisters would've been silenced indefinitely.

Once they were farther away, I asked, "When the other team leaves without a word, does that mean you won?"

"Let me demonstrate how you know you've won," Mom said and began to shout, "Woo-hoo! Yay! Hoorah!" Then she jumped and cheered and laughed and whooped loud enough for the defeated team to hear.

We all laughed with her and I gave her a hug. "That's a good one, Mom."

"They really are terrible sports, aren't they?" Derek said.

"I'll say," Mom said.

"I loved watching you, Claire," Cameron said, "because you clearly love the sport. But they were so sour. It made it difficult to enjoy playing with them."

Claire shrugged. "I will say, I quite enjoyed watching Bitsy when she was aiming the arrow and letting it fly. She's not bad. But she doesn't have any fun at all."

"It's kind of sad," I said.

"I blame her mother," Mom said.

"Oh, her mother is definitely to blame," Gwyneth agreed. "Horrible old sourpuss. Always was."

Mom helped pack up Claire's equipment. "The problem is, they're still staying in your home."

"It might be bearable," I said. "After all, they don't come out and mingle much."

Gwyneth gave Claire a warm hug. "You were fabulous, Claire."

"Thanks, Auntie."

"Well, I've worked up a thirst," Dad said. "Can I buy anyone a victory beverage?"

*D*erek and I decided not to join in the après-archery festivities. We needed to hunt down more books.

"Let's start in the library," I said.

"Sounds good, darling," Derek said. "Gwyneth would like to help us."

"Oh, that's great," I said. "The more, the merrier."

She showed up a minute later. "What's the plan? How can I help?"

"Mom was in here a couple of days ago, and we saw a stack of books that Olivia claimed were books on finance. I'm looking for that stack and also looking for any Christmas books that might've been misplaced."

"Got it," Gwyneth said. "Finance and Christmas. So I should look behind the books on the shelves and under the counters and other places that might be hiding a book?"

"Exactly," I said, feeling relieved that I didn't have to explain too much. "You get it."

She laughed. "I used to get paid to find things. I was awfully good at it."

"You still are," Derek said.

"And so are you," she said with a wink.

I smiled at them both. "You two must've been so much fun to work with."

"We still are, kiddo," Gwyneth said. "So let's get to work."

"All right. How about if we each take a wall?"

"Seems as good a plan as any," Gwyneth said. "But what I really want to do is ride that ladder."

I laughed. "That will be our reward."

Gwyneth glanced at Derek. "She's a strict one."

"Yes, so behave yourself."

She saluted smartly. "I'm going to start on this row of shelves right here." She walked over to the first row of shelves on the right-side wall.

"All right," I said. "I'll start on the left side. Derek, do you mind starting on the back wall?"

He smiled at me. "Whatever you say, darling."

"Thank you."

We worked quietly for ten minutes, then Gwyneth said, "I think I've found something."

"Really?" I said, and walked quickly over to her side. "What is it?"

She had her arm bent at an awkward angle as she reached behind a row of books. She slowly lifted her arm and came up with a book.

"What is it?" I asked.

She stared at the cover. "*A Christmas Carol*." She turned it over. "It's rather posh, isn't it?"

"I'll say it's posh," I said, taking the book and giving it a quick examination. The book was covered in red leather with an inlaid painting of an old-fashioned Christmas tree. It was luminous. "It's supposed to be worth twenty-five thousand pounds."

"It's very handsome," Derek declared. "I can see why it's worth so much money."

"Well, I'm very proud of myself," Gwyneth said. "Not bad for an old-timer."

"You'll never be old," Derek said.

"He's right," I said. "You're perfect."

"I like her," she said to Derek.

"And so do I," he replied.

"I like you guys, too." But I couldn't resist turning to the title page to learn about the book. From first glance, it was in extraordinary condition. I guessed that it was a first edition, dated 1843. I would look it up later online. On a cursory look-through, I saw a number of charming color illustrations. "I'm getting chills just holding this."

"I'm guessing we found the big daddy of them all, didn't we?" Gwyneth said.

"Yes!" I laughed. "This is the big daddy. Thank you so much for finding it. I hope you didn't hurt your arm too badly."

"I'll never play cricket again, but it was worth it."

"That's terrible!" I laughed again and grabbed her in a major bear hug. "Thanks."

"You're a good girl," she murmured, and patted my back.

"Shall we keep going, or are you ready to quit while you're ahead?"

"Let's keep going," Gwyneth said.

"Absolutely," Derek agreed. "I'm determined to find another one."

I didn't say anything to that, but the fact was that Derek and I were still living with that image of Willy sprawled in that closet. I sighed inwardly and went back to work doing the same thing as before, checking behind books and feeling underneath the counters. On a whim, I checked Olivia's desk and found the drawers locked. I wasn't surprised, but it still made me suspicious. Of course, I'd been suspicious of her right from the start. She had a vertical file on her desktop with notebooks and folders, and I imagined they were full of library and book ordering information, but I thumbed through them anyway, just in case.

And that's where I found it.

It was a thin book, barely half an inch thick, which made sense since it was just a short story, but a classic, nonetheless. The book was about eight inches tall and five inches wide. It was threadbare with a faded cover and half the spine in tatters.

I pulled out the folder that I'd found the book in and skimmed through the contents. There wasn't much: just a few pieces of paper with scribbled notes and numbers.

"I'm sorry it's in such terrible condition."

"What, love?" Derek called from across the room.

"Sorry, I didn't realize I was talking out loud. Anyway, I found another book. I think you'll both be interested to see it."

While they hurried to see what I'd found, I gingerly opened the book. A bookmark fell out of it and I set it on the desk.

"What have we here?" Gwyneth said, staring at the pitiful old book.

"It's *The Gift of the Magi*," I said.

"That's right." She shook her head. "Can you believe what bad shape it's in?"

"You never know," Derek said. "One man's treasure, et cetera."

"I suppose." Gwyneth carefully picked up the book. "As you can see, it's falling apart."

"I know."

"I thought it would be a fun book for Claire to read," Gwyneth said. "But I never would've expected anyone, especially Matilda, to consider it a great treasure."

I took it and examined the back cover, which was ready to fall off the hinge. I carefully turned a page or two. "Hey, look. It's even got writing on it."

At my words, Derek and Gwyneth stared at each other. "No way," she said.

"Come on, now," Derek protested. "It's impossible."

I laughed. "You guys, chill out. It's not the same as the *Rebecca*. Look, it's a couple of letters and a row of numbers. Hardly a secret code."

"And what's this?" Gwyneth asked, holding up the bookmark.

I shrugged. "It was stuck inside the book."

"Don, look at this."

Derek glanced at me, and we both realized Gwyneth had used his fake spy name. "Let me see," he said.

She handed him the bookmark, and I looked at it, too. There was one word written on it in blue ballpoint pen: *Octillion*.

"May I see the book again?" he asked.

I handed it to him, and he turned to the last page and studied the row of two letters and numbers. "Twenty-eight digits total," he murmured.

"An octillion," Gwyneth said.

"Is that what it is?" I said.

"That's according to the US definition," Derek said. "May I see that paper with the scribblings?"

"Of course." I handed him the lined paper. "You guys are freaking me out a little."

Gwyneth patted my shoulder. "Oh, we're fairly freaked out ourselves, sweet girl."

"Darling, do you have your phone with you?"

"Of course."

"Look up the IBAN code for Mauritius."

"Mauritius? The country?"

"Yes, the tiny island country in the middle of the Indian Ocean."

"Okay. And I'm just checking the spelling of the other thing. Is it I-B-A-N?"

"That's right, love."

"What does it mean?" I asked as I googled it.

"It stands for International Bank Account Number."

"Ah, good to know." My search came right up and I read it aloud. "The Mauritius country code is M-U."

He sucked in a breath and let it out slowly. "Thank you, darling." Then he stared at Gwyneth. "Looks like our little librarian had just about figured it out."

We sat in the blue parlor and continued working out this puzzle. "So, the younger Kerr girl gave the book to the vicar for the church's charity auction," Gwyneth explained. "Then I ended up buying the book because Claire had enjoyed the story when she was a girl."

"Right, and then Claire took it and put in the castle library," I said, "which probably made all sorts of sense at the time."

"Until it was stolen," Gwyneth said. "Or so we thought."

Derek frowned. "Turns out, Olivia the librarian had it hidden away the whole time while she tried to figure out what it all meant."

I smiled at them. "That's what librarians do."

"Yes, indeed they do."

For a change, I was drinking hot tea with milk, which sometimes tasted wonderful, but only when I was in England or Scotland. Same with Scotch. I rarely drank the stuff at home. Go figure. "So, what's on that page of scribblings?" I asked.

Derek pulled the sheet out of his own folder that he'd asked Mrs. B for after we left the library. "Among several nonsensical items, there are a list of mail carriers with numbers behind them, such as Royal Mail-X, DHL-X."

"What does the X stand for?" I asked.

"It stands for the number of characters in each carrier's tracking number."

"So, if you have the octillion number and the mail carrier number and the country code, you can theoretically call up a bank in Mauritius and give them all that info, and they'll send you whatever you have in your private bank account?"

"Something like that," Derek said. "Very good, darling."

"Here's something else I know," I said, feeling a bit smug. "The Kerr family traveled to Mauritius for Bitsy's summer vacation."

"How do you know that?" Derek asked.

"Claire told me. You should ask her all about it."

When Cameron and Claire joined us, our little group expanded by two.

"What are we doing?" Claire asked.

"Did I wake you?" Gwyneth asked.

"It's all right, Auntie. I was taking a little victory nap after the archery tournament."

"You deserved it, and I apologize for waking you. But it's rather important, I'm afraid."

She hunkered down next to her aunt. "What is it?"

"Can you tell us about Bitsy and her family taking trips abroad during their summer breaks?"

When she glanced at me, I said, "I told them about Mauritius."

"Ah. Yes, they traveled quite a lot during summer breaks to all sorts of exotic locales while the girls were growing up. All over Europe, of course, but they also made a big point of bragging to the rest of us about places like Mauritius and Madagascar and Zimbabwe and Uganda to see the great apes. Hong Kong one year. And another time they even went to Kuwait."

"Kuwait," Gwyneth murmured, and gave Derek a quick look.

"Is that significant?" I asked.

"It's just another country with a particular banking code," Derek explained. "I think we have it right with Mauritius, though, given the two-letter country code written on the bookmark."

Claire stared at all of us. "You all seem to know what you're saying, but to me, you've suddenly begun speaking in formal gobble-dygook."

I laughed. "That's what it sounds like, but I think I'm beginning to get the hang of it."

Derek sat back in his chair. "So, tell us about the late Mr. Kerr."

Gwyneth began. "He was an important man in the village. A banker. He was personally in charge of the bank accounts of a lot of people and many of the bigger businesses around town."

"So, why do you think he had an IBAN?"

"Maybe he didn't trust his own bank," Claire said. "Although, you have your money in that bank, don't you, Aunt Gwyneth?"

"It's the only game in town, frankly. But working in London and traveling extensively, I've become quite a bit more diversified than that one little bank."

"Very good," Derek said. "What about you, Cameron?"

"My money's scattered all over the highlands, which is to say that I'm also diversified."

"Now I'm going to ask for the truth," Derek said. "Is it because you didn't trust Mr. Kerr? Or his bank? Or did you simply want to put your money in other pots, shall we say?"

"I have other pots, including cattle and farming. But frankly I haven't trusted him since his wife established that ridiculous women's group. He was quite a force behind the group."

"Matilda and her two sisters started it," Gwyneth said. "But he was involved from the start. I'm not sure why."

"Is one of Matilda's sisters Olivia's mother?" I asked.

"Yes."

"What a family," I muttered. "And now Matilda happens to have a book in which her husband wrote IBAN numbers with the country code of Mauritius." I shook my head in disgust.

"And she's simply dying to get ahold of that book."

Derek sipped his drink. "Meanwhile, that librarian of yours has broken the code and might even be getting the money wired to her account at this very minute."

"Let's hope that's not true," Cameron said.

"It's not," Derek admitted. "But she's getting close."

I frowned. "If someone does get the money, would it all go to Matilda Kerr? Her husband is the one who wrote all this information down in the book."

"So, her husband had a secret bank account in Mauritius," Derek said. "He was also the president of the local bank here. Was he making enough money to open a foreign bank account?"

"That sounds like a job for one of those covert government agencies you two used to work for."

Derek gave Gwyneth a look. "I'll be making some calls this afternoon."

Gwyneth smiled. "I'll be joining you."

"That's going to be fun," I said.

"But what shall we do about Olivia?" Claire asked.

"The good news is, we have all her notes." I flashed her a wicked grin. "Right now she's probably chomping at the bit to get back into the library."

"I'm not sure if it's good news for her, though," Claire said. "Because she's never getting into our library again."

"That's my girl," Gwyneth said.

Claire stood. "I hope we'll talk about this some more, but right now I've got to get ready. I'm expecting at least eight to ten more people to arrive in one hour for dinner and a wake."

Chapter 11

When we walked downstairs with Mom and Dad an hour later, there was a tuxedoed waiter standing at the door to the dining room.

"Roy?" Derek said. "Is that you?"

"It's me, Commander," he said, looking abashed.

"What are you doing in a penguin suit?"

Roy Turnbull, Cameron's part-time security guy and driver, wore a very nice tuxedo and shrugged self-consciously. "Mrs. B asked if I would fill in for poor Angus. I couldn't say no."

"That's sweet of you, Roy," I said.

"Och. I was happy to do it. Especially with the extra folks staying over. And the boy is too shattered about Willy to do any real work."

"Poor Angus," I said. "It's just terrible."

Cameron walked up just then and shook Roy's hand. "Thank you for stepping in, Roy."

"It's my pleasure to help out."

Cameron and Claire were about to lead our mini-procession into the dining room when the doorbell rang.

I glanced up at Derek. "More police?"

"Perhaps."

One of the other attendants walked briskly to the front door and opened it to reveal a nice-looking man in his thirties standing next to the vicar.

"Vicar, welcome," Cameron said, trying for joviality. "We're about to sit down for supper. Won't you join us?"

He looked chagrined. "I dinnae mean to interrupt your meal."

"'Tisn't a problem," Cameron insisted. "Come in. And who is this?"

"Let me introduce you to Archie Brown." The vicar turned to Archie. "Archie, this is Laird MacKinnon."

"You look familiar," Cameron said, not bothering to correct the vicar for using his title. "I must've seen you around the village."

"Aye, I grew up here," he said. "But I'm just back from Edinburgh after two years working in a law firm. My parents are Stewart and Maggie Brown."

"Och." He scratched his forehead. "Of course I know Stewart and Maggie." He swept his arm to usher them inside. "So, you're young Archie."

"Aye, but not so young these days."

Cameron chuckled. "You're welcome to come in and have supper with us."

"Thank you, sir."

"Thank you, Cameron," the vicar said. "We're honored to join you on this solemn occasion."

Cameron led the way into the dining room, where Mrs. B and her troops were already setting places for the new visitors.

"Hello, Vicar," Mrs. B said. "It's nice to see you."

"And you, Mrs. B. Something smells wonderful."

"It's Tamara's special sirloin stew. And it is indeed quite wonderful."

"Might Tamara be joining us tonight?" Archie asked. "It's been a while since I've seen her."

Mrs. B frowned. "I'm not certain she'll have time to join you, but I'll pass along your regards."

"Please do."

Mrs. B indicated which chair the vicar should take. "Please have a seat, Vicar."

"Thank you, ma'am."

The seat happened to be right next to Fluff, who was already seated. As she watched the vicar approach, she seemed to bubble over with excitement to have the vicar seated next to her.

"And, Archie, won't you sit here?" said Mrs. B.

"Thank you kindly, Mrs. B."

Archie sat across from the vicar. A minute later, Bitsy walked into the dining room. Archie immediately stood.

"Archie!" Bitsy cried. "Is it really you? What are ye doing here?"

"I came along with the vicar," Archie said. "I had no idea you'd be here. You're looking quite lovely this evening."

"Thank you, Archie." She continued looking for her seat, taking it slow and easy so everyone could get a look at her.

"He's a flatterer," Matilda murmured for Bitsy's benefit, although everyone could hear. She gave the young man her version of the evil eye, which was pretty scary as far as I was concerned. Matilda was seated directly across from Archie and seemed determined to listen to every word he uttered.

Bitsy looked around for the right place to sit, and Archie indicated the only empty seat, right next to him. He pulled out the chair. "Please sit here."

Bitsy practically galloped to it and flopped down, then turned to Archie and actually batted her eyelashes at the young man. She was probably trying for demure, but there was too much calculation in her attitude to pull it off.

"How long have you been back?" she asked. "I haven't seen you at the pub."

"Bitsy, mind your manners," her mother hissed. When her daughter ignored her, she apparently decided that subtlety be damned, and jerked her head in Cameron's direction. "There are others at the table to whom you may wish to speak."

She obviously meant Cameron, and now it was becoming clear that Matilda and Fluff hadn't come to take Bitsy home from the castle. They hadn't come to celebrate Hogmanay. They were here to join the assault on Cameron until he surrendered to Bitsy.

It was so obvious and pathetic I wanted to laugh. Was it really so important that her daughter get her hooks into the Laird? What was I thinking? Of course it was!

The vicar looked down the table at Claire. "Do you know yet when you'll be able to be married?"

Claire glanced at Cameron, hesitant to speak in front of the assembled crowd. I couldn't blame her, given the attitude of some of the ladies of the village and the fact that at least one of the old battle-axes, Matilda Kerr, was seated at the table. But Claire forged ahead. "With the sad news of Willy's death, we're not certain how soon we'll have our ceremony. I know it's thrown everyone's schedule off, but I do hope you'll still be available to officiate?"

"But of course!" the vicar practically sputtered. To think that he would miss the nuptials of Laird MacKinnon and his Lady? Why, it was sure to be a highlight of his career.

Matilda scowled at the man, but he paid no attention.

"Vicar," Fluff said. She was probably trying to whisper, but that squeaky little-girl voice of hers could carry into the next county. "Did you think about what I asked you the other day?"

The man turned six shades of red and coughed.

He was saved from answering the question when Mrs. B led a procession of servers into the room. Each carried a large platter or a tureen, and they began to place the platters down the center of the table so that everyone could easily serve themselves.

"The tureens contain an excellent stew prepared by Chef Tamara. The platters hold potatoes and other vegetables as well as a lovely salad. Please enjoy."

"Thank you, Mrs. B," Cameron said. "And please pass along our special thanks to Chef Tamara. Everything looks wonderful."

She gave Cameron a brilliant smile, then left the room. The servers stayed on to help serve the guests. Once everyone had a bowlful of stew and a plateful of the assorted accoutrements, Cameron clinked his knife against his wineglass.

"I'd like to suggest a moment of silence in honor of our friend Willy Smith, who died yesterday."

Within a few seconds, everything quieted down and we all bowed our heads. After a minute, Cameron clinked his glass again. "Thank you. Later on, I would invite each of you to please give a brief reminiscence of Willy Smith. For now, though, please enjoy your meal."

There was more silence while everyone took their first bites.

"This is delicious," I said, and several others agreed wholeheartedly.

"The meat is so tender, it practically melts in my mouth," Mom said.

"And the veggies are cooked to perfection," Dad added.

The quiet conversation grew louder as we all began to talk with our friends and neighbors. Everyone tried to keep the tone down, except for Fluff, who only had one level of talking, and that was *loud*.

Bitsy, meanwhile, listened rapturously to Archie's soft tones. He was only speaking to her, and I wondered what that was all about. Had they been a couple? Were they still? Did Mama approve?

"Everything is delicious," I said to Claire.

"I know. Tamara is such a godsend."

I noticed Matilda was staring at her older daughter, and her face was growing redder. Apparently she didn't approve. After another minute, she grew almost apoplectic as she continued to watch Archie and glare at Bitsy, who seemed to not be following her rules.

Perhaps Bitsy considered them not rules but mere guidelines.

Sophie winked at me from her side of the table, and I wondered what mischief she was up to.

"Archie," she said loudly.

Distracted by Bitsy's intense whispering, he had to look around to see who was calling him. Sophie waved to get his attention.

"Ah, Sophie." He grinned at her.

She smiled. "Isn't this stew heavenly?"

Now he looked a bit confused. "Aye, it is. Everything is delicious. I'm very thankful to our host and hostess for allowing me to join them this evening."

"You're welcome, Archie," Claire said.

He smiled at her but then turned back and gazed at Sophie with a look that could only be described as starry-eyed. I wondered if he had always had eyes for her. That wouldn't make Bitsy happy, but it made me smile.

"Everything is delicious and it's because of the new chef," Sophie said, directing her comment to Archie. "Tamara is the chef here at Castle MacKinnon."

"That's what I hear," he said. "She was always a good cook, but her talents have improved greatly, wouldn't you say?" He directed the question to Bitsy.

Bitsy choked on something, and Archie began to pound her back until she finally stopped coughing. He handed her a water glass and turned to look at Sophie.

I caught Dad's gaze and grinned. "This is fun, isn't it?"

"A barrel of laughs," he said, and raised his glass in a toast.

I would have to remember to ask Sophie what the deal was with Archie and everyone else. She seemed to be the official repository for everything that had ever happened in Oddlochen. After all, she was a bartender. They knew all and saw all.

Especially in a small town.

I glanced at my mother, who sat on the other side of Derek. "Are you having a good time, Mom?"

"Of course. Everyone is lovely, the food is exceptional, and the human dynamics around this table are fascinating, aren't they?"

"They are. Later tonight we'll have to sit down with Sophie and get everyone's origin story."

"Won't that be fun?" She sipped her wine. "We could do it right here and now, but I believe there would be carnage."

I laughed. "You're so right."

"A mother never gets tired of hearing those words."

I was still laughing, until Matilda made a noise that sounded like she'd coughed up a hairball. It could happen, given that cats did live here. But I looked around to see what might've upset her. And there was Archie, holding Bitsy's hand while he whispered something profound in her ear.

Mom was suddenly compelled to interfere, thank goodness. "So, Bitsy," she said, loud enough for everyone to hear. "How did you and Archie meet? Did you go to school together? What are your plans?"

Matilda was still coughing, but she managed to say, "I beg your pardon. That's none of your business."

"Oh, Matilda," Mom said, waving her hand at the woman. "I can understand why you're a protective mama with your two beautiful daughters. I'm the same way with my girls. But I just love meeting new people and making new friends. So I'd love to hear about you two." And with that, she gave Bitsy and Archie her complete attention.

Kate Carlisle

"Um, er," Archie said.

Bitsy jumped in. "Archie was the smartest student in school. He excelled at everything. None of us were surprised to hear he was accepted into law school. In London of all places."

Archie gazed at her somewhat adoringly. I couldn't tell if he was actually smitten by her or just happy that someone was familiar with his educational background.

"That's impressive," Claire said.

"Speaking of London," Matilda said. "Bitsy, didn't you and Cameron drive to London together a few years ago?"

"Yes, Mother."

It was Fluff's turn to cough and she held up her napkin. The way her shoulders were shaking, I knew she was laughing.

Cameron looked momentarily mystified, then said, "Oh, that's right. I actually drove Bitsy and three of her friends to London for one of those courses you were taking." He looked at Bitsy. "What was it? Cosmology?"

She looked appalled that he would ask, but I was genuinely impressed. "You studied astronomy?"

Bitsy looked flummoxed.

"It was cosmetology," Fluff corrected. "You know, hair, nails, skin care."

There was complete silence for a long moment, and Bitsy looked as though she were the one going nuclear.

"But that's wonderful," Mom said. "I wish one of my daughters could do my hair and nails. It's a very important aspect of hygiene and self-care, and a really fantastic way to help other women. Don't you think so, Bitsy?"

"Do you have a salon?" I asked.

"Yes," she said with a sniff. And she was back to her snooty self. "Bits and Bobs, on the high street."

"And she's a businesswoman!" Mom said to Matilda. "You must be so darned proud."

*B*y the time dessert was served, I was exhausted by all the tension flowing through the room. However, to borrow a phrase, I was so darned proud of my mother for turning that potential disaster with Matilda around. But exhausted or not, I was determined to keep the energy going so that Claire and Cameron wouldn't be forced to do it themselves.

I kept up my end of the conversation until it was time to leave the dining room. I whispered to Claire, "Is there a powder room nearby? If not, I'll just run upstairs for a minute. I just need to wash my hands."

"There's one down here. I'll show you." Instead of turning left to return to the blue parlor, she turned right and took me down another corridor that ran along the stairway leading up to the Laird's suite. A few yards farther and I saw the door marked LADIES.

"I didn't know this was here," I said. "Very convenient."

"Isn't it?"

I started to push the door open but stopped when I heard voices on the inside.

"What do you think you're doing?"

Recognizing Matilda's voice, Claire and I slowly backed away.

"Honestly, Mum, I'm trying to get close to him, but his stupid girlfriend is glued to his side. And that other girl, the one who whinges on about books? She won't shut up! And Cam is all, 'Oh, you're so clever and you make books.' Yuck. And then he's all about Claire, 'You're so beautiful, I can't wait to marry you.' Makes me sick."

"I'm not even talking about them," Matilda whispered loudly

enough for us to hear through the door. "I'm talking about you flirting with Archie Brown right in front of the Laird."

"I wasn't flirting. He's just a . . . a friend."

"I know you're lying because you're wrapping your hair around your finger."

"I'm not lying!"

"Mum's right," another voice chimed in. "You're lying. You always wrap your hair like that when you lie."

Claire and I frowned at each other. "Fluff," she whispered, and I nodded.

"You're going to ruin everything," Fluff said. "If you don't get your act together, I'll take over. I could win him quicker than you anyway. You're getting to be an old cow."

"Haud yer wheesht, young lady!"

That was Matilda, and I almost laughed because I remembered a waitress in Edinburgh telling the cook to do the same thing.

"Yeah, shut up, Fluff," Bitsy griped.

"Both of you, watch your mouths," Matilda said, then spoke so low that it was hard to hear. But I managed to catch most of it.

"I've one thing to say," she said. "And then I want to get out of here. Honestly, sneaking into the loo is so déclassé."

Claire rolled her eyes and I almost burst out laughing.

"All right, Mum," Bitsy said. "What is it?"

"I've done my best to make that woman persona non grata in Oddlochen," Matilda said slowly. "Nobody in town will take her business now, so it's working according to plan. I doubt she'll even make it to her so-called wedding."

"I did my part," Fluff insisted. "I almost killed the silly wench with my cupping glass."

"But ye missed," Bitsy said, her voice taunting.

"I won't miss next time," Fluff said, and I could swear it sounded like a threat aimed at her sister. "Next time I'll hit the mark, and we won't have to deal with her anymore."

"Your sister has the right of it," Matilda said. "You missed, and besides, I never said anything about getting violent. We have other ways. So, Bitsy, now it's your turn. And it's time to raise the stakes."

"How am I supposed to do that?" Bitsy whined.

"By remembering your duty to your family and to your father."

The two girls sighed dramatically and in unison replied, "Yes, Mum."

Matilda continued in that same harsh tone. "You, Bitsy, were born to marry the Laird. Daddy raised you to be the Lady of Castle MacKinnon. Don't. Blow. It."

"I won't, Mum. I was just chatting with Archie because I haven't seen him in a while. I'm totally determined to follow our plan, and I will get him, I will."

"Get him?" I whispered. I assumed she meant the Laird.

"How did Archie even know to show up?" Matilda asked. "Was he invited here to screw things up for us?"

"Don't be so paranoid, Mum. He came with the vicar."

"Who was invited by me," Fluff said. "But I didn't know anything about Archie coming along."

Claire's eyes went wide, then she shook her head in disgust. She pointed toward the foyer.

Yes, it was time to get out of here.

We tiptoed past the loo, then raced to the blue parlor, where Claire shut the door. "I'm going to be sick to my stomach."

"I don't blame you. Eavesdropping outside of the loo is so déclassé."

She giggled. "They're just so awful."

"They're also vicious and conniving. You've got to convince Cameron to get them out of the house."

She sighed. "He's allowing them to stay because he's a good man who follows the old traditions. But this is beyond ridiculous."

"Do you want me to talk to him?" I asked.

The door opened and Cameron, Sophie, Derek, Dad, and Mom walked in.

"Well, that was entertaining," Dad said, and headed for the bar.

"I've come up with a few activities for tomorrow," Cameron said.

"Good," Mom said. "We don't want to have to sit and stare at them all day while they plot your demise."

"You have no idea," I said.

Cameron gave me an odd look. "What do you mean?"

"I mean, we just overheard the three Kerr women in the ladies room plotting to snag you. And by 'snag,' I mean get rid of Claire and get you and Bitsy married."

"Ridiculous," Cameron said angrily.

I turned to Derek. "By the way, Fluff's the one who threw that glass cup at Claire and nearly hit her in the face."

"You heard her admit it?" Derek asked.

"Right out loud," I said, then rubbed my arms from the chills gathering there. "She's creepy."

"I would have to agree," Claire said, folding her arms tightly across her chest.

I watched as Derek stood and walked out of the room.

"This is getting old," Cameron said. "They don't have the power they think they have, but I'm sick of them hurting Claire. I'll tell them to leave tomorrow."

"But—"

"No, Claire, this is emotional blackmail."

"He's right about that," Sophie said.

Cameron nodded at Sophie. "We've had to put up with their

bullying and lying just to appease some of the old cranks who think they can keep our future children from attending a wonderful school? It's ridiculous!"

Claire threw her hands up in frustration. "What can we do?"

Cameron shrugged. "I'll threaten to pull their leases. Half of those club women have husbands that are interested in leasing our land to grow crops and raise cattle. This is business. And that's how we'll handle it."

She stood and moved to him. He grabbed her and kissed her.

"Thank you," she said.

"And not a moment too soon," I said.

"Tell us more about the conversation in the ladies room," Sophie insisted.

"According to Matilda," I said, "it seems that every woman in town is on board with trying to get rid of Claire."

"I'm not," Sophie said. "And neither is Tamara or Mrs. B, along with every other level-headed woman I know."

"But if the conversation we just heard is anything to go by," I said, "they really do intend to have Bitsy snag you."

He laughed cynically. "Bitsy was flirting with Archie at dinner."

"Yes," I said, "and her mother was livid. She was yelling at her in the ladies room. We overheard them."

"Those two girls seem so young," Claire said.

"They're probably not much younger than you," I said. "But they're so immature."

"That they are," Cameron agreed.

"Tell us more," Mom said.

I gave them a brief rundown of what the women said.

"Bitsy is a real puzzle," Mom said. "She doesn't seem attracted to Cameron at all. She was much friendlier to Archie than to Cameron or any of us."

"You'd think she would suck up to us," Dad said, "since we're Cameron's friends. Right?"

"Yes." Cameron nodded thoughtfully. "She's not at all friendly to any of you. Or to me, for that matter," he added with a half laugh. "She's actually quite rude."

"Bitsy might be rude," I said, "but Fluff is downright scary."

"What did she say?" Cameron asked.

"She threatened Bitsy, her own sister, that if she didn't get her act together, Fluff would take over, because she's younger and prettier and smarter."

Cameron shook his head in disgust. "This is farcical. And it's dangerous. They'll leave tomorrow."

I said, "Matilda told Bitsy to remember her duty to her family and her father. Told her she was born to marry the Laird."

"That's right," Claire said. "We heard Matilda tell Bitsy, 'Your father raised you to be the Lady of Castle MacKinnon. So don't blow it.'"

"Her father?" Cameron's eyes narrowed at the words. "Mr. Kerr was always very friendly to me. Treated me like a . . ." His eyes widened.

"Like a what?" Dad said. "Like a son-in-law?"

"You're exactly right, Jim." Cameron pointed at Dad and swore. "He used to take me fishing, and we went hunting a few times, too. In fact, Mr. Kerr taught me how to shoot. My own father was too busy doing other things."

"Well," I said, sitting on the edge of the big blue chair, "Mr. Kerr apparently fed his girls a lot of nonsense about one of them marrying the Laird. And Matilda seems hell-bent to make his wishes a reality. With Bitsy."

"I really think Fluff might be more dangerous," Claire said.

"They're out of here tomorrow," Cameron said flatly. "And then I'll call a meeting of the town council. And set down the new rules."

"Hallelujah," Sophie said.

"And one more thing. Tomorrow night we're getting married."

"Double extra hallelujah!" Sophie cried.

"Yes!" Claire said, and jumped into Cameron's arms.

Everyone was quiet for a moment as we all felt a collective sigh of relief and happiness.

"Sophie, are you on board with this?" he asked.

"Got my phone tree lined up and ready to go," she said.

"Please let them know that there'll be plenty of food."

"Important note," Sophie said, typing it into her phone.

"That'll bring in the crowds," Dad said approvingly.

After a few seconds, I said, "I'm going to go find Derek and tell him the good news."

Dad was behind the bar, pouring himself an IPA. "He might be upstairs with Gwyneth."

"They've been putting their heads together a lot," Claire said. "I think they're up to something."

"Oh yeah, they are," I said, thinking of the IBAN situation. "I'm going to go find him, and then I'll be back."

"Okay, sweetie," Dad said. "We'll be here."

"I'll go with you," Mom said. "I'm going to run upstairs for a minute."

We walked past the great hall and into the foyer. Matilda, Bitsy, and Fluff were still chatting with Archie and the vicar. None of them paid any attention to us, which was just fine.

I glanced up the stairs and saw Derek standing at the top landing. I waved and he waved back. Gwyneth was right behind him, telling him something.

Derek turned to say something to Gwyneth, who stopped and seemed to wobble, then began to fall backward. She screamed and then disappeared out of sight!

"Gwyneth!" Derek shouted.

The heavy tree began to fall over.

I started to run for the stairs, but suddenly we all heard a horrible screeching sound. "Yeouwll!"

"What the hell was that sound? Derek?"

The tree crashed to the floor.

"Oh my God!" I shouted as decorations rolled across the carpet and fell step by step down the stairs.

"Derek?"

"I stepped on the cat's tail," he said in disgust. "I thought it was Gwyneth."

Claire had followed me out to the foyer. "Where's Aunt Gwyneth?" she shouted.

"She seems to be buried under this tree."

"I'm here," Gwyneth said, her voice muffled and sounding far away.

Buried under the Christmas tree?

"Auntie!"

Suddenly a tiny black-and-white creature came racing down the stairs to freedom. Robbie the cat! The poor thing had been in the middle of the madness up there.

"Somebody help the cat," I cried.

"I've got him," Claire said.

"I've got to get upstairs," I said. "They need help."

I took one more step up, and suddenly my worst nightmare came alive. Everything froze inside me, and I screamed like I'd never screamed before.

Chapter 12

"Get out of the way!" Mom shouted. "It's a bat!"

It came swooping down from somewhere up above, and it flew right at me, wings flapping, like the worst horror movie I'd ever seen. I shuddered and screamed, then dropped down and curled up in a ball. I leaned against the stairwell and rocked myself and prayed that hundreds of bats weren't about to lunge at me and pounce if I lifted my head.

I had faced down guys with guns before and women with knives and other really bad people who wanted to kill me. But a flying bat was somehow worse than all of that. It was horrifying! I was actually wrapping my hands around my neck because, you know, they bite your neck!

"Sweetie, are you all right?" Mom was patting my back and trying to lift me up.

"I–it's a bat."

"Oh, it's flying around here somewhere. I think it's more afraid of us than we are of it."

"Are there more of them?"

"Nope, just the one. It's really small."

I felt pretty silly now, but I was still shaking. I forced myself to look up and saw Dad waving something in the air, trying to smack the bat. Was it a broom? And meanwhile, he was laughing like a loon. Not that I'd ever actually heard a loon laughing, but I could imagine it sounded very much like my father just now.

"Jim, stop that! Come and help Brooklyn."

Oh jeez. So much for heroically facing down men with guns. I had now shown the world my true self. I was a cowardly meatball who couldn't deal with a really small flying creature. Okay, yeah, it actually looked like something out of *Dracula*, which was a movie that always haunted me. But Mom was right. It was tiny. Which meant that I was bigger than the bat. But still a meatball.

I sat on the bottom stair and looked around, still flinching at the slightest movement. "Where's Derek?"

"Here, darling," he said, sounding as if he had just come off the polo fields and was ready for a refreshing cocktail.

"Are you all right?"

"I'm fine, love. Still trying to get Gwyneth untangled from this diabolical tree."

"I can help."

"No, stay downstairs. The tree has blocked the hall, and it's difficult to—oh, hell."

"Yeooow!"

"Good grief!" I screamed a little. "What was that?"

"I just stepped on the darned cat."

"But the cat's already down here," I said.

"Well, clearly there's more than one cat."

"Which cat is it?" I asked from my safe little perch on the stairs.

"It's a big, fat, furry gray cat," he said.

"Not important right now," Gwyneth moaned.

I had to agree with her. Finally I pulled myself up and stood on the stair, looking around, but still flinching at every movement.

"I'd like to get this thing off me," Gwyneth said.

I began to slowly climb the stairs to see what was happening and figure out if I could help in any way.

Derek had angled his way over to the tree, which really did block the entire hallway outside of our rooms. He would first have to pick up the tree, but Gwyneth seemed to be tangled in branches and covered in ornaments and a string of lights.

Cameron passed me and dashed up the stairs. Derek shouted, "Grab a branch from your side, and I'll do the same from this side."

Together, the two of them were able to heft the tree and stand it up against the far corner. Derek reached down and pulled Gwyneth up. She was still tangled in a string of lights but didn't look too damaged.

"Well, that was fun," she said, and bent over to shake some of the pine needles out of her hair.

"Are you all right, Auntie?" Claire called from the stairway near me.

"Other than dying of sheer mortification, I'm fine."

"Nobody saw anything," I assured her. "Your kick-ass reputation is intact."

"You're a liar, aren't you?"

"Maybe," I admitted.

"I appreciate that in a friend." Gwyneth brushed more needles off her sweater, then straightened up and looked around to see Derek and Cameron moving chairs to block the tree from falling again. "Thank God for big, strong men."

"I'll drink to that," Claire said.

Gwyneth squinted to see. "Is my niece drunk?"

I glanced back at Claire. "Possibly. It's been a long evening."

．．．

I woke up the next morning and turned to Derek, who was awake and checking his cell phone.

"A lot went on last night," I said.

"Really?"

I glared at him. "You're kidding, right?"

He laughed. "Yes, darling. There was a lot that went on."

"So, who was that other cat?" I asked. "It was gray, so I know it wasn't Robbie or even Mr. D, who rarely ventures out from his home in the north wing."

"I haven't the faintest idea. But he'll probably turn up eventually."

"I suppose so."

He snorted. "But with everything that went on, you're most worried about the cat?"

I chuckled. "I guess I should be worried about the bat, too. But only in regard to getting it out of the castle ASAP."

"I'm concerned that Gwyneth might've tweaked a muscle or two during her unfortunate ordeal."

"Oh, I can't believe I didn't mention poor Gwyneth before the cat!"

"I won't tell her, but you'll owe me."

I laughed. "I'll pay any price. But I do hope she didn't injure herself."

"I seriously doubt it. She spent almost forty years as a covert operative. She was drilled on all 322 proper ways to fall safely without injuring oneself."

I laughed. "It was clearly useful. The drilling, I mean."

"And despite those drillings, I think it's fair to say that last night was a disaster."

"But also pretty funny."

"There were some lighter elements," he allowed. "But still disastrous for the most part."

I would try not to think about the bat.

I climbed out of bed and opened the drapes to take in the beautiful view of Loch Ness and the hillside behind the castle. I could see one of the archery targets still set up and ready for someone to play a round.

"Where's the other target?" I didn't remember moving it into the garage yesterday. But maybe Claire and Cameron had taken care of it.

I stretched and bent down to touch my toes. I'd barely done any exercise except climbing up and down stairs. "Nothing wrong with that," I argued under my breath.

"Who are you talking to?" Derek asked.

"Myself."

"Ah."

I went back to the window to enjoy the view while Derek bounded out of bed and went to brush his teeth. That's when I realized that the missing target wasn't exactly missing. The second hay bale had fallen on the ground, and the white bull's-eye cover was spread across the grass.

Or was it? It almost looked like someone was using it as a blanket. On the freezing cold grass?

"Derek, something's wrong out there."

He turned off the water and came to the window. "What is it?"

I pointed. "Do you see the bull's-eye cover lying on the ground?"

He stared for a long moment. "I'll get dressed and we'll go check it out."

On the way downstairs, we ran into Cameron and Claire, who were going to breakfast, and we told them where we were headed.

"I'll come with you," Cameron said.

Claire took his hand. "Me, too."

Halfway to the garage, it became obvious. At least, to me.

"There's a body under that cloth," I said as chills began to slither up my arms and across my shoulders.

Cameron whipped around and stared at me. "That's impossible."

"Who's been out here?" Claire wondered, then walked a few feet past the scorer's table. "Isn't this the bow I strung for you?"

"Yes. And that's my quiver." I started to pick it up, then left it. But I grabbed the scoring pencil we left on the little table and used it to open the bag just enough. "The arrows are missing."

"Someone came out here and took a few practice shots," Derek said.

Cameron nodded. "That's what happened."

"But they upended the second target," Claire said. "And the bull's-eye cloth is all wet from the dew on the grass. Who would leave it there?"

"Maybe it got tangled up in something," I said, then stopped walking. I hated being right about things like this. "Oh no."

Derek noticed at the same time and pulled his gun. "Cameron, get Claire back in the house."

"No way," Claire said.

I looked around. "We're sitting targets out here."

"No, we're not." Derek continued walking while turning in a circle, staring in every direction. "There's nobody nearby."

"Okay," I said.

"This is a nightmare," Claire whispered.

"It'll be over soon," I said. "But we need to see who it is. Derek will cover us. When we find out who it is, we'll go back in the house and call the police."

"The voice of reason," Derek said. "Let's move."

The four of us walked slowly toward the target cloth and recognized the shape of a body underneath. And I could see thick strands of blond hair. It wasn't long, like Olivia's, but shoulder length, like . . . Bitsy's.

"You don't have to look, Claire."

"Yes, I do," Claire said. "We have to know what happened. This is our land. These are our people."

"That's right, love." Cameron hugged her tightly.

Cameron carefully lifted one corner of the cloth. Bitsy lay on the grass, her arms splayed out awkwardly. An arrow protruded from her heart.

"That was a good shot," Derek muttered.

I looked up at him. "The only person good enough to shoot that arrow didn't shoot that arrow."

"I know."

"Do you have your phone?" Derek asked Cameron.

"Yes."

"You should call the police. Or Silas. Yes, you should call Silas. He'll know who to talk to."

"All right."

"Tell him to meet us and come armed."

Barely four minutes later, Silas drove up with two other men in an SUV.

Claire grabbed my arm. "How could this have happened?"

"I think you know, but I'll tell you what I think. Someone used the bow and arrows you set up for me. I'm guessing it was Bitsy, and it looked like she took some practice shots. Then she went to retrieve the arrows and someone else shot her in the heart. Then they covered her up and walked away."

Claire shook her head but couldn't say anything.

"Who in this town is good enough to make that shot?" I asked.

Her eyes started to water. "Me."

I grabbed her hand. "I already know it's not you, so don't say anything crazy like that again."

"Then who?" she demanded.

I suddenly had one thought. "Olivia?"

"Can she even shoot a bow and arrow?"

"She grew up here," I said. "She might've been good at archery. I'll bet the kids who went to Atherton Academy all took archery. Bitsy couldn't have been the only who was any good."

We both thought about it for a moment, and then Claire said, "We need Sophie."

"You're right. Is she coming by?"

"She'll be here in a little while. I'm sure she'll already know about Bitsy when she gets here." She frowned. "Bad news travels fast."

"Who else was an enemy of Bitsy's?" I wondered.

"I don't know her well enough," Claire said. "I'm sorry. I'm sure she has many wonderful friends."

"But at least one vicious enemy."

Claire and I sat in her suite drinking coffee and waiting for a report from Derek. I wanted to know when the police arrived.

"They'll probably blame me," she said.

"Maybe, but they'll be wrong."

There was a knock on the door. "I'll get it," I said, and jumped up to open the door.

Gwyneth stood there wearing what looked like a bulletproof vest over a bulky sweater and cargo pants in a camouflage pattern.

I held the door open and she walked in.

"You look like G.I. Jane, Auntie," Claire said.

She winked at her. "Good thing I still have my flak vest. And it still fits. Comes in handy." She gave Claire another look. "Maybe you'd better be wearing this thing."

That wasn't a bad idea, I thought, but Claire simply wrapped her arms around Gwyneth. "I love you, Auntie."

The Twelve Books of Christmas

Gwyneth rested her head on Claire's shoulder. "When this day is over, we'll start getting you married."

"Thank you." She kissed her cheek. "That's the best plan I've heard all week."

The MIT team arrived and spoke first to Cameron, Silas, and Derek. Bitsy's body was carried off the field and held inside one of the empty garage bays until the Inverness coroner arrived. Then the crime scene team began combing the archery field for evidence.

My mom and dad had chosen today to go to Cawdor Castle, a formidable medieval castle near Inverness that had beautiful gardens and lovely walkways. Dad was psyched that the castle was actually mentioned in Shakespeare's *Macbeth*, and Mom had heard great things about the café. I couldn't be happier with the news, and I knew that Timothy would keep an eye out for them. And most importantly, it would keep them away from having to deal with another dead body and two frantic women.

Gwyneth and I had unofficially declared ourselves the protectors of Claire. When Sophie joined us, she made it clear that she was on the protection team. Not that Claire couldn't defend herself in a fair fight or even an unfair fight, but when it came to Matilda and Fluff, she would get our protection regardless. Those women were mean!

Derek reported that both Kerr women started screaming at the front door and screamed all the way out to the archery field. I couldn't blame them; their best girl was gone. Derek had to stop them, and they began kicking him and scratching his face. Cameron had to pull them off and several constables came running.

"Please be careful," I said, when he called. I was still worried for his safety. I mean, sure, he had a gun, but those women had lethal nails. And they could bite.

"I will," he said.

"Are they still out there?"

"No. Two constables took them inside to their sitting room and locked them in. Cameron insisted they be guarded because they're a menace to everyone here today."

True, I thought, but again, I couldn't blame them too harshly. They'd just lost a loved one. "Okay. Keep in touch."

An hour had passed and I was getting antsy. "I'm going to go to the library and look for more books to while away the time."

"Do you want my flak jacket?" Gwyneth asked.

"That's very sweet, but I think I can make it from here to the library unscathed. Call or text me if you need anything. And please stay close to Claire."

"You know we will."

*A*s predicted, I made it to the library, locked the door, and spent two quiet hours looking for books. Meanwhile, Derek called to report that the police were interviewing every single person in the castle.

They took a really close look at Claire, who was declared by some to be the best archer in the house, if not the entire village. But they also spent time with me because I had accompanied Claire out to the field to set up the archery games.

"I shot arrows back in school," I said, "but it's been many years since I had anything to do with the sport."

They were much more deferential to Gwyneth and Derek, aka the professionals. It always made me happy when police and others showed Derek respect by calling him Commander. And of course Cameron was interviewed, but as Laird MacKinnon, he, too, was considered above reproach.

Once they were finished with the interviews and the body was taken to the morgue at Inverness, Assistant Chief Constable Rory

Logan sat in the dining room to speak with the people they considered the castle family. Cameron and Claire, Gwyneth, Derek and me, and Sophie. Mom and Dad showed up halfway through the discussion, so they heard some of the news. I was just glad that they hadn't seen the body.

The conversation turned into a bit of a lovefest when it became obvious that the police recognized that none of us had killed Bitsy. We made it clear that we were all anxious to find out who'd done it.

"We'll help in any way we can," Cameron said, and the rest of us nodded in agreement.

"I want to take a moment to thank you for your cooperation," Rory Logan said. "I know it's been a trying time for you, what with two deaths and multiple visits by the police."

"Thank you, Assistant Chief Constable," Cameron said. "That goes for you and your team for making it relatively painless for us, despite the fact that Bitsy's family and Willy's family will never recover from these tragedies."

"Can you tell us how she died?" Claire asked.

"Yes." She pulled out a sheet of paper. "Elizabeth—Bitsy—Kerr was pronounced dead this morning from an arrow that was shot through her heart."

"Good heavens," Mom said. This was the first they'd heard about the cause of death. We all looked at each other and shook our heads in horror and sadness.

The remaining police left sometime that afternoon with their evidence bags and information, leaving a trail of fingerprint dust and lots of worried faces.

We gathered, as usual, in the blue parlor to discuss our next move.

"I think I'd like to go for a walk," Mom said.

"I can dig that," Dad said. "Anyone else? Gwyneth?"

"Why, yes, I'd love to join you."

I noticed Gwyneth and Derek exchanging glances, then Gwyneth stood.

"Then we'll be off," Mom said.

Had Derek assigned Gwyneth to watch over my mom and dad? I was definitely okay with that. The woman had survived the great Christmas tree fall of the year. She could certainly handle getting my parents out and back without any mishaps. I hoped.

"Have fun," I said, and Mom bent over and kissed my cheek.

"You know we will."

"I should get back to the pub," Sophie said. "But I'll be back in a few hours."

"I'm so glad," Claire said.

"Unless you'd all like to come to the pub."

"Oh, let's do that," Claire said. "I'll let Mrs. B and Tamara know."

"They'd probably love a night without all of us underfoot," Cameron said.

"And they've got a wedding to prepare for," I reminded them, and got a grateful smile from Cameron.

"Then I'll see you all later at the pub," Sophie said. "I'll reserve your favorite table."

"Thanks, Sophie," Claire said.

*T*hat afternoon I found two more books in the library and ran upstairs to show Claire.

She gazed at them fondly. "I always loved this one," she said, holding up the thin copy of *The Little Match Girl*. Then she laughed. "*How the Grinch Stole Christmas!* This is an old favorite of mine."

"Mine, too. I was surprised to see it on your list because it feels so American."

"Oh, we love the Grinch over here, too," she insisted.

"At this point it's a classic."

"So, some of the books were really here all along," she said, shaking her head in amazement at our luck in finding them. "Do you think Olivia stashed them away all this time, waiting for the right moment to take them out of the castle and sell them?"

"I can't think why she wouldn't just take them instead of hiding them. None of it makes sense."

*D*inner at the pub that night was subdued. The entire village had heard the news about Bitsy, and everyone was quietly playing the "Who Did It?" guessing game.

At our table, we weren't playing that game.

Claire was particularly sensitive to the fact that people might think she was the best archer in town and, therefore, a killer.

"We know you didn't do it," I said, "so let's figure out who did."

"Has anyone seen Olivia around?" I wondered aloud, not for the first time. "Is she any good at archery?"

"She grew up here, didn't she?" Mom asked. "It seems that everybody knows everyone in town, and they all went to school together. So if Bitsy was the archery queen, who was her competition?"

"And they were cousins, remember?" I said. "Which is something I'm continually blown away by."

"Good point," Claire said. "I'll ask Sophie. If she doesn't know, she'll know who to ask."

"I'll go with you. I have some questions."

We waited a few minutes until Sophie could stop and talk. First, we asked her about archery. "Who else is good at it?"

She placed two IPAs in front of us, and we both thanked her.

"So," she began, "do you only want archery, or do you want to know other stuff?"

"I'd love to know all the men who dated Bitsy and, well, throw in Fluff, too." I took a sip of my beer. "And I'd like to know who else they dated, because it might give us a clue about who was jealous of whom or who the friends and enemies are. Every little bit of info helps."

Sophie thought about it for a minute. "So, you think that if Bitsy was flirting all night with Archie, there might be someone secretly jealous enough to hurt her?" She grinned. "Archie's a good friend, but I probably wouldn't kill the woman if he looked at her."

"What do you mean by 'good friend'?"

She laughed. "I'll never tell."

"Okay," I said. "It seems like everyone knows everyone in town, and at least half the people seem to have access to the castle and the grounds. So, where do we start?"

"Well, 'tis a small town we live in, so it's safe to say that everyone has dated everyone else at some point or other."

"Oh, that's a big help." I laughed.

"Aye." Sophie grinned. "Well, we can start with dinner last night. There's Archie, who used to date Bitsy, and while they were dating, he used to meet Tamara here in the back room."

"Tamara the chef?"

"And I think he might've even dated Fluff a time or two."

"Good heavens."

She laughed. "Aye, indeed. And Angus dated Fluff, as well, and I think he dated Bitsy, too."

"Wow, everyone gets around, don't they?"

"That's a small town for you." She took an order for a lager from a woman at the end of the bar, then came back. "Where was I?"

We laughed. "I think you were talking about Fluff."

"Right. So, Angus dated Fluff, and Fluff used to date Willy, too. Oh. And Bitsy dated Willy, too. In fact, those two were hot and heavy for a long time. That was right after Willy broke up with . . . hmm."

"Who?" I asked.

"Sophie?" Claire said. "What's wrong? Who did Willy date?"

She blew out a heavy breath. "Before Fluff and Bitsy, Willy used to date Olivia."

"Of course!" I said. "That's why Willy and Angus were always hanging out in the library."

"They seemed to have quite a rivalry going for a while," Claire said. "But they were mates to the end." She frowned at the memory. "I'm so sorry about Willy."

On the ride back to the castle, I sat next to Claire. "I can't tell if Sophie's information was helpful or not. It seems like everyone in town has dated everyone else at some point or other."

"Yes, we didn't get too far with that." Claire let go a long sigh. "I asked Cameron not to send Matilda and Fluff home until tomorrow. I'd really like to help them in some way."

"I think they're beyond help, honestly. They'll have to make it through these hard days ahead. You expressing sympathy might even make it worse. They're really quite contrary people, unfortunately."

"You're probably right," she said. "Still, it would be good to do something."

Back at the castle, we discovered that Matilda had taken a sleeping pill. Cameron told Fluff that it was fine for them to stay over while her mother was in her precarious condition. So the two Kerr women spent their last night in the green parlor, but Cameron also insisted that one of the policewomen stay with them.

"It's not as though they're under house arrest," he explained. "But those two women even had the impulse to attack Derek, so if they're staying here, I want a member of law enforcement to stay with them."

Everyone signed off on that arrangement, and the policewoman agreed to sleep in the lounge chair, claiming that she was the world's lightest sleeper and would wake up at the slightest sound.

"We'll lock our doors," Cameron said, "and you all must do the same."

"Sounds like a plan," Dad said.

"Oh, sweetie," Mom said, slipping her arm around Claire's waist. "I'm so sorry you're going through all this when you should be spending your time enjoying your new married life."

"We'll get there soon," Cameron said, "and then we'll have the rest of our lives together."

"That's lovely," Mom said.

We said good night to everyone and walked with Mom and Dad up to our rooms.

"I want to hear you turn the lock in your door," I said to Dad before he closed it.

"Okay, but then I want you to send us a text that you locked yours."

"It's a deal."

Sometime in the night, Derek and I heard the sound of crashing pots and pans. It wasn't chains being dragged or howling mountain lions, but we both went running out of the room. The clanging continued, accompanied by some woman swearing like a dockworker.

We stood in the hall for a moment while we gauged where it was coming from.

"It sounds like the north wing," Derek shouted, pointing in that direction.

"Claire and Cameron are in the north wing."

"Let's go," he shouted, and we went running down the stairs, through the foyer, and up the other set of stairs to the door of the Laird's suite.

"Claire!" I cried. "Are you all right?"

Claire shouted from down the hall. "Over here."

"It's okay," Gwyneth called. "I got her."

"Let me go, you silly old goat."

"That's Matilda's voice," I said, completely mystified.

Derek and I walked down the hall, where Gwyneth held tightly to the ends of a thin rope that she'd tied around Matilda Kerr.

"Where'd you get the rope?" Derek asked.

"I brought it with me," Gwyneth said. "You never know. It's high-quality braided cotton rope, suitable for all sorts of household activities, including tying up thieves."

"Oh, shut up," Matilda grumbled.

"You were after the book, weren't you?"

"It's mine. It belongs to me. And you wouldn't give it back."

"Believe it or not, I was about to give it back to you tomorrow."

She wore a look of shock combined with distrust. "Why would you do that?"

"Because it's yours, Matilda. To be perfectly honest, the book went missing, and we only just found it this morning. I'll give it to you tomorrow morning. Now go back to sleep. You could get hurt roaming around this great big place by yourself."

I turned to Cameron. "Did the policewoman wake up?"

"I don't believe so. And Fluff is apparently still asleep."

"Fascinating," I muttered.

"So, my homemade alarm worked," Gwyneth said, grinning.

"We heard it all the way over on the other side of the castle," I said.

"Excellent." She slapped her hands together, a job well done.

"Hey, we heard it, too."

I turned and saw my mom and dad padding down the hall, looking sleepy eyed but interested.

I frowned at Matilda. "I can't believe you thought you could sneak all the way over here without getting caught."

"And then she tried to sneak into my room," Gwyneth added.

Claire smiled. "Perhaps she didn't realize that you spent most of your life as a covert operative."

"It's not something I've advertised in the *Daily Bugle*," Gwyneth said.

"Mother?"

"Fluff!" Matilda groused. "Go to bed, Fluff."

Fluff rolled her eyes. "Is this about that stupid old book?"

"Of course it is, and it's your fault. You gave it to the vicar to sell it in the auction. You have no idea of its worth."

"It's a ratty old book, and I certainly did give it to him. And the vicar was really impressed with my charitableness." She wound a strand of hair around her finger. "I think he might want to ask me out."

Matilda sighed, then shook her head. "Come on, let's go to bed," she said, a bit more gently than before.

Derek said, "We'll follow them downstairs and back to their room."

Cameron nodded. "I don't think she'll make any more trouble tonight. But thank you."

As we walked through the foyer, Dad said, "I can't believe she was trying to sneak into Gwyneth's room."

Mom looked at Dad. "Got to admit, I did not see that one coming."

Chapter 13

We woke up early and dressed quickly, then met Mom and Dad in the hall. The four of us walked downstairs and found Cameron and Claire in the breakfast room getting ready for another hearty meal.

"I'm going to gain a thousand pounds," Mom grumbled.

Dad grinned. "But what a way to go."

A minute later we were filling our plates with eggs and bacon as Mrs. B walked in with a plate of homemade doughnuts.

I blinked. "Doughnuts?"

"See?" Mom said with a look that said, *What'd I tell ya?*

"Thank you, Mrs. B," I said, grabbing a cruller. It was my personal favorite kind of doughnut, although I liked all types. Because they're doughnuts. Come on!

"It's a big day," Mrs. B said.

Claire blushed. "It surely is."

"Oh, sweetie," Mom murmured, scooting up closer to me. "I wanted to read you this fun text from Ginny and Charlotte."

"Oh yes, read it to me."

"Here goes. 'Becky, hope you're all having the best time. Are you using your new wand? Hope it's bringing you joy and serious protection. Charlotte can't stop talking about sweet Charlie. She says, "Hope we can visit the pretty kitty when you get home." Miss you, xoxo.'"

"Oh, that's sweet," I said. "They most definitely can visit anytime. Charlie enjoyed that little girl."

"They're really good people. I hate that they lost their husband and daddy."

"Do you know how it happened?"

"I don't know all the details, but he was sick for a long time."

"How sad."

Mom sipped her coffee. "They're going to love their gifts from Scotland."

"I'm sure they will."

"What's happening with Matilda and Fluff?" I asked Cameron.

"The policewoman took them home."

"They're not here?" I asked. "Your home is back to normal?"

Claire laughed. "I wouldn't go that far, but yes. And you are free to do whatever you want today. But tonight at eight o'clock, we're having a wedding. Sophie already sent out the notices."

"Yippee! Hooray!" I said. "Good decision."

"I'm so happy for both of you," Mom said. "It's been a long slog."

"I couldn't have put it better myself," Cameron said.

After breakfast, we went back to our room. Derek wanted to take a few minutes to call his parents down in England. He smiled ruefully. "They're so close and yet so far away."

"Please give them my love. I hope we'll see them soon in Dharma."

"I will. I'll find you when I'm finished."

"Okay. I'll be out walking."

It was probably too cold to be out walking, but I could see a couple of Cameron's men digging something up on the hill beyond the garage. If they could take the cold, so could I. Besides, I was so insulated by the thick parka, silk underwear beneath my heaviest jeans, socks and boots, wool scarf, ski cap, and all the rest, I shouldn't have been able to even feel the cold.

I started to walk toward the archery range but instead turned and headed for the path around the loch. I didn't believe in ghosts, but I had to admit I was having uneasy thoughts about the archery range. It was to be expected, I suppose, when you found a dead body right there. Uneasy thoughts would be the least of it! But there was something. I couldn't quite put it all together, but I knew I was forgetting something I heard or something I saw. And maybe a nice, peaceful walk near the water would stir some memories.

It was so beautiful out here and, yeah, freezing cold, too. But I concentrated on the view and wished I had brought Cameron's binoculars with me. I'd be able to get a closer look at the incredible ruins of Urquhart Castle and the other sights along the opposite shore.

Instead, I kept seeing Bitsy under the cloth, and I wondered who would shoot her in the heart and then place that cloth over her. They would've had to remove the cloth from the hay bale, and that wasn't so easy to do. But they took the time to do it, so what did that say about the killer? They were a nice person? Except for that pesky killing? Or they didn't want her to freeze? Even though she was dead?

It was befuddling.

And it wasn't like the cover-up would fool anyone. We noticed the cloth on the ground right away and went to check it out. So, maybe they just covered her up as an act of kindness. Which was beyond psycho, right? Kill and be kind. That did not compute.

I was obviously getting lost in all of this, except that I still knew that I'd heard or seen something. I would just have to rack my brain to figure it out.

When I got back to our room, I was ready for a nap. There was something about the combination of a walk in the freezing cold and a big breakfast that made me want to crawl back into bed and curl up and sleep.

"Come look at this," Derek said. He stood by the window with the curtain pulled back a few inches.

"What is it?"

"There." He pointed, and we both stared out at the archery field by the garage.

Someone was practicing their skills out on the archery range. So, not everyone worried about ghosts, I suppose. "Who is that? It can't be Claire. She would be way too creeped out to come here only one day after finding Bitsy's body."

"That ski mask she's wearing is effective," he said. "I can't tell who it is."

"I almost walked over to the archery range but decided to head for the loch instead. I didn't see anyone out there."

Derek mused, "I wonder if Cameron lets anyone from the village practice archery out here."

"Whoever it is, they're good."

"She's hitting bull's-eyes every time," Derek said.

That's when we looked at each other, then grabbed our heavy jackets.

"Let's go," he said.

As we jogged down the stairs, I said, "It supports one theory that there are plenty of others in the village who are good at archery."

"True," he said. "And knowing Cameron, I'm certain he'll allow anyone to use the archery equipment. Just as he does with access to the loch."

"And the castle library," I added.

We got to the front door and rushed outside. We looked down the drive and saw the woman fifty yards away. We started to run.

She didn't realize we were trying to catch up with her, so she took her time and was just reaching the car she'd parked next to the gardening shed. When she heard us call to her, she turned, removed her ski mask, and I saw her face.

"Hey, Fluff," I said.

"Hello."

"I'm really sorry about Bitsy," I said.

She shrugged. "Yeah. My mum's totally tweaked."

"I can imagine."

"She just died on the archery field, so we were surprised to see you out there," Derek said.

She sniffled, and I couldn't tell if she was going to cry or if she'd simply been standing out in the cold for too long. "Coming here was sort of a personal memorial to my sister."

"That's sweet," I said. "You're a really good archer."

"Aye, I know. I don't get a chance to play too often, but I thought about all of the Laird's equipment and figured I'd come over."

"Do you know a lot of people who are into archery?"

"Aye, many of my schoolmates enjoy it. But like I said, we don't often get the chance to play."

She was being almost cordial, so I didn't want to spook her. I said, "I know you'd be welcome here anytime."

She rolled her eyes. "Huh. We'll see about that."

I guess I pushed her over her limit of cordiality.

She shoved her key in her car door lock, opened the door, and climbed in. She shut the door without saying another word and drove off.

We started to walk back to the castle, and I stopped. "Oh my God."

"What is it?"

I paced across the drive and back. "I just remembered what I was trying to think of."

"What is it?"

I shook my head, annoyed with myself. "Remember when Matilda was going on and on about how Bitsy was the class champion and the best in the school and how nobody else was as good as Bitsy was?"

"How could I forget?" he said.

I smiled. "Right. Well, I heard Fluff mutter, 'I was.' Something like that. In other words, Fluff was as good as Bitsy was. But her mother didn't care. Bitsy was her mother's favorite. And it made me feel sorry for Fluff, thinking she must've lived her entire life in her sister's shadow. Matilda allowed Bitsy to be the queen of the house while Fluff was nobody."

Derek's eyes narrowed. "Do you consider that a motive for murder?"

I stared at the ground, then up at him. "I don't want to believe it."

"It's a pretty odd family," he argued quietly.

"I know. But I can't help thinking, my sisters occasionally drive me up the wall, but it doesn't mean I would ever hurt them, let alone shoot an arrow through their heart. Jeez."

He shrugged easily. "Frankly, I'm inclined to believe anything about that family."

I leaned against the wall of the gardening shed. "How do we prove it?"

Now he grinned at me. "*We* don't prove it. The crime scene investigators will prove it. The fingerprints will prove it."

I blew out a breath. "You're right. But maybe we should call Assistant Chief Constable Rory Logan." I liked saying her whole title along with her name. "She might like to know what we've discovered."

"Good idea."

"I imagine Fluff will probably show up for the wedding since the whole town will be here, and she'll get to wear a fancy dress."

"If she does, I might bring up the fact that she's as good an archer as her sister was. Maybe better."

"She might enjoy that little touch of glory, but I doubt that'll cause her to confess." I thought about it. "You might want to do all that while her mother is standing nearby. Oh, wait. Her mother will never show up to Claire's wedding."

He took another look down the driveway. "We'll see."

"Maybe we should suggest to Cameron and Claire that they invite the Major Investigations Team to the wedding."

"I'm pretty sure they've already thought of that."

I spent another few hours in the library and found two more books, both shoved behind other books. I could no longer believe Olivia's claim that she surveyed the shelves for a half hour every day. I also thought my own eyes might be a little suspect since, when I first walked into the library, I thought it was spotlessly clean and organized. I guess it was true on the outside, but upon taking a closer look, there were problems.

The books I found were both clean copies in good condition. One was an absolutely beautiful copy of *Little Women* by Louisa May Alcott. The other was a charming first edition of *The Tailor of Glouces-*

ter by Beatrix Potter. Both of these weren't exactly considered Christmas books by most, but each of them had an element of the holiday, so I considered them eligible for that category.

The door opened and I froze, expecting Olivia to walk in at any moment. But it was Derek, and I couldn't help but smile.

"Hello, darling," he murmured. "You look pleased with yourself."

"I am. I'm also very pleased to see you. What have you been doing since I've been ensconced in here?"

"I've been helping Cameron and his men arrange the great hall for a wedding."

"Yay! Sounds like fun."

"Indeed, it was. They're planning for quite a crowd."

"They're probably expecting the whole town and half of the county besides."

"Probably so. By the way, your mother asked me to tell you that she might stop in to give you a hand."

"Oh, that would be great." I was watching as he moved around the room, going from bookshelf to bookshelf, running his fingers along the spines of the books. "You look like you've got something on your mind."

"I do have something to tell you," he said. "You missed a bit of excitement a few minutes ago."

"Oh, darn. What happened?"

"A young man came to the door asking to see Cameron. I was standing in the foyer with him, so I heard the conversation."

"Who was it?" I asked. "And why are you giving it such a buildup? I'm starting to get very tense."

"That's probably a good thing," he said. "Because the young fellow was Rudy Smith. He's the brother of Willy."

"Oh." I felt my shoulders fall, and I moved to the nearest chair at the library table. "I'm so sorry. What did he say?"

"He told Cameron that the police brought Willy's coat home to the family after going through and checking for evidence. You know, stray hairs and such."

"Did they find anything?"

"They did, speaking of stray hairs. They found a long strand of blond hair."

I gasped. "Olivia."

"Precisely."

"Are they picking her up? Have they arrested her?"

"Cameron was just on the phone with Assistant Chief Constable Logan. She told him they haven't found her yet, but assured him that they would. But there was another interesting item found in the pocket of Willy's coat."

I started to laugh. "You sound like an old-time detective who's about to reveal all the secret clues to a captive audience."

"I'm pausing for dramatic effect. Just sit and listen."

"Yes, my love." But I was still laughing on the inside.

"In Willy's pocket was a torn piece of MacKinnon stationery."

"Oh, that's good," I whispered.

"Written on the stationery were the letters M–U."

I gasped again. "Wait! No way! The bank code for Mauritius? Willy knew about the octillion scheme?"

"It would seem."

"But wait. Were they written in Willy's handwriting? I mean, it's only two letters, but still. They might be able to tell."

"His brother confirms that it was Willy's handwriting. Apparently he was left-handed, and his letters had a rather radical slant."

I clutched my arms and rubbed briskly. "I've got chills. The good kind. This is incredible." I gasped. "Derek! The letters! Willy didn't write zero-one or O–I. He was trying to write *Olivia*, but he died before he could even get to the third letter in her name."

He nodded. "That makes sense."

I reached out for his hand. "Poor Willy."

Derek pulled me into a hug. "All we can do is give him justice, darling."

"And we will," I vowed.

Derek left me to my work and went to tell the investigators what we had realized. There was no doubt that Olivia killed Willy Smith. It was just too bad Olivia wasn't a champion archer, because then we could pin Bitsy's death on her as well.

"That would be way too neat and tidy," I muttered as I searched another shelf. I was up on the ladder now and going for the top shelf behind the Christmas tree. I was seeing more and more of Olivia's spotty cleaning efforts. She was good at keeping the shelves at eye level clean, but up here, there was plenty of dust and even a cobweb or two. That was unacceptable.

If Olivia wasn't such a rude bully to her employer as well as a cold-blooded murderer and a knife thief, she would still have been fired for the crummy dusting job she did.

Derek called me. "I have a short break while Cameron talks to the vicar." We discussed the octillion issue for another few minutes, and I told him my theory, that Willy had happened to come into the library while Olivia was working out the bank codes from *The Gift of the Magi*. He saw all her notes and he probably demanded to get in on the action since he and Olivia had dated. They could use the money to leave town and get married.

"Olivia never would've gone for that," I said.

"No, you're right," Derek said.

"It wouldn't be enough for her."

"I'm going to go talk to Cameron and get the police on the phone. I have no doubt that they'll be in complete accord with your theory," he said.

"It's a good one," I said.

A minute later, we ended the call, and I continued my search of the top shelf. I was feeling pretty good about solving the mystery of Willy's death. I knew it wouldn't bring much peace to his family, but it might bring some small amount of closure to know the truth.

The door creaked open.

"Mom? I'm back here."

There was no response. "Mom?"

I heard the click of the door lock.

Okay, I'd been in scary situations before, and I didn't feel like getting caught in another one. Especially as I was stuck on top of a ladder behind a Christmas tree. Memories of last night's Christmas tree fiasco floated through my mind as I slipped my cell phone from my pocket and quietly sent a text to Derek. Help. Now.

I just hoped he would read it quickly.

"Who's there?" I called.

Still no answer, but I thought I knew who had snuck in here.

And suddenly she was standing right under my ladder. "Surprise!"

I jolted and screamed. I couldn't help it. She really snuck up on me.

"Olivia! Wow, you scared me. What're you doing?"

"I just stopped by to pick up some papers I left on my desk. What're you doing?"

"I'm looking for lost books."

"Aye. Never give up, do ye?"

"Not usually," I said. "Do you need help finding your papers?"

"No, I know right where I left them."

I nodded. "That's good."

"But they're not there." She gazed up at me. "Do you know what happened to them?"

"Me? No." I smiled down at her, but I figured it was a little thin. "I'm just in here looking for books."

She suddenly grabbed the ladder and shook it. I screamed again and was barely able to hold on. "Stop that!"

"Where are my papers? My notes?"

"I have no idea what you're talking about."

"Liar!" She shook the ladder and then pushed it hard. I clung to the top step as the ladder flew halfway around the room on the track. When it slowed down, I grabbed on to the nearest bookshelf.

"You're nuts!"

"Are you scared?"

"Of you?" I laughed. "I don't think so."

"You should be."

"You're right. I should be, because you're a witch and a bully and a thief, and you're stupid."

"I'm not stupid!" she shrieked.

"Oh, but you are a witch and a bully and a thief."

"Shut up! You'll be sorry! Everyone here will be sorry!"

She was shouting so loudly that she probably couldn't hear the tiny clicking sounds that told me that Derek was using his picklocks to get in here. *Hurry up, please,* I silently implored him.

That clicking sound gave me a great big load of courage, and I said, "So, you stole the book and got the codes to steal whatever was in Mr. Kerr's bank account in Mauritius. Did Willy want to get in on the deal? Is that why you killed him?"

She stared at me. "How do you know all that?"

I almost laughed. She'd basically just confessed to murder and embezzlement, or robbery or whatever you called stealing from someone else's foreign bank account. "You're not as slick as you think you are."

She began to scream and shook the ladder so forcefully that I was afraid I'd fall and land on her head.

Which gave me another brilliant idea. But first, I had to know. "Do you like archery?"

She shook her head in confusion. "Why does that matter?"

"Because your cousin Bitsy was killed yesterday when an arrow was shot through her heart. I was just wondering if you had anything to do with it."

"I hate archery. It hurts my hand."

"Yeah, I get that. So, who do you think killed her?"

She shrugged and seemed to ease her grip on the ladder just slightly. "If it has anything to do with archery, then you'd have to look at Fluff. She was the best in her class for years. And she hates her sister. She hates her mother, too. We all do. Matilda's a raging rocket, but then, so is Fluff. Believe it or not, Bitsy was the only normal one in that family."

"What do you mean, 'rocket'?"

"Psycho, like, totally off her nut." She frowned, considering. "Bitsy managed to survive a couple of odd accidents in the past that had no explanation, but Fluff was always right there, pretending to mind her own business. So, who knows, aye?" Olivia chuckled. "I guess I ought to give Fluff one feather in her cap, and that's because she's good for a laugh when we're out getting steamed. But otherwise, she's got her priorities all screwed up. At least I'm motivated by money, which makes more sense, don't you think?"

"Right. Good to know."

"Right. But Fluff. She's mad. I mean, angry all the time. Can't blame her, though. Her mom is Team Bitsy all the way. That's gotta get old, aye?"

I couldn't believe we were having a semi-normal conversation in the midst of Olivia trying to seriously injure me. Any second now, she would flip, though, and I needed to be prepared. I grabbed hold of the top step and waited.

The door swung open and Derek charged into the room. Olivia screamed again and shook the ladder. I grabbed the nearest group of books and flung them down on top of her.

She screamed even louder as the books conked her on the head. "Stop that!" She covered her head with her arms, but I kept grabbing the biggest, thickest hardcovers and flinging them down at her. Finally she ran away from the ladder and right toward the Christmas tree.

"Not again!" I shouted. "Not the tree!" I jumped down, landing on my hands and knees, hard enough to make me yelp in pain but close enough to grab Olivia's ankle. She tripped and fell, just missing the Christmas tree.

Derek ran over and pulled Olivia up from the floor.

Cameron and Claire were right behind Derek. Cameron took Olivia and drew her hands behind her back. She struggled violently, but Cameron was too strong for her. "We need some handcuffs."

"Mrs. B will have zip ties," I said, and felt quite brilliant for thinking of it.

Claire shouted, "I'll get them," and ran out of the room.

Cameron easily subdued Olivia despite her screaming and wriggling to get free.

"Pay attention, Olivia!" Cameron shouted. "You're fired!"

"You can't fire me!" she cried. "I quit!"

I almost laughed at that. Fluff wasn't the only one who was off her nut. I didn't have to ask what that meant.

Derek reached for me. "Once again, you're surrounded by your weapon of choice."

"Books?" I blew out a breath. "They seem to work for me."

"Here are the zip ties," Claire said, sounding winded from running the whole way.

Silas walked in behind Claire, holding out a pair of handcuffs. It figured the head of security would have all the right equipment, but he still took the plastic ties from her. "I can take it from here."

"You'll call the police?" Cameron asked.

"Already done. They'll be here momentarily."

"Thank you, Silas," Cameron said.

"Aye. Don't you have a wedding to get ready for?"

"Aye, we do. And I expect you to be there."

"Wouldn't miss it for the world."

As Silas led Olivia out of the library, Claire stared at Cameron. "Now can we get married?"

He laughed and shouted, "Yes!" He grabbed her, whirled her around, and then kissed her soundly.

And Derek and I both shouted, "Watch out for the Christmas tree!"

Chapter 14

It was a beautiful wedding. Over three hundred people attended, and there wasn't a dry eye in the place.

Sophie, Gwyneth, and I helped Claire get ready, and she looked more gorgeous than I'd ever seen her. Her dress was vintage lace over a silk satin slip. It was tasteful and sexy and simply beautiful.

"I'm not going to cry," I said.

"Your eyes are a bit damp," Sophie said.

I chose to ignore her.

"We have one more little surprise for you," Gwyneth said, holding a box out for her.

"What is this? I already have everything I could possibly want."

"Well, this is a little extra," Gwyneth explained. She opened the top and lifted the beautiful old wedding veil that Claire's mother had worn.

"You found the veil," she whispered. "How in the world?"

"Actually, I *won* the veil at the church auction."

"That's impossible. It's my mother's wedding veil."

"Apparently she had loaned it to a friend who never returned it, and it sat in that family's attic for years until they decided to clean out the room and donate everything to the church auction."

"And since you were in charge of donations, you found it."

"I had it cleaned and starched just a bit so that it falls perfectly." She held it out. "Would you like to wear it?"

Now Claire was tearing up.

"Don't cry. You'll ruin my perfect makeup job." Sophie moved in with a tissue and blotted up the tears.

"I don't know what I would do without you," she said to Sophie, then looked at Gwyneth and me. "Without all of you. Thank you so much."

The veil went perfectly well with her mother's wedding dress, and once I had texted Derek that the bride was on the move, we helped her down the stairs.

I could hear the beautiful strains of . . . I gasped and stared at Claire. "What in the world? Is that 'Love Shack'?"

"It's one of our favorite dance tunes," Claire said. "We decided to camp it up a bit. And honestly, isn't everyone a bit tired of hearing *Pachelbel's Canon* for the three hundredth time?"

"Right on, my girl," Gwyneth said, already moving to the awesome beat of the B-52's.

"I'm impressed," I said. "And my parents are probably in there somewhere getting their groove on. Be afraid."

"Let's get this party started," Claire said.

And with that, we headed for the great hall.

The vicar looked very handsome in his well-fitted suit, but standing next to Cameron and Derek, he could hardly compete. But he still looked good. They really were two—okay, three—of the best looking men in Scotland.

Sophie and I preceded Claire, and we made it to the altar without stumbling once. I walked over and stood with Derek. Sophie followed and stood on my other side.

As everyone started to settle, I leaned closer to Derek. "Is that Fluff sitting over there on the left side, six rows from the back?"

He searched the area. "That's her."

"We both know she killed her sister."

"Yeah, we know it."

"The police need to get her out of here before she makes more trouble." He pulled out his phone and sent a text. Then he leaned over to whisper to Cameron, who whispered something to the vicar.

I gave Derek a look, and he said in hushed tones, "The Major Investigations Team is still here processing Olivia." He took my hand, and we smiled and listened to the B-52's and watched the crowd.

There was suddenly a commotion at the door, and I looked up and saw Assistant Chief Constable Rory Logan standing with two of her constables.

"What is it?" Cameron asked loudly. "Do you need to talk to me?"

"I'm sorry to interrupt the proceedings, Yer Lairdship, but I'm here to arrest one of your guests."

"Please proceed, Assistant Chief Constable," Cameron said.

"Appreciate it," Logan said. And she and her men traipsed down the aisle and stopped at Fluff's row.

Fluff stood and screamed, "I didn't do it!"

"Haud yer wheesht, girl!" Matilda barked. "What's this all about?"

"Fleur Kerr, you're under arrest for the murder of Elizabeth Kerr."

Matilda's mouth dropped open. "You?"

Fluff shook her head vehemently. "I didn't do it!"

"You killed my Bitsy?" Matilda whispered. "Our best girl?"

"I'm your best girl!" Fluff shrieked, then simply stared at her mother. "It was never going to be my turn, was it?"

Matilda seemed to deflate. She just kept whispering, "You killed our best girl. Our best girl."

"Oh, shut up, Mummy," Fluff muttered.

Matilda stared at her daughter and I recognized that look. It was fear. Matilda was afraid of Fluff. I couldn't blame her.

The police managed to pull Fluff out to the aisle, handcuff her, and lead her away. But before she left the great hall, Fluff stopped in the middle of the aisle. She turned, raised her cuffed wrists, and pointed at Claire. "I was top bowler on my cricket team six years in a row. I could've killed you with that cupping glass."

"But you missed!" I shouted, then stared at Derek in shock. "Sorry. That was rude."

"No, it wasn't," he said. "You were right."

I shook my head in disbelief. "I heard her say it in the ladies room, but I never thought she'd confess it in front of the entire town. I kept wondering how I could prove it, but now I guess I don't have to."

"No, she did that herself," Derek said, still watching the drama. "She really could've killed Claire with that glass cup. And apparently she was going to keep trying."

Cameron strode up the aisle and out of the hall to speak to Assistant Chief Constable Logan. After a moment, Cameron walked away, and the constables led a still struggling Fluff out of the castle.

Cameron stopped and whispered something lengthy to Derek, then finally continued down the aisle to start the wedding ceremony.

"What did he say to you?" I asked.

"He said he asked the assistant chief constable if they were arresting Fluff based on hearsay evidence or if they had actual proof of her guilt."

"Good question," I said. "What did she tell him?"

"Fluff's partial fingerprints were found on each of the arrows, including the one they pulled out of Bitsy."

"Ugh," I muttered.

I wasn't sure what Matilda would do when she heard that detail, but at this point, she knew she couldn't stay. She stood and followed the police out of the hall. I had to admit, I felt sorry for the woman, even after all the damage she'd done to Claire. That look in her eyes said so much, but I didn't want to think about it. I didn't want to feel sorry for her.

It was good to know that Derek and I had been right about Fluff. But it made me wonder how one extended family had managed to raise two women, Olivia and Fluff, who both turned out to be killers. I remembered that Fluff had actually set her sights on the vicar, and I had to shake my head. *Dream big, girl*, I thought.

We were all still distracted until Cameron finally asked everyone to please allow the ceremony to continue. And slowly everyone did as he asked.

The vicar began. "Dearly beloved, we are gathered together here in the sight of God and in the face of this company to join together this man and this woman in holy matrimony, which is commended to be honorable among all men and therefore is not by any to be entered into unadvisedly or lightly, but reverently—"

"Yeeoowl!"

The vicar halted midsentence and looked around.

"Now what?" I whispered, glancing up at Derek.

His eyes narrowed in speculation. "That's a cat."

"Please proceed, Vicar," Cameron murmured.

But just then, heavy boots sounded at the doorway and everyone turned to see a distinguished older gentleman walk into the hall. He was dressed in formal wear that almost exactly matched Cameron's elegant tuxedo. And he carried a cardboard packing box.

The music stopped.

Cameron took a step forward, and when he spoke, his voice was incredulous. "Father?"

There were gasps throughout the hall, especially from me. Well, and Claire, and others. Gwyneth didn't look surprised at all.

"Hello, my dear boy," the elder Laird said. He smiled at Claire. "Hello, young lady. My dear Claire." He took her hand and shook it gently.

I watched Claire. She might've stopped breathing but then sucked in air as tears erupted from her eyes.

Next to me, Sophie muttered, "Damn it, there goes her makeup."

I laughed quietly as tears threatened my own makeup.

He turned to the vicar. "Beg pardon for the interruption, Vicar. It appears that I stepped on the damned cat's tail again. Ye'll pardon me French."

Then he turned and faced the crowd. "Hello, my friends."

There were shouts of greeting and "Aye, Yer Lairdship." And one old gentleman shouted, "Looking spry, ain't ye?"

Cameron walked slowly toward his father and shook his hand. "I'm glad you made it."

"I dinnae want to miss it," he said. "But I dinnae want to arrive too early, so I camped out upstairs. Hope I didn't cause too much of a ruckus."

"Almost every night," I muttered.

He heard me and laughed! Pointing at me, he said, "Ye're a feisty one, ye are."

"Yes, she is, Your Lairdship," Derek said in an annoyingly serious tone.

The old Laird chuckled at that.

"But Father," Cameron said. "It appears that you have a box full of . . . kittens?"

"Kittens?" Claire said. "I've got to see this." She walked down the aisle and stopped next to Cameron. He took hold of her hand, and both of them looked into the box.

"Aw," Claire sighed. "They're such wee ones, aren't they? I count eight of them, and they're each completely precious."

"Ye're a love," the Laird said quietly. "Aye, these rascals been hiding in your wall over on the east side. For weeks now."

"That's what woke us up every night," I whispered to Derek.

He must've heard me again, because he said, "What ye heard was their ma'am whinin' every night and movin' them from place to place, as it never failed but that some human would get close enough to her hidey hole to disturb her. She had to protect her babies, don't ye know?"

"Did you fall down one night?"

He huffed. "Tripped over her damned tail, didn't I? Bloodied my hand." He glanced at the vicar. "Pardon me French."

I glanced up at Derek and he nodded. So, the Laird must've grabbed the wall panel and left that streak of blood on there. Another mystery solved.

"What made the chain sound?" I asked, since it was becoming clear that the wedding ceremony was on hold.

"Och! That's the old dumbwaiter. The chains were rusted and barely moved when I first got here. But I fixed it up well enough to deliver me supper each night. But aye, it makes a racket, don't ye know!"

"Yes, I know." I took a step forward. "May I see your kittens?"

"I'll bring 'em to ye," he said, and proceeded down the aisle until he was standing next to the vicar. I came up close and looked inside the box.

301

"Oh, they're beautiful. Half black-and-white and half fuzzy gray darlings. How old are they?"

"Seven weeks by my count," he said. "Almost old enough to start weaning, I'd say."

I whipped around and found my mother in the crowd. Grinning, I nodded at her and she nodded back, then pointed her two fingers at her eyes and then at mine. So, we were on the same page. If the kittens were already weaned, we'd be able to take one or two home with us. Perhaps as a gift for Charlotte? My heart was pounding with excitement. We would have to call and check with Ginny first, but a sweet kitten would make a perfect gift for a little girl. Along with the stuffed kitten and a pretty tartan scarf I'd bought last week. And a couple of books, of course.

"Now I've taken up enough of your wedding time," the old Laird said. "Let's get on with it, and we can talk later."

So, the wedding ceremony continued, and it was lovely. Before I knew it, Cameron was kissing his bride, and then they were playing the recessional, which was, of course, Bruno Mars's "Marry You."

The crowd was laughing and crying and cheering as the couple ran for the door.

Everyone agreed it was the most exciting wedding they'd ever attended. The food was carried in by all of Mrs. B's helpers, and it looked absolutely delicious.

Our little group gathered near the huge Christmas tree—I prayed it wouldn't fall over—and congratulated the happy couple.

The old Laird was there, too, and the box of kittens was placed on a table nearby for everyone to ooh and aah over.

"Where's the mother cat?" I asked the elder Laird.

"I ken she's nearby. She won't go far away from her bairns. It was her tail I tripped over on the way into the great hall."

"Then she'll show up eventually."

"Aye." He looked at Claire now. "I have another gift for ye, but I left it in the library."

"Oh. I can go get it," said Claire.

"Nae, Claire. I'll just tell ye. I saw that young library girl doing some odd things, so I took a few books and hid them in places. I think she was planning to steal some of them. So I took them from her hiding places and put them in my own."

"That was your doing?" I asked. "I've found some of them, but not all."

"Aye, so I saw," he said with a wink. "The rest are in a box under the counter on the east side of the room. You know they're all Christmas stories, and those are my favorites."

"That's what I hear," I said. "They're some of my favorites, too."

Claire sighed and slipped her arm through the elder Laird's. "You've brought us so many gifts, and that's one of the best."

"Right here and now," the Laird said. "This is one of the best gifts of all."

I smiled at him. "I would have to agree."

"So, Father," Cameron said. "Are you thinking of staying for a while?"

He took a deep breath and let it out slowly. "If ye'll have me, I'd like to stay. Permanently."

Cameron looked gobsmacked. "You'll stay?"

"If it suits ye."

Cameron grabbed him in a big manly hug. "It suits me fine."

"And what about your beautiful new bride?"

"It suits me, too," Claire said, and hugged him.

"Me, too," I said without thinking. But the rest of the group happily repeated the same thing.

The old Laird turned and winked at me.

The mom cat made her appearance just then and circled the elder

Laird's ankles. "Aye, there you be. This is the saucy little minx that brought us these lovely kittens." He picked her up and nuzzled her.

The cat was almost twice the size of the sleek Mr. D and the dapper Robbie. She was a long-haired gray and very friendly, obviously.

"She has two different colored eyes," I said. "That's so cool. And she's a big girl. And very pretty."

"Aye, she is," he murmured, and ran his hand along her spine, making her purr. Then he turned to Cameron.

"As ye ken, son," he began. "I've lived much of the last few years in the company of wealthy women. I've loved them all in my own way. But frankly, I'm tired. I want my home, I want to get to know my beautiful new daughter-in-law." With a twinkle in his eye, he added, "And I want grandchildren."

Cameron grinned at Claire. "We'll do what we can to oblige, Father."

"Absolutely, yes," Claire said, holding both Cameron's hand and the elder Laird's. "I can't wait to get to know my new father-in-law. And I want you to get to know me, too. And our children."

And once again, there wasn't a dry eye in the place.

Epilogue

Several days later, Claire and Cameron drove into town and two hours later returned with some news. By now, since we felt like family, we all gathered at the front door as they walked in and demanded to know what happened.

"I know it's barely noon," Dad said. "But I'm happy to pour some toddies if desired."

Claire laughed. "Oh, Jim, I wish you were staying longer. We could use more of your humor and honesty around here."

"Well, thank you, sweetie," Dad said. "But was that a yes to the cocktail question?"

We all laughed, including Cameron and Claire, and Cameron said, "Let's go to the blue parlor and chat."

We followed him down the foyer hall and into the blue parlor, a room that had become like a second home to all of us.

"What happened?" Derek asked. He had an idea of what Cameron had gone to the village for, but was unclear on the outcome.

At that moment, Mrs. B entered the room with a large carafe of coffee and all the accoutrements that went with it, along with a bowl of everyone's favorite biscuits.

"Thank you, Mrs. B," Claire said when she had set everything out on the coffee table.

"You call me if you need anything else," she said, and shot Cameron a look of concern before she left the room.

So, everyone knows that something has happened, I thought.

"What happened?" Derek asked.

Cameron took his time pouring coffee for Claire and himself. Then he leaned against the bar and said, "It went well."

"What does that mean?" Dad wanted to know.

Cameron laughed. "I don't blame you for your suspicions."

"Hearing something like that," Dad said, "I'm inclined to think they told you to get out."

"But we don't believe that," Mom said, patting Cameron's shoulder. "So, what happened?"

Cameron said, "I'll give you the bullet points."

Dad nodded. "That works."

"First," Cameron began, "the Oddlochen Women's Club is hereby disbanded."

"What?" I said, maybe a little too loudly.

"That's right," Claire said with a grin. "It was explained that there were some bad seeds among the hierarchy who led the club astray."

"You can say that again," Mom grumbled.

"And what about the town council?" Gwyneth asked.

Cameron sat down in the blue chair, rested his elbows on his knees, and held his head in his hands.

"What's wrong?" I asked. "Were they mean to you?"

"In a manner of speaking," Cameron said.

Claire slapped his knee. "Don't tease them." She looked at each of us and said, "They've elected Cameron president of the town council. And they want me to form a new women's group that will include weapons training."

I laughed. "That couldn't have been the men's idea."

"No," Claire said gleefully. "The women are dying to throw knives. And axes!"

"I like the sound of that," I said.

"This could get ugly," Gwyneth warned with a half smile.

"I won't let it," she said, holding her hand up in a pledge. "They were all so lovely, and I understood that it was mainly those three women that caused all the trouble for us. Turns out, nobody much cared for them anyway. But I did insist that they all support Matilda in her hour of distress. One of her daughters was killed and the other is going to prison. She needs the support of her friends."

"That is amazingly generous of you," Mom said.

Gwyneth nodded. "I'm very proud of you."

Claire held her coffee cup in both hands. "I know how it feels to be on the outside looking in. And that's what I read in Matilda's eyes when she walked out of the great hall after Fluff was taken away. She looked so . . . lonely."

I had seen that same look in Matilda's eyes. It felt like desolation to me, but loneliness was a close second. And there was fear in there, too. Not for what might happen to Fluff but for what Matilda had felt when she was with her younger daughter.

"I think she was actually afraid of Fluff," I said. "Even Olivia said that there was something odd about that girl."

"Maybe that's why she showered all her affection on Bitsy," Claire said.

Derek nodded. "Quite possibly."

"Perhaps being supported and included in the new women's group will help her get through this," Gwyneth said.

"I hope so," Claire said.

The elder Laird stood in the doorway. "I heard what you did, Claire. It was admirable of you."

"Thank you, Poppy."

"Ah," I whispered, and smiled, remembering the night of the wedding when Claire had asked the Laird how he would like to be addressed by her. She had suggested Father or Laird, but instead of suggesting one or the other, he'd told Claire and all of us a story about an old friend from years ago whose grandchildren had called him Poppy. The elder Laird had so enjoyed the cheerful, lively sound of it very much.

After only one day, I realized that the name suited him down to his toes.

It was clear to all of us that there was a lot of love and happiness in the castle, and I couldn't help but attribute some of that good feeling to my mother. After all, the day after the wedding, Mom went into witch mode to perform what she liked to call her "Wing-Ding-Whoa-Nelly-Whopper of a Happiness Spell." It took her all over Castle MacKinnon, shaking her stones, whipping her wand, and chanting her favorite words of joy. She filled every room with abundance and love, and left each and every corner smelling as sweet as the roses that grew along the path to the loch.

The following week, Derek and I landed in San Francisco with Mom and Dad and two adorable kittens, one black-and-white and one fuzzy gray with two different colored eyes. We drove Mom and Dad home to Dharma, then we all went over to Ginny's house and presented the new kittens to Charlotte, the darling little girl who had won our hearts from the very beginning.

ACKNOWLEDGMENTS

There are several people I must thank for their extraordinary help and support on this book.

To my brilliant executive editor, Michelle Vega. Thank you for your relentless positivity and faith in me, no matter how deep into the woods I find myself.

Thank you to my superagent, Christina Hogrebe at Jane Rotrosen Agency, for always having my back and never letting me down.

To my enthusiastic and awesome team at Berkley, including Annie Odders, Elisha Katz, and Yasmine Hassan, who work so hard to make my books shine. And many thanks to Daniel Craig for my exceptionally gorgeous book covers!

Muchas gracias to my plot-group pals, Paige Shelton and Jenn McKinlay, for the plotting and the laughter and the good times. You guys make life worth living!

And as always, love and thanks to my husband, Don. You are my rock.